SPARK

Spark

Harry Bucknall

Matador
9 Priory Business Park,
Wistow Road, Kibworth Beauchamp,
Leicestershire. LE8 0RX
Tel: 0116 279 2299
Email: books@troubador.co.uk
Web: www.troubador.co.uk/matador
Twitter: @matadorbooks

ISBN 978 1 83859 509 8

British Library Cataloguing in Publication Data.
A catalogue record for this book is available from the British Library.

Printed and bound in Great Britain by 4edge Limited
Typeset in 11pt Adobe Garamound by Troubador Publishing Ltd, Leicester, UK

Matador is an imprint of Troubador Publishing Ltd

Contents

PART ONE

PART TWO

PART ONE

CHAPTER ONE

The Boat

Musa Ali Abubakr finished the fourth rakat of the Salat al-Zuhr noon prayer. The Salat al-Zuhr was the second prayer of the day and the last of Musa's life.

Musa rolled up the prayer mat and placed it next to his mobile phone on top of an empty bookshelf. The second-floor, one-bedroom flat, just off the Kilburn High Road in north London, was sparsely decorated. Apart from the prayer mat and phone, it bore few signs of its current occupant.

There were two messages on the phone, both of which Musa had read several times. The first was an SMS from his cousin Tariq. It read, "Arrived Zuwara. Waiting for boat. Will be together soon, Insh'Allah. T."

So, Tariq had made it to Zuwara. Good. Musa thought of his own time waiting in the Libyan fishing port a hundred or so kilometres west of Tripoli, crammed into a run-down, ramshackle, concrete hovel. Waiting.

Zuwara was the middle of the journey. It was a staging point, a place where hope and despair mixed on equal terms. It was one of a hundred towns and villages along the north African coast where men, women and children from all over Africa and beyond gathered, hundreds of thousands of them, hoping for passage across the Mediterranean, dreaming of a better life, reflecting on what they had left behind, and thinking of those who had already died on the journey. To a million desperate eyes staring out from a desolate north African coast, the deep aquamarine of the Mediterranean promised renewal.

Musa's own journey had started almost a year earlier in the town of Wad Madani on the banks of the Blue Nile, south of Khartoum. A payment of five thousand dollars to a local broker was supposed to guarantee him passage all the way to Italy. Yet when he turned up at the collection point on the first night of his odyssey, the driver demanded three hundred dollars.

Initially, Musa was one of five in the back of a white, twin cab, Toyota Hilux pickup truck, but by the time they passed Khartoum, eleven migrants were hanging on for dear life, with a further six packed into the twin cab.

At some stage they crossed the border into Libya, not that border guards were an issue. There weren't any. On a map, the border was a dead straight line, one of the many geometric abnormalities drawn by former colonial powers in Africa. In reality, it was a howling wilderness.

Two thousand kilometres and five days bouncing along desert tracks later, Musa arrived in the isolated town of Al-Jawf where they swapped vehicles. The new driver took a roll call, one of several on the journey. Checking names was a critical part of the migrant audit trail, proving the migrants had paid a bona fide broker who was part of a genuine smuggling network. There were plenty of opportunists pretending to be honest brokers, dangling the promise of a new life, ready to dupe you, take all your money, and leave you to an uncertain fate. No name on the roll call, no further passage. That was the harsh reality. They left Al-Jawf one light. A young girl from Khartoum was not on the list. She belonged to the smugglers now and would have to pay her way to freedom with the only asset she had left.

From Al-Jawf, the reduced group of sixteen was driven to Waddan, a nondescript oasis town in the middle of Libya. As the crow flies, it was only nine hundred kilometres, but the drive must have been at least fifteen hundred. The second leg of the journey was much the same as the first, except Musa had to pay the driver two hundred dollars and the Hilux was red.

One of the two infants got sick and cried from dehydration and hunger. Pleas to the driver to stop so they could all get food and water went unheard. He didn't care. He was on the clock. By the time they reached Waddan, the child was dead.

Fifteen of them made the next leg of the journey to Zuwara. A high percentage, Musa discovered, after hearing story after story told by fellow migrants waiting for the boat.

Musa opened his eyes and glanced around the bare London flat.

The boat. Despite having paid the full fare to the broker back in Sudan, Musa had to wait more than a month before he got the text message from Mustafa, his pre-arranged smuggler. After what seemed like an interminable wait, everything happened very quickly. Late one night, Musa followed the SMS instructions and went to a large, open-sided, tin shed on a beach on the outskirts of town. There were fifty migrants there when he arrived, but by midnight there must have been two hundred.

Musa hoped there weren't more than two hundred. His five thousand dollars was supposed to guarantee an upper limit for the crossing. The boat was an eighteen-metre, wooden fishing trawler, though trawler made it sound a lot more solid and stable than it actually was. It wasn't unusual to cram over three hundred people into these sea-weary old craft.

Everything was a market. Even in the most dire and desperate of human circumstances, the market ruled supreme. Maybe the

5

desperation made the market inescapable. And the maths was simple. Two hundred people each paying in the region of five thousand dollars generated one million dollars.

One million dollars. That was first class. If all you could afford was a few hundred to a thousand dollars for the journey to Europe, you would be packed like sardines into the cheapest boat the smuggler could lay his hands on. This was a margin business, and even at the cheap end of the scale, three hundred and fifty migrants could generate over quarter of a million dollars for the smuggling network.

Musa read Tariq's text again. "Arrived Zuwara. Waiting for boat. Will be together soon, Insh'Allah. T."

His thoughts drifted back to the tin shed, a half-moon night, and a disorderly sea of people funnelling into a bottleneck, their names ticked off a list for the last time.

Musa prayed Tariq would not have to wait so long. He shouldn't have to. Musa had seen to that. The agreement was that Tariq be found as safe a berth as possible within days of arriving in Zuwara. And for Tariq the entire journey from Wad Madani all the way to the UK was free. There was a price to pay, but it was a price Musa had been prepared to pay for years.

The second message on Musa's mobile was on the HiddenChat secure messaging app. It was a simple, smiley emoji. It was the instruction to move.

Musa went into the bedroom and stood in front of the wardrobe. From the two oval mirrors on the wardrobe doors, two young men with tight, curly black hair, and panda-like shadows encircling almond eyes stared back at him. But Musa didn't see the physical features, he had no use for vanity. He saw a deep, inner strength, a conviction, granted him by the grace of Allah.

Musa opened the wardrobe doors and looked at the only item of clothing hanging on the rail. Then, carefully, very carefully, he put on his suicide vest.

He felt calm, in control, at peace. He was sad he wouldn't see his beloved Tariq again. Inseparable as children, playing for hours on the banks of the Nile, their friendship embodied a time of simple innocence, a time long since lost to the modern world.

Shortly after noon on a cold, overcast Tuesday in April, an unremarkable twenty-two-year-old man from Sudan walked out of his second-floor, one-bedroom flat in Kilburn, and began the final leg of his journey.

CHAPTER TWO

Undercover

One thousand eight hundred kilometres south, south east, Lucinda Spark took a deep breath and strode into the lobby of the Hotel Hanifa. She dropped her bag on the X-ray machine and walked through the scanner, setting off the alarm. A bored-looking security guard, slouched in a white, plastic chair, nodded nonchalantly for her to pass.

A man in his mid-thirties was at the reception desk, arguing over the room service bill. Next to him, his young son was standing on tiptoes, reaching for a stack of tourist brochures on the desk and pushing them onto the floor one by one. Sitting on her own, oblivious to his actions, the boy's mother adjusted her hijab and continued scrolling through the thousands of pictures on her phone.

The only other person in the hotel lobby was two hundred and seventy pounds of muscle turned to fat and squeezed into a cheap, brown suit. He had been staring at Lucinda with expressionless eyes the moment she entered the hotel.

Lucinda held his gaze for a second, then turned left into the darker atmosphere of the hotel's Chopin coffee lounge. She paused to let her eyes adjust and approached the only occupied table.

'Hakim Nasri? Ann Edmunds. Thank you for meeting me.'

'A pleasure, Miss Edmunds. Please, sit.'

Lucinda took a mobile phone and a business card from her bag. The phone she put on the table, the card she handed to Nasri. She placed her bag on the floor to the right of her chair.

Nasri held the card between the thin, bony index finger and thumb of his left hand. The pristine card gleamed against Nasri's dark skin and thick mat of hair between his knuckles.

'Ann Edmunds. Legal Counsel,' Nasri read out loud, looking up at Lucinda. 'Please, turn off your phone, Miss Edmunds.'

Lucinda picked up her mobile and held it so Nasri could see her right swipe to "power off". She put the phone back on the table.

'Let me be frank,' said Nasri. 'I don't normally take meetings with strangers, but I agreed to meet you as a courtesy to Karim Ahmet. He is a respected man here in Tunis and he was most insistent.'

Nasri beckoned a hovering waiter to approach. The waiter's black shirt, black pyjama trousers, and gaudy black and gold paisley waistcoat suited the surreal atmosphere of the coffee lounge. Karim had set up the venue. A nondescript, three-star hotel. A sensible choice, there were no prying eyes. And no security cameras. None that worked, anyway.

'Coffee,' ordered Nasri. 'What will you take?' he asked, turning to Lucinda.

'Single espresso,' replied Lucinda, noticing how nervous the waiter seemed and that he refused to look Nasri in the eye.

Lucinda sat up straight and pushed her shoulders back. 'Karim has been a friend of ours for quite some time,' she said. 'He is a kind and astute man.'

'And what is it you and those you represent want, Miss Ann Edmunds, Legal Counsel?'

Nasri stared at Lucinda, leaving the question hanging in the air, half enquiry, half threat. She guessed he was mid-forties, maybe

9

fifty. His short black hair was tinged with grey at the temples and beginning to thin a little on top. A week-old beard, and tired, dark grey suit would have suggested a mild, mid-ranking government official, but for one thing. Nasri had piercing green eyes. Intense, alert, they brought his face alive.

The waiter in the waistcoat returned. In one fluid movement, he poured thick, black liquid from a golden coffee pot into a porcelain cup, raising the pot high above the cup allowing the coffee to breathe as it flowed like a torrent, before bringing the pot down until it touched the lip of the now full cup. Not a drop spilled. The waiter put the cup in front of Nasri, still avoiding eye contact, and then served Lucinda the espresso. The logo on her cup said Lavazza. Not Lucinda's favourite brand, but pretty good, assuming the coffee inside was actually Lavazza.

'As I believe Karim told you, I represent the Martin brothers. Fifteen years ago, they inherited a small business started by their father and based in east London. Today, they not only have extensive business operations across the entire capital, they also have interests in most of Britain's major cities, either directly or through affiliates.'

Lucinda could smell the black depth of Nasri's coffee, but she also detected a hint of orange blossom. She picked up her cup and drank the shot of espresso. Still not her favourite, but definitely Lavazza.

'My employers have watched the growth of your business in Britain over the past few years and believe there are areas of mutual interest. In short, Mr Nasri, they would like to discuss a relationship, perhaps even a partnership.'

Nasri held up his hand. 'Miss Edmunds, I am aware of the Martin brothers, both their business and their reputation. However, my interests in the United Kingdom are relatively small, and, forgive me, I do not see how a relationship with the Martin family would help me or be in their interest.'

Lucinda looked at Nasri and felt the heat from his piercing eyes. She had been instructed not to push Nasri too far, this was a technical operation. Let the mobile phone do its work and get out of there in one piece. But what use was the phone information if Nasri didn't feel threatened? It would give an address book of numbers to run down, but nothing earth-shattering. This was a perfect opportunity to rattle the cage and shake out some real intelligence.

Everything up until this moment had been easy. Well, not easy, but certainly conventional. Recruitment, training, Lucinda had passed all the tests, both theory and practical, with ease. She was the stand-out candidate in her year. Now, on her first undercover assignment and for the first time, she had a real decision to make. A decision that could influence the course of events.

A bead of sweat slid between her breasts and was absorbed by the bridge of her bra.

'Mr Nasri, may we talk frankly?'

'I expect nothing less.' Nasri took a sip of his coffee and pushed the cup to one side.

'You are being modest about your UK interests, Mr Nasri. You run a human trafficking organisation with major hubs in Tunisia, Algeria and Libya. There are two main strands to your business. The first is facilitating the transit of as many illegal immigrants to Europe as possible. Even though the overall number of immigrants has fallen in the last couple of years, last year your organisation smuggled in the region of 50,000 people to Britain alone. That is an impressive number, particularly when the going rate can be as much as fifteen thousand dollars per person.'

Lucinda paused, trying to gauge the effect, if any, her gambit had had.

Expressionless, his green eyes focused on Lucinda, Nasri said, 'Continue.'

Lucinda leaned forward. 'We are not interested in the first strand of your business, except perhaps in that it might provide the finance for the services we propose. It is the second strand that interests my employers.'

'And you are about to tell me what that is, Miss Edmunds?'

'Hidden among the migrants are terrorists, sent to Britain to carry out attacks. We think it's an excellent business model. I must confess,' continued Lucinda, not allowing Nasri time to interject, 'we do not know if there is an ultimate architect behind the attacks, driven perhaps by an ideological Islamic struggle, bent on exporting the war to the West. Nor, Mr Nasri, do we care. The motives are not our concern. We see a business opportunity, and that is what my employers would like to discuss.'

Exhaling as gently as she could, Lucinda sat back in her chair. There was no going back now.

Nasri tapped the table with the fingers of his right hand. 'Continue,' he said.

'If I may, and please don't take this the wrong way, when people blow themselves up in the heart of London, that gets my employers' attention. It's their town. They want to know who is behind it and how these operations are planned and supported. Our 'investigations' have led me here to you, Mr Nasri. The Martins believe your support network in the UK would benefit from a little local content.'

'Miss Edmunds, you tell an interesting story. I do not admit to any of your allegations, but, just for the sake of argument, why you don't you tell me what your employers propose.'

Growing in confidence, Lucinda began to feel in control of the conversation.

'Please, Mr Nasri, don't think I am making any allegations at all. I want to be clear we make no criticism of your activities, merely that we believe we can improve your efficiency by working together for our mutual benefit.'

Nasri remained motionless, inscrutable. Lucinda couldn't read his emotions, but she had his attention.

'Let me give you one example,' continued Lucinda. 'In London, you mostly use an Albanian crime syndicate to provide logistics support. Rented accommodation, safe houses, et cetera. We know the Albanians well. They are direct competitors who have recently become somewhat of a nuisance to the Martins. We expect their operations to suffer some serious setbacks in the coming months. We propose taking over their role. You will quickly see we have access to considerably more resources, including a vast portfolio of real estate. But our unique selling point is our relationship with the Metropolitan Police. We can leverage this relationship and guarantee your activities remain very much under the radar. We can provide these and other facilitation services across the UK.'

Nasri picked up the business card, rotating it between his fingers.

'Miss Edmunds, I think perhaps this is enough for a first meeting. Should I decide to meet you again, you will hear from Karim Ahmet.'

It wasn't a suggestion, it was an order. Trying not to look disarmed, Lucinda smiled and said, 'Mr Nasri, I hope you don't feel I have been too direct. I know there are certain customs that should, in an ideal world, be observed. But, likewise, we are keen not to waste time. I hope you understand.'

'But of course,' replied Nasri getting to his feet. 'It was a pleasure to meet you.'

Lucinda got up, put her mobile phone in her bag and shook Nasri's hand.

'I look forward to hearing from you,' said Lucinda. Nasri nodded and sat back down.

As Lucinda turned and left the Chopin coffee lounge, she could feel her heart beating hard against her chest. She had kept admirable control of herself, but now her mind was racing. She

13

couldn't, in all honesty, be sure what Nasri had made of the pitch, he was difficult to read, and he had brought the meeting to an abrupt end. But surely it would elicit some reaction? A flurry of phone calls that could open up at least part of the operation, lead to intelligence that could reduce the number of attacks.

Adrenalin-fuelled and walking a little too quickly through the lobby, Lucinda saw the cheap, brown suit following her with his eyes, but he was just Nasri's goon-come-driver. He was no threat.

She also noticed for the first time the hideous painting on the wall beside the reception desk. A green and yellow Impressionist meets Jackson Pollock monstrosity, cut into four equal squares with an inch between the constituent parts. Where did hotels get this stuff? Did they all go to the same place? Smiling to herself, she made a mental note to log on to CheapHotelArt.com.

Lucinda stepped out of the Hotel Hanifa into the spring warmth of Tunis in April. She noticed a taxi parked on the side of the road and thought nothing of it. She noticed the individual on the other side of the street, leaning against a wall, arms crossed, staring straight at her, and thought nothing of it. She did not notice the bulge on his right hip, barely disguised under the tail of his thin, blue shirt.

CHAPTER THREE

Murder and Mayhem

George Oluwale was struggling to pin a black flag into the wall of his ground-floor, studio flat just off Streatham High Road, south London.

White writing in Arabic across the top of the Islamic State flag declared, "There is no God but Allah", and at the bottom of the flag three words written in black on a white circle proclaimed, "Allah Messenger Mohammed".

George's phone beeped.

'Fuck,' he shouted, and turned to pick up the phone, the flag draping to the floor, held in place by a solitary drawing pin.

George tapped the icon of the secure Invisible Ink messaging app and read the message he knew would be from Abu Issa.

'Are you ready my brother?'

'I am ready brother,' George typed in reply.

'Midday. Bayswater Road. Peace be upon you. I will be with you all the way.'

Abu Issa kept typing. 'One more thing,' followed by more typing. 'No video.'

'No video,' replied George and closed the app.

Abu Issa sat back, hoping George was telling the truth, but knowing he wasn't. Issa had found George two years earlier in an internet chat room sympathetic to the Nigerian militant organisation Boko Haram. He was classic fundamentalist fodder. Sixteen, impressionable, and angry with everything and everyone, with no idea why.

Like many young men around the world, George was poorly educated, unemployed, and looking for something to believe in, something to belong to. A cause. A purpose. He had access to a global community through the internet, which just made him feel all the more alone and disenfranchised. He had few prospects and even less hope.

Issa had spent the last two years grooming, coaching, at times fathering George. George's anger had been difficult to channel. A problem child, reflected Issa, thinking of the many charges he had brought to this final point in their lives. And like children, no matter how similar their DNA, they were all unique, all needing a different level of care. Issa thought fondly of them all.

George pinned the flag back on the wall, pushing so hard the pinhead created an imprint in his thumb. He turned on the video of a second mobile phone. He had gone through the message a thousand times in his head and now he didn't have time to do it or him justice.

But even if he couldn't leave the message to the world he wanted, he was going to leave a message. Fuck Abu Issa. This was his decision. His act. The world would know who George Oluwale was.

Wearing a black and white cotton Shemagh wrapped around his head in the Middle Eastern style, a camouflage T-shirt, and black cargo pants, George stared into the camera.

'You will know my name, but you do not know me or all those like me. We are lions of the Caliphate and we are among you infidels. You see us, but you do not see us. With the grace of Allah we will slaughter all the unbelieving Kafir. The Zionist Jews will perish and Palestine will be free. Africa will be free from your imperialist domination and we will bring down the weak, corrupt, white-loving governments that steal our wealth. The spark has been lit and we will bring the fires of Dabiq to your homes and burn the Crusader armies. Allah will come upon you from where you do not expect. Allahu Akbar. Allahu Akbar. ALLAHU AKBAR.'

George stopped the video and left the phone on the table. He took off the Shemagh, put on a black, hooded jacket, pocketed his other telephone, took one last look around, and walked out of the flat, turning right towards Streatham High Road.

Lucinda plucked her mobile phone from her bag and dialled a local number.

'Firas, tell me we got it.'

'It's downloading now. He has a basic encryption tool, but it didn't take me long to crack. We've already got Nasri's entire address book, and it looks like we will get all his text messages as well as the metadata from all the calls he has made.'

'Yes!' exclaimed Lucinda, looking skywards and closing her eyes for a second.

'Firas, get the numbers on cover as quickly as possible. Start with the most recent ones he has called.'

'Er, thank you for telling me my job, Spark,' replied Firas with a smile in his voice. 'I've been doing this a little longer than you. You're the rookie, remember?'

'I know, I know. I'm sorry.'

'What's the plan?' asked Firas.

'I'll come to the Embassy now, have a first run through the data with you, stay tonight, then fly back to London tomorrow,'

Lucinda replied. 'And I'm true to my word, Firas. I told you if this worked, I would buy you dinner, and buy you dinner I will. But you're the local, so you choose the place.'

Lucinda heard the beep of a new message in her inbox.

'Cool. See you soon, Spark,' said Firas and rang off.

Lucinda opened the text message. It read, 'Your mother deserting me again. Ten days in Geneva. At least I have the vegetables for company. Call her. Dad x.'

There were many advantages to Lucinda's mobile phone. It looked like an iPhone, it talked like an iPhone, but it was in fact a state of the art, bespoke model, custom-made by the Secret Intelligence Service's Directorate of Science and Technology in a laboratory buried deep in the bowels of the MI6 building on the banks of the River Thames.

One of the main features of the phone was that it could clone any digital media device within five feet. Even when it appeared to be switched off.

A second, no less important, feature was the programmable sim that allowed ten numbers to be active on the phone at once. The clash of personal and professional worlds on one phone was still a little weird to Lucinda, a feeling exacerbated by messages from her father.

Smiling to herself imagining her father deep in conversation with the tomato seedlings, a sixth sense made Lucinda turn around. She was being followed. And this time she did notice the barely concealed weapon under the thin, blue shirt.

Triacetone triperoxide – TATP – is a good news, bad news explosive. The good news is all the ingredients are readily available in high street shops. The bad news is the finished product is extremely volatile. The good news is TATP does not contain nitrates, making it difficult for some scanners to detect. The bad news is it is extremely volatile. The good news is it is relatively easy to initiate and does not require a detonator. That's because of the bad news.

Not for nothing is TATP known among bombmakers as the Mother of Satan.

Three stops. No change. The doors closed and the underground train pulled out of Kilburn Park station. Musa Ali Abubakr, wearing blue jeans, trainers, a baseball cap and black leather jacket zipped up to his neck, was sitting in the middle of the carriage. He closed his eyes, thought of Tariq, and smiled.

Lucinda kept a steady pace, the thin, blue shirt staying thirty yards behind her. She was calm. There was no need to panic. She would go to the hotel, collect her bag and grab a taxi to the Embassy. After a quick debrief, she would leave straight for the airport and catch an evening flight out. Firas could see to that.

Lucinda turned right into Avenue Habib Bourguiba and continued straight towards the hotel. She passed café after café, there must have been a thousand people within a fifty-metre radius, sitting in the sun drinking coffee, unaware of the unfolding mini-drama.

She contemplated entering the Cathedral of Saint Vincent de Paul, it had been on her list of sites to see, but she dismissed the idea as absurd. What would that gain her? Not sanctuary, certainly.

A klaxon blast diverted Lucinda from this thought and she narrowly avoided being run over by the city tram as she crossed the tracks into Avenue de France.

The Hotel Royal Victoria was fifty metres ahead. Her tail had closed the gap and was no more than fifteen metres behind her. Still no need to panic. It was broad daylight and Lucinda could see three armed police officers on the other side of the street.

Parked on the corner of Rue Mongi Slim in a direct line with the hotel was a black Audi A4. The driver was behind the wheel, but a second man was standing by the open, rear passenger door watching Lucinda as she approached.

There was no doubt in her mind. She was being shepherded to the car. Police or no police, she would never make it to the hotel. God knows where they planned to take her and what they wanted to do, but it presumably involved some pretty robust questioning. Something Lucinda was keen to avoid.

Taking no more than a second to consider her options, Lucinda crossed the road and walked through the Porte de France, one of the gates to the old city. She avoided the hotel to her right and turned left into the Medina.

At first, Lucinda thought she had made a big mistake. The narrow market streets were packed. A sea of humanity moved with its own glacial momentum. Porters blocked her path, meandering through the streets wheeling flatbed carts and upright, Sydney trolleys. It was impossible to force the pace.

Every good known to man was on sale. Clothes, shoes, fake designer bags, wallpaper, plastic flowers, children's toys, tinsel. Tinsel in April?

Market traders advertised their wares, shouting to be heard over each other. They competed with tinny microphones blaring out recorded sales pitches.

Mass movement and three-hundred-and-sixty-degree noise hemmed Lucinda in. A riot of smells added to the sensory invasion. Burning incense, herbs, spices.

Lucinda shuffled on, her feet stuttering. She looked back. At least her pursuers faced the same inexorable tide. And the crowds gave her some safety in numbers.

She needed a plan. Time to call Firas. She ducked into a corner store packed floor to ceiling with glass lights and wall clocks, all gold and silver.

'Firas, I'm being followed. Clear intent to pick me up. Hotel blown.'

'OK,' replied Firas, 'don't panic and remember your training.'

'I am not fucking panicking,' snapped Lucinda, 'I'm calling to tell you plan B. I'm going to lose these guys, then come to the Embassy as planned. I think I should fly out tonight.'

'Makes sense. I'll sort your flight. See you here when you can make it. Be careful, Spark,' said Firas and ended the call.

Lucinda put her phone back in her bag and her mind to the problem of losing her tail. She looked up and froze, taking a moment to register what she saw.

The thin, blue shirt was standing on the threshold of the store, staring at Lucinda. His pistol, which Lucinda recognised as a 9mm Croatian HS-9, was drawn and he was holding it by his side. The second man from the Audi was next to him, holding an AK-47.

Lucinda had no time to think. They raised their weapons. She threw herself to the floor behind what little cover she could find a split second before a hail of bullets strafed the store, shattering the glass lights and clocks in an explosion of noise.

Instinct honed by training enabled Lucinda to hit the floor just in time. Others were not so lucky. The storekeeper was cut to pieces by shards of flying glass. A little girl and her mother lay face down, pools of blood seeping round their already lifeless bodies.

Lucinda scrambled down the aisle on all fours, praying there was an exit at the back of the store. It was her only hope.

Her would-be assassins crunched over the glass, stepped over the mother and her little girl, and raised their weapons again.

George Oluwale walked out of Lancaster Gate tube station and turned left onto the Bayswater Road. He hated everything he saw.

The green grass and tall, imposing trees of Hyde Park were nothing more than symbols of imperial power. A fake garden in a fake city planted on the blood of martyrs. He hated the occupants of the flash cars that sped past him in a bubble of their own wealth. Bankers, lawyers, they knew nothing of this world. Nothing. But soon they would know.

George turned into Clarendon Place. The door of a white Transit van opened and a man in his early twenties got out. He held the door open as George climbed into the driver's seat. They didn't exchange glances and the man disappeared, absorbed by London's anonymity. George pulled the door shut and put the van into first gear.

Soon they would know.

There was an exit. Lucinda flung the door open, turned right and sprinted down a quiet side alley. She turned right again at the end, doubling back on herself. She was in the fish market area of the Medina and thankfully the street was not too packed. Lucinda kept running.

Her next decision was simple enough. Get out of the Medina, or go deeper into its heart.

Go deeper.

Left, right, left, right at pace was the only thought in Lucinda's head. She had to buy some time, put some distance between her and her attackers. There was no way she could lose them by blending in. The black trouser suit and white blouse had been perfect for playing the part of a legal counsel, but in the crowded alleyways of the old city she stuck out like a sore thumb. Her auburn hair, swept back and tied in a plait, not to mention the two-inch, business heels, didn't help either.

Deeper and darker. Into the heart of the Medina where the

maze of streets was enclosed by low, arched ceilings blocking out the sunlight.

No sign of her attackers.

Lucinda made a call.

'Hey, Spark, don't tell me…' Firas managed before Lucinda cut him off.

'Bastards tried to kill me. I'm OK, somewhere in the bloody Medina.'

'OK. Go to Safe House Blue. I'll be there in fifteen minutes. And for fuck's sake, make sure you lose them.'

Musa opened his eyes just as the train lurched into the tunnel between Maida Vale and Warwick Avenue. Images from his childhood and the journey to the UK flashed before him, spliced together and projected onto the walls of the tunnel, framed by the windows of the train, which carried him faster and faster into the darkness.

Natural light broke into the maze up ahead. A way out. Lucinda ran towards the light and found herself in the outer courtyard of the Zaytuna mosque. She was still in the middle of the Medina, but the mosque was at least a landmark from which she could get her bearings. If she turned left after the mosque and went as straight as possible, she should emerge on the west side of the Medina, the right side for Safe House Blue.

Lucinda looked back to check she was still in the clear, missed her footing and twisted her ankle in one of the drainage channels that ran down the middle of the cobbled alley, there to sluice away the rubbish at the end of a day's trading.

Fuck.

Storekeepers sat on stools outside their shops, smoking, chatting on their phones, ignoring Lucinda as she tried to walk off the pain.

Leather. The smell of polished leather. Handbags, belts, leather poufs. Saddles and bridles in two shops on the right and then light. Bright light. Daylight. Lucinda was out of the Medina.

George pulled away from the first set of traffic lights at Marble Arch. His phone rang. With his right hand on the wheel, George picked up the phone with his left and put it to his ear.

'Coming to Oxford Street now.'

'Paradise is yours. Allah is waiting for you,' encouraged Abu Issa.

'Allahu Akbar,' replied George.

Abu Issa hung up, kicked a stone into the River Euphrates and watched the ripples fan out and disappear before walking back through the date orchard to the air-conditioned comfort of his villa.

George dropped the phone onto the passenger seat and accelerated towards Oxford Street.

The tube train doors opened and Musa stepped onto the platform. He followed the signs indicating the main National Rail concourse at Paddington Station. Hordes of people pushed past him, bustling back and forth. Musa was in a different dimension, walking in a different world, his feet not touching the ground.

As he reached the middle of the crowded, enclosed tunnel, chosen for maximum destructive effect, Musa Ali Abubakr unfastened the zip of his leather jacket and initiated the chemical fuse.

He whispered 'Allahu Akbar' and closed his eyes a second before ten pounds of TATP exploded in a blinding flash. Nails and ball bearings packed in his vest were forced down the tunnel at a velocity of fifteen thousand feet per second, killing and maiming everyone in their path.

On Oxford Street, just outside Selfridges, George yanked the steering wheel left and mounted the pavement. The van jumped violently as George hit the accelerator and started to run down pedestrians indiscriminately.

The first few victims had no idea what had happened, smashed to death by the front of the van, their limbs snapped, their bodies crushed. As people began to realise what was happening, they froze in terror, easy victims for George as he swerved left and right. The van flew across the Duke Street intersection, running down a cyclist before mounting the pavement again. George fought to keep control of the Transit.

Workers on a break, shoppers, tourists were all now beginning to flee, their frozen terror turning to panic as they ran across the road, ran into shops, ran anywhere to try to avoid the madness.

At Stratford Place, the windscreen of the Transit shattered and George felt a sudden fire of pain in his left shoulder. He lost control of the van and ploughed into a lamp post, stopping dead a few yards short of the Disney store. George threw open the door.

'On the ground. Now!' screamed one of the two armed police officers.

Before George could pull the knife from the waistband of his trousers, two rounds from a Heckler and Koch MP5 tore through his heart.

The sign on the glass doors of the IT repair shop on Avenue De Bab Djedid said closed, but Lucinda walked straight in and locked the doors behind her. She went to the other side of the cashier's desk and pulled the curtain back. Firas was already opening the door to the back office.

'Quick. Inside now,' said Firas, his voice calm but commanding. Firas drew the curtain, locked and bolted the door, and looked at the CCTV monitor.

'No sign of them, but let's not fuck about,' said Firas. 'You're on the 19.20 to Paris. Orly. Here's a clean passport.'

'Thanks,' said Lucinda. 'I still can't figure out…'

'Fuck. They're here.'

Lucinda looked at the monitor and saw the two familiar faces.

'We don't have long,' said Firas, kicking a rug and revealing a metal trap door. 'Go along the tunnel till the first set of metal steps. They come out in the back of a tea shop in Rue El-Hadjamine; it's two streets from here. You'll be seen, but we're beyond that now. There's a white Kia parked outside. Keys in the exhaust. Baseball cap and sunglasses in the glove compartment. You can abandon the car at the airport. Go.'

'You've got to come with me, Firas.'

'I've got shit to destroy here. Don't worry, I won't be far behind you and I can look after myself.'

As Lucinda swung her legs through the trap door, she heard the glass of the outside doors shatter. She looked back at Firas, who had put two incendiary grenades on the table and drawn a 9mm Glock 19 pistol from the holster on his hip.

'Go,' ordered Firas.

'Good luck,' replied Lucinda. 'Don't stay long.'

Forty-five seconds later, Lucinda was in the back of the tea shop. She neither saw nor cared if anybody noticed her. She walked out onto the street, fished the keys from the exhaust, started the car, and drove off.

She couldn't tell if she heard or felt the explosion first. Involuntarily, she ducked down in her seat and hit the brake pedal hard. In the rear-view mirror, she saw a ball of flame and a thick, black, mushroom cloud of smoke. Lucinda prayed Firas had got out in time, but something in the pit of her stomach mocked her prayer.

Across Central London time stood still. The sound of panic and first responder vehicles filled the air.

Without knowing it and without knowing each other, Musa Ali Abubakr and George Oluwale had conducted the most successful, high-casualty, coordinated suicide attack on the streets of Britain since July 7, 2005.

CHAPTER FOUR

Headquarters

By the time Lucinda walked along Millbank her Segafredo double espresso from Gianni's on Horseferry Road was no longer hot. She took a seat on the low, concrete wall by the Vauxhall Bridge Road bus stop and drank the tepid coffee. She needed a moment to herself before entering the lion's den.

It was 7.30 am and the first proper spring day of the year was making itself felt, at odds with the mood of the capital. On any other day, London would have embraced the bright, clear sky and light breeze which made the leaves on the trees rustle in unison. A day that finally consigned winter to memory. But today, less than twenty-four hours after the attacks, London was struggling, and not yet ready, to return to normal. The streets were filled with emergency services. The wailing and screaming of sirens split the air. There was an urgency and edginess to the heartbeat of the city.

Lucinda stared at the bronze sculpture in one of those little bits of green that made the capital so special. An abstract bronze by Henry Moore. She always saw human bones, a hip joint, balls and sockets protruding yet fused together. But there was also an elephant, sometimes a whale, and, strangest of all, this most earthly, organic of abstracts had an industrial quality. It was one of her favourite pieces.

Her focus shifted beyond the sculpture, across the Thames, to the headquarters of the Secret Intelligence Service, SIS. Hauled back to reality, she stood up, dumped the empty paper cup in a bin, climbed the flight of steps, and turned left onto Vauxhall Bridge.

The ebb tide revealed the muddy banks of the Thames, a breakfast table for the seagulls. Like many of London's bridges, the traffic lanes had been divided, a metal barrier separating the motor vehicle from the bicycle lane, a counter-terrorist more than a safety measure. At the end of the bridge to her right, the gull-wing rooves of the St George Wharf apartment complex dominated the blue skyline.

To Lucinda's left, the office. About as secret and now about as iconic as the Lubyanka, the old Moscow headquarters of the KGB, the MI6 building had attracted numerous nicknames and descriptions over the years. To some, particularly its earliest inhabitants dragged unwillingly from their previous headquarters in Century House, it was Ceausescu Towers, to others a Mayan temple. To Lucinda, the honey-coloured granite made the building more reminiscent of an ancient Mesopotamian temple, a Sumerian or Assyrian ziggurat. The green, triple-glazed windows, tempested against electronic attack from hostile intelligence services, complemented the temple-like design.

Lucinda entered via the riverside pedestrian gate and took the lift to the fourth floor. The open-plan office, home to the Counter-Terrorism Department, was already over half full. Lucinda nodded good morning to several colleagues, one or two of whom she noted were keen to avoid eye contact, and sat down at her desk.

She didn't have time to open her computer before the door of the glass-walled corner office opened and Cristine Laird appeared.

29

'Spark. My office now,' barked Laird, turning back to her desk and leaving the door open.

Steeling herself for the confrontation, Lucinda closed the door of the office and took a seat on the opposite side of the desk from her boss.

'What the hell were you thinking?'

Before Lucinda could get a word out, Laird held up her hand and continued, 'I don't want to hear it, Spark. I have a dead agent, a safe house destroyed, the Tunisian government asking all sorts of questions. Not to mention one very pissed off Karim Ahmet accusing me of abusing his generosity and putting him in a difficult position. You, Spark, have put me in a difficult position, and I am the one who has to clean up your mess, and all this on the same day as one of the worst attacks in our history. Do you have any idea how incompetent this makes the Department look?'

How incompetent it makes you look, thought Lucinda.

Cristine Laird was a difficult woman at the best of times. Diminutive in stature at five feet three, she compensated for her lack of physical presence by being a bully. She had a Margaret Thatcher outside the doors of Downing Street look, all power suits and steely eyes. Her brunette bouffant hairstyle hadn't changed in living memory. It was known by her colleagues as one of the few certainties in the intelligence world. Horn-rimmed spectacles held round her neck by a beaded, metal chain and the daily pussy-bow blouse completed the prime ministerial, headmistress image.

Laird was ambitious. There was no question in her mind she should be the next head of the Service. She managed up, ensuring throughout her career those above her always valued her work, even if that meant treading on the careers of equals and those below her.

Supremely bright, Cristine Laird was, as far as her staff could tell, the most unpopular Controller of Counter-Terrorism in the Department's history.

'The Chief is apoplectic with rage,' continued Laird. 'I had to spend an hour calming him down last night. Forty-one dead so far and several hundred wounded, by two men we have never heard of. Not a sign of them on the Watch List. And then your fiasco in Tunis. The only saving grace is that the Chief is in with the Prime Minister and will be in and out of emergency COBR meetings all day.' Laird clipped the "R" of COBR with a tight roll, denying space for the "A" erroneously added by some wag of a journalist way back in the mists of time. 'He will be too busy to see the likes of you, Spark. What the hell were you thinking?'

'Ma'am…' Spark tried to intervene, but Laird was far from finished.

'You were given a simple task, but for some reason best known to yourself you decide to go beyond your – by me – specifically instructed remit–'

The phone on Laird's desk rang and she snatched the receiver.

'Yes,' she growled.

'Ah, yes, Daisy, of course,' Laird continued in a more conciliatory tone and hung up.

'Turns out the Chief is in his office and he wants to see you. Put your pads on, Spark, is my advice.'

Four minutes later, Laird and Lucinda entered the outer office of the Chief of the Secret Intelligence Service, more commonly known by the letter "C".

'Morning Cristine, morning Lucinda. You can go straight in.'

Daisy Thorn, the Chief's personal assistant, was dressed in an immaculate white blouse and black pencil skirt with black, slingback shoes. Her shoulder-length, jet black hair was swept back and tied up in a bun, not a strand out of place. In her early forties, she was on her third Chief, the current incumbent her favourite.

'Thank you,' replied Laird, without looking at Daisy once.

Daisy raised her eyebrows conspiratorially at Lucinda as the two exchanged glances.

31

'Ah, Cristine, Spark, come on in.'

Sir Philip Colville-Browne was sitting behind an enormous, early nineteenth-century, mahogany empire desk. The red leather surface was gilt-edged with a crossband pattern. A thick, leather blotter was in the middle of the desk. On the left, there was an in-tray and, on the right, an Emeralite banker's lamp with green shade and brass stand. Nestled underneath the lamp were two telephones, the only concession to twentieth century technology. The desktop computer and suite of monitors were relegated to a second desk off to the right.

Sir Philip's predecessor had favoured a minimalist look, all sharp glass edges and chrome, a modern look for a modern service, but within a week of moving in Sir Philip had got rid of all that "modern muck" and returned the office to a style that to his mind spoke of stability and strength. Behind him, four paintings commemorated the Duke of Marlborough's victories at the battles of Blenheim, Ramillies, Oudenarde and Malplaquet in the War of the Spanish Succession.

'An interesting twenty-four hours for all of us, especially you, Spark,' Sir Philip began. 'I think we can agree that time is of the essence, so why don't you tell Cristine and Spark what you have just told me, Ramesh.'

Sitting at a round meeting table by the window was Sir Philip's chief of staff, Ramesh Varma. In front of him was a pile of papers, each one stamped Top Secret Umbra Strap Three, one of the highest classifications of British Intelligence.

Glancing at his mobile phone, Varma said, 'The fatality count now stands at forty-three, with over two hundred wounded, at least fifty of whom are in critical condition.'

Varma was self-assured, matter of fact, and a brilliant chief of staff. A third generation British Indian, he was often, only half-jokingly, referred to as the poster boy for SIS diversity. A first-class degree in Philosophy, Politics and Economics from Balliol

College, Oxford, however, suggested the Service still had some way to go to overcome its elitist image.

Within a month of becoming Chief, Sir Philip had plucked Varma from the Central and Eastern Europe Department to replace the outgoing chief of staff, Bill Tanner. It was a meteoric and well-deserved rise.

'We have very little information on either Musa Ali Abubakr or George Oluwale,' continued Varma. 'They are clean skins, not on any Watch List, either ours or the Europeans'. Suffice to say neither we nor the Security Service are in the PM's good books today.'

'Let's refrain from comment for the time being, shall we?' interrupted Sir Philip.

'Sir,' replied Varma, picking up one of the classified papers. 'So, what do we know? Abubakr was twenty-two and Sudanese. Oluwale, eighteen and Nigerian. Both have been in the UK for about a year, but there is no immediate evidence to suggest they knew each other. However, the attacks were clearly coordinated so they were not lone wolves.'

'Which begs the obvious question,' interjected Sir Philip.

'And there we have our first proper lead, the mobile phone recovered from the van Oluwale was driving. It is not unusual for a terrorist to be in contact with someone right up to the moment before an attack. A cyber coach. Someone whose role is to groom and guide the attacker, often over a considerable period of time. And in this case, that "someone" is a man called Abu Issa. No doubt not his real name, and no doubt his phone is now dead. We have the techs downstairs seeing what they can extract from Oluwale's mobile. First indications are that Abu Issa is in Syria, but nothing more specific than that at the moment. The fact of Abu Issa points to the Islamic State, who have already claimed responsibility in several of their traditional media outlets,' concluded Varma.

'What else?' asked Sir Philip.

'The Metropolitan Police are working on a list of all known associates of Abubakr and Oluwale. I should get that shortly.'

'Working assumption on how Abubakr and Oluwale got here?' Sir Philip swept his hair back from his forehead. It was one of his perpetual mannerisms.

'Given their respective nationalities, working assumption is that they came by boat from North Africa, probably via Italy.'

'Which brings us to you and Tunis, Spark,' said Sir Philip, looking at Lucinda and indicating with a gesture for Varma to continue.

'It looks like we have some good intel from Hakim Nasri's phone. Good job, Spark.'

Laird flashed a look at Varma, unable to hide her contempt.

Varma returned the briefest of smiles and continued. 'In the ten minutes after Spark's meeting, Nasri made three calls and sent five texts, all to numbers in his contacts list. The bad news is we didn't manage to get the numbers on cover in that time, but the good news is we have the meta data and the guys downstairs think they should be able to retrieve the actual voice and texts. Given time.'

'If they don't know already, impress upon the boys downstairs how imperative it is we get that data. And in terms of time, I'd like it ten minutes ago. What do we have?'

'The texts may not be that interesting. All five were to North African numbers, two in Tunis, two in Libya, and one in Algiers. We'll see, but I suspect they were to members of the local smuggling network and then probably one text to give orders on what to do with Spark. The calls are more interesting. One, as you would expect, was to Karim Ahmet. The second was to a Syrian number, and the third, most intriguingly, was to an Iranian-registered mobile phone.'

'So,' said Sir Philip, leaning forward, putting his elbows on the desk and clasping his hands together. 'Ramesh, get that list of known associates from the Met and give it to Cristine to run through our databases. Regular liaison with MI5 and chase the boys downstairs. Cristine, everything you have on African smugglers and links to the Middle East. There is nothing to prove a connection between Nasri and this Abu Issa, but the circumstance is strong. And I want to know who this Iranian is.'

'Yes, Chief,' replied Laird. 'I agree with the possible connection between Nasri and Abu Issa. I want to prioritise Issa's location and once we have that, I have a number of assets in place in both Syria and Iraq who may be able to shed some light. One more thing, sir, do you want to bring the Americans on board?'

'Much as I would prefer to keep this in-house,' replied Sir Philip, 'we need all the help we can get. I will talk to Langley, you make sure the numbers get to the NSA. Oh, and GCHQ of course.'

'Very good, sir.'

'Right, I've got another COBR meeting in an hour and I want to be able to give the PM something. Let's get cracking.'

Varma collected the papers on the table and stood up.

'Thank you, Ramesh, thank you, Cristine,' said Sir Philip, issuing the gentle instruction for them to leave.

'Spark, you can stay behind.'

Lucinda had been standing close to the door, careful not to utter a word. Now that they were alone, Sir Philip beckoned her to one of the two chairs on the other side of his desk.

'How are you, Lucinda?' asked Sir Philip, sweeping his errant hair back into place.

Lucinda knew not to be disarmed by the Chief using her first name. Sir Philip was a political appointee, not a career Service man. Previously Permanent Secretary at the Home Office, where he had earned his knighthood, the Prime Minister had handpicked Sir Philip to head MI6. The rumour mill had gone into overdrive at an outside appointment. The new Chief was here to cut staff numbers, rein the Service in, politicise it and make it a willing servant of the PM.

In his first week, he did something no other Chief had done before. He walked round every single office and introduced himself to every single employee. Not only did he know everyone's name before meeting them, he also knew what they did, and the value of their work. When Sir Philip looked into your eyes, you felt valued, trusted. He was instantly popular.

'I'm angry, sir,' replied Spark. 'And I blame myself. I was sure I had lost my tail, but they found the safehouse. Maybe I didn't lose them. Maybe Firas…'

'Maybe,' interrupted Sir Philip. 'But it is entirely possible they knew the location of the safehouse beforehand. Every town and city in the Middle East and North Africa is little more than a big village. Everybody knows everybody else's business. Be angry, but don't blame yourself.'

'Thank you, sir.'

'You have the potential to be an excellent intelligence officer, Spark. And listen to me carefully, Firas will not be the only colleague who is killed during your career. The world is uncertain enough, but now you work for the Service, you live on shifting sands. All your certainties are gone. And the trick, though easy to appreciate, is difficult to achieve. Believe in what you are doing and know why you are doing it.'

'I do, sir, and I know exactly why.'

'I know you do, and there are few better reasons than yours. Right, I need to have a little think about where to send you next. Don't worry,' said Sir Philip, holding up a hand, 'you will still be in the thick of it. That, Spark, is all for now.'

And with that, Lucinda got up and left C's office.

CHAPTER FIVE

Mentor

Lucinda emerged from a twenty-minute shower, her skin tingling from the heat of the water. She half-dried herself and wrapped a towel around her body so that it hung from above her breasts to halfway down her thighs. She took a second smaller towel and in one fluid movement wrapped her hair in a giant white turban.

Barefoot, she walked downstairs and headed for the drinks cabinet. She took out a cut-glass, Bohemian crystal tumbler and went to the kitchen where she found a fresh lime and cut off the end. Lucinda stroked the inside of the end slice around the rim of the tumbler. She got three ice cubes from the freezer and dropped them in the glass, savouring the sound as they clinked and crashed into place. She cut another slice of lime and dropped it on top of the ice. Returning to the drinks cabinet, Lucinda reached for the bottle and poured two fingers of Plymouth Original gin. Pausing, she added another dash of gin before mixing in the tonic, holding the can high and pouring the tonic directly onto the ice, listening to the cubes crack and split.

Lucinda sipped the gin and went back upstairs. She placed the tumbler on the bedside table and looked in the full-length mirror.

She removed the smaller towel and rubbed her hair, first with the towel and then with her hands. Her still wet hair cascaded down her back between her shoulder blades, the natural wave already visible.

Lucinda removed the second towel, letting it fall to the floor. She stared at her naked reflection. She was twenty-eight years old. She was young, fit and strong. Her shoulders were perfectly balanced, with distinct trapezius and well-defined deltoid muscles. Toned biceps and triceps further emphasised Lucinda's upper-body strength.

Her stomach was flat, and when she looked in the mirror Lucinda could see the taut strength of her abdominal muscles, but she was pleased there was no sign of a six-pack.

Lucinda was not vain, but she loved her bottom, tight and firm, as it deserved to be with all the training. She thought perhaps she could work a little more on her thigh and calf muscles, but that was to be critical.

Lucinda's strength was framed in elegance. A slender neck and tapered waist defined her feminine power. It was her body and it did exactly what she commanded it to do.

She tilted her head sideways and felt the tiny indentation in her right temple, a reminder of that terrible day six years ago. She lifted her right breast and ran her index finger along the one-inch scar, noticeable only to the most assiduous of lovers.

She took another sip of gin and lay on the bed.

Lucinda brought her left leg towards her, letting it rest at a forty-five-degree angle. With her right hand she stroked her flat stomach. She directed her fingers over the neat line of pubic hair and continued downwards, one gentle movement over her labia until she reached her perineum. She pressed with her middle finger, the softest of pressure, and brought the finger back up, parting her lips at the base of her pussy.

Lucinda closed her eyes as she felt the warmth and wet. She

entered herself, just for a second, before she guided her finger up to her clitoris. Lucinda groaned, turning her head into the pillow, making tiny little circles with the tip of her finger.

The phone rang.

Jolted back to reality, she looked at the phone display, took a large sip of gin, and sat up on the edge of the bed.

'Hi Mum.'

'Hello, darling. How are you? Why haven't you called? It's just dreadful. Those poor people. How many dead now?' launched her mother, not drawing breath.

'I know, sorry. I think the count is fifty, maybe more. I left messages with Dad and Louisa, but we're kinda busy at the office, as you can imagine,' Lucinda replied. 'And anyway, Dad told me you're in Geneva. Big meeting?' said Lucinda, shifting the subject.

'Nothing so exciting, and it seems totally irrelevant now. They asked me to stand in on a conference panel. Last minute cancellation, so as usual they drag me over here. Are you in London?'

'Yes,' Lucinda answered. 'I've been in the office all week and I guess we'll be tied to our desks for a while now.'

The lies started small, they always did, and Lucinda, like everyone else, told herself they were necessary to protect her family, just as much as they were necessary to protect her country. The Service now allowed its personnel to tell immediate family members they worked for MI6, but what exactly they did remained a secret. A secret that over the years became clothed in layer upon layer of obfuscation and deceit.

'And I'm out tonight. Dinner with Miles.'

'Ah, the mysterious Mr. Miles. Are we ever going to meet him?'

'How many times have I told you it's not like that?' replied Lucinda. 'And I'm late, and Miles is never late. I have to go. I will call you in a day or so, I promise. Hope it all goes well in Geneva. I love you.'

'Love you too, darling. Bye. And don't forget–' Lucinda never heard the final words as she put her phone back on the bedside table.

Thirty-five minutes later Lucinda was standing outside Randall & Aubin's in Brewer Street, Soho, number two in the queue for a table. The spring day had given way to a cool night. There was a hint of drizzle in the air, but the wait was unlikely to be long.

No sooner had Lucinda looked at her phone to confirm Miles was late, than she saw him ambling across Wardour Street.

Lucinda smiled as she always did when she saw Miles Cavendish, one of the most comforting presences in her life. Miles had been one of Cristine Laird's predecessors as the Service's Controller of Counter-Terrorism. He had been at the helm when the Twin Towers were attacked on 9/11. Originally a Russia expert, he had cut his teeth when the Iron Curtain hung between East and West. He had long since retired from government, but still got called back to consult on various issues, including cybercrime, on which he had become a world expert. He also helped mentor new recruits to the Service. Apart from her father and Sir Philip, Miles Cavendish was the only man who made Lucinda feel stupid.

He was wearing a light-beige trench coat with matching light-beige weather-proof trilby. He looked every unconscious inch the tinker, tailor Cold War spy. Miles was a big man, just shy of two hundred and eighty pounds. His arms didn't quite walk in sync with his legs, and his feet pointed outwards as he walked, which made for the rolling gait of a mildly inebriated penguin.

'I'm late,' Miles apologised. 'Blame some idiot from the Home Office who likes the sound of his own voice too much.'

Doffing his hat, he kissed Lucinda on the cheeks and said, 'Great to see you.'

'And you, Miles,' replied Lucinda, giving him a hug. 'Back in service?'

'Yes, for my sins, and I'll tell you all once we get a table. Looks like we're next.'

A Brazilian waitress in a tight-fitting white shirt, and black trousers, showed them to a corner table at the back of the restaurant. She had a forest of tattoos, a sprawling, indecipherable motif on her chest, half-hidden by her shirt, and a series of symbols and words on both forearms. A rose sprouted from her collar onto her neck. Her dark hair was tied up to control the curls and to emphasise the large, hoop earrings. She was beautiful, a fact not lost on Miles.

'Not your type, Miles,' joked Lucinda as they settled in.

'I think it's the other way around. Only the men will be interested in me here. Oh, the curse of being heterosexual,' sighed Miles. 'We need a drink.'

Lucinda never drank gin when she was out. Gin and tonic had become the trendy cocktail of choice over the last few years, with hundreds of artisan gins flooding the market. All botanicals and herbs, served in ridiculous goblets with far too much ice, juniper berries and God knows what else floating around only to get stuck in your teeth. To Lucinda, gin wasn't a cocktail, it was a drink. They agreed on a bottle of the 2015 Domaine Vacheron Sancerre.

'How are the oysters?' asked Miles, flirting with the waitress, whose name he had discovered was Luna.

'I would have the French Rock, I tried them at lunch. They taste like sex,' replied Luna with a wink.

'In that case, I'll have three of the French, and three native. Not sure my heart can stand that much sex.' Lucinda ordered the moules marinière, followed by the sea bass, Miles the lemon sole.

'Will you stop now and talk to me?' chided Lucinda. 'What are you doing at work?'

'Security Service called me up. You know MI5, they want to make sure, and let me get this right, they "are optimally organised to counter the current threat picture". I mean for Christ's sake, we went through all this after 9/11. It staggers me, our inability to learn lessons. Mind you, keeps me in a job and on a very good day rate at that.'

'Who would like to taste the wine?' asked Luna, placing a wine cooler on the table and opening the bottle.

'He will,' replied Lucinda.

Miles made a circular motion with the glass, the wine rising and falling at the side, creating a whirlpool. He poked his nose into the glass but didn't taste the wine.

'Excellent, thank you,' Miles smiled at Luna. 'You know,' he said, turning to Lucinda, 'you should try the Sancerre Rouge from Vacheron. It's fantastic. Now, tell me about Tunis.'

'It was a disaster,' said Lucinda as Luna brought their starters and wished them bon appetit. 'I mean the meeting with Nasri went well, we got the intel, and it's good intel, but then...' Lucinda's voice tailed off.

'I know, and you blame yourself for Firas. That's natural. But, as I am sure Sir Philip told you, there's no way of knowing if they followed you or, as is more likely, if they knew the location of the safe house already.'

'Either way, Firas is dead, Miles.'

'Yes, and heartless though it may sound, he knew the risks. And so do you, Lucinda. The North African angle, and wherever it leads, is critical. Well over half a million migrants have crossed from Libya to Italy in the last few years, and that's even with the Italian government trying to stem the numbers. And there are another million or so poor souls in miserable conditions in camps across North Africa waiting to make the journey. A million. This is not going to stop any time soon.'

Miles paused to concentrate on his oysters, starting with the French Rock, adding a squeeze of lemon and some of the accompanying mignonette sauce.

'With luck the data from Hakim Nasri's phone will lead

42

somewhere. Then there's the cyber coach, Abu Issa. Delicious, thank you,' said Miles as Luna removed the plates from the table.

'And apart from advising the Security Service on how to organise themselves, what else are you working on?'

'An artless change of subject, but because I know you are interested, I will tell you. I'm writing something on Russia's closed cities. You know the sort of thing, Arzamas-16, Petropavlovsk-Kamchatskiy-25, and all the other equally romantically named cities.'

Wishing them bon appetit again, Luna delivered the main courses with a smile and turned her attention to a rowdy party of five that was settling down at one of the tables in the middle of the restaurant.

'They were established by Stalin as scientific and weapons research centres. One-industry towns. Well, two actually, and that's one of the fascinating elements.'

'How so?' asked Lucinda, infected as ever by Miles's enthusiasm.

'People were force-migrated to towns created out of nothing in the middle of nowhere. Factories churned out a military product, but also a civilian product. My personal favourite is the Nizhniy Tagil tank factory, which, in addition to building tanks, as you would suspect from the name, also made fridges.'

'Armoured, I presume.'

'Don't joke. When I lived in Moscow, I had a fridge from Nizhniy Tagil. The compressor motor fired up every twenty minutes twenty-four hours a day. Sounded like the 70th Motor Rifle Brigade traipsing through my flat on their way to invade Afghanistan.

'Anyway, no one's really done the subject justice, certainly not in English. What the towns were then, what they have become since the fall of the Soviet Union. Fascinating human stories set against a backdrop of economic decline. Of course, research is proving to be a little tricky, but I think I may have an in, an old opposite number of mine.'

'Something tells me you'll manage to get the access, Miles.'

'Let's hope so. Bugger, is that the time? I'm afraid, my dear, I have to go back to Thames House, where the Security Service awaits.'

'Right now? There's still a little left in the bottle,' said Lucinda, reaching for the Sancerre.

'Wrap-up of the day. Got to go. Mind you, I probably won't get a word in edgeways if that idiot from the Home Office is still there.' Miles stood up to go. 'Follow the numbers in Nasri's phone. At least one of them will take you to the right place. If you need help, call.'

'I will, and it was great to see you. No, I've got the bill, it's my turn, Miles.'

'Thank you. And I'm sorry to run out on you,' said Miles, bending down to kiss Lucinda, 'but the two boys at the table behind us seem keen to keep you company. They've been ogling you the whole time.'

Eyes in the back of his head, thought Lucinda as she watched Miles leave the restaurant and amble off in the direction of Westminster. Lucinda finished her glass of wine and asked for the bill.

'Well, I wouldn't leave you stranded like that. Bloody rude. Come and join us. I'm David and this is Ronan. And you are?'

'I am tired. And I am going home. But thank you,' said Lucinda.

'C'mon, one drink,' said the one called Ronan. 'It looks like you need cheering up.'

'Goodnight,' replied Lucinda. 'Enjoy your dinner.'

'You could be missing the night of your life, with me obviously, not him,' said one of the two, Lucinda not registering or caring which.

Funny, she thought to herself as she left the restaurant and felt the soft drizzle of rain against her cheeks, how men always thought they could chat and charm her into bed. As if they were in charge. Just boys being boys, but if she was going to sleep with someone, it would be her decision. It always was.

A Tupperware sky lay low over London, a milky-grey lid sealing the city, locking out yesterday's promise of spring. Lucinda closed the front door of the house on Maunsel Street and turned right towards Vincent Square. She hunched up against the morning chill and tightened the belt of her navy-blue raincoat.

For such a short walk, there were numerous ways to get to the office. If Lucinda turned left out of the house, she could go all the way down Horseferry Road and then along Millbank. If she was running late and didn't have time for breakfast, this route had the advantage of passing by Gianni's where Lucinda could grab a coffee. Alternatively, she could cut Horseferry Road short and take any number of smaller streets behind the Tate Britain museum.

Today, she turned right so she could walk past the green of the Vincent Square cricket pitches. The only disadvantage of this route was at some point she had to walk down Vauxhall Bridge Road, one of Central London's uglier arteries.

As she crossed Vauxhall Bridge, her phone beeped.

'Come straight to my office when you decide to come in.'

It was 7.10 am. Lucinda shook her head.

Six minutes later, Lucinda walked into Cristine Laird's office without knocking.

'Good morning, ma'am.'

Laird looked up from the mound of papers covering her desk, her horn-rimmed spectacles perched on the end of her nose. She

45

had tired eyes. 'Morning, Spark. Sit down.' The tone was at least civil.

Lucinda, still wearing her coat, took a seat.

'If it was up to me, Spark,' Laird sighed, sitting back in her chair, 'I would banish you to the basement and the archive department for the rest of your miserable career. But it seems the Chief has a soft spot for you. God knows why. What do you know about Iraqi Kurdistan?'

'Semi-autonomous region in Northern Iraq. Capital Erbil, often referred to as Hawler,' replied Lucinda, ignoring Laird's vote of confidence. 'Claims to have the oldest, continuously inhabited citadel in the world, something like 6,000 years. Saddam Hussein gassed the town of Halabja during his Anfal campaign. Late eighties, eighty-eight I think, part of the Iran-Iraq war. Thousands killed. Made semi-autonomous after Gulf War One with the help of the Coalition and the imposition of no-fly zones. A strong partner in the fight against ISIS. Held an independence referendum in 2017 which led to a significant deterioration in relations with Baghdad. One interesting fact is the Kurds, and I mean all the Kurds not just the Iraqi ones, but the Turkish, Iranian and Syrian, are the largest ethnic group in the world not to have their own state.'

'Quite,' replied Laird, impressed against her better judgement. 'The last few years have been a disaster for us in the Middle East. Russia and Iran have outwitted the US geopolitically. We have next to no influence in Syria, which Moscow and Tehran now have under wraps. Iraq is run by the Shia establishment, which if it doesn't quite do Tehran's bidding, then it's near as dammit.'

Laird took off her glasses. They dangled round her neck at the end of their beaded, metal chain. 'The Iraqi Kurds are one of our few remaining friends in the region. And we – and when I say we, I mean the Yanks – need our military bases there. With the independence referendum, the Kurds went rather off-piste.

46

Can't blame them, but it wasn't what we wanted and it soured our relationship a bit. But they are a key ally and we don't want to lose them. The good news is we have leverage. They are surrounded by enemies. If there is one issue that unites Turkey, Iraq, Syria and Iran, it's their hatred of the Kurds and their fear of an independent Kurdistan. We need to be right in the middle of it, propping the Kurds up, limiting Tehran and Ankara's footprint, and keeping the bloody Russians out.'

'We don't have anyone in Erbil, do we?'

'No, we don't. Thanks to these perpetual cuts, we are pretty thin on the ground. The Station in Baghdad is run by Alan Hollister, but he's pretty much a one-man band. We do have a listening station up there though. Hollister will read you in.

'Your job, Spark, is to go to Erbil and gather intelligence. And listen to me,' Laird emphasised each of her words, 'this is a classic intelligence officer mission. As an IO, you will have a specific set of intelligence requirements against which to collect. You will stay within the bounds of those IRs. Is that understood?'

'Yes, ma'am, understood,' replied Lucinda, managing to keep the irritation out of her voice.

'Good. Details on your desk, but this, in a nutshell, is the brief. One, current political situation in Kurdistan, in particular the relationship between the major parties. Who's in, who's out, who are the people we need to get to? This is a base requirement to support the Ambassador in Baghdad and Consul General in Erbil. Two, Iranian influence in the region. There are numerous Shia militias in the area that have been part of the fight against ISIS. Despite being brought under the banner of the Iraqi Armed Forces, they do pretty much what they want when they want and report to Tehran not Baghdad. Half of them are commanded by individuals officially classified as terrorists. This is a more dynamic requirement. We believe the Iranian number Nasri called is related to the Shia militia. Seems odd, I know, and we need to run that to ground. Three, ISIS renaissance. The Caliphate may be gone, but ISIS is far from over and they are taking advantage of the current security vacuum to launch a comeback. Clear?'

'Clear,' answered Lucinda. 'I assume I won't be declared as an SIS officer attached to the Embassy?'

'No, you will not.'

'What's my cover, ma'am?'

'We will keep your Legend,' replied Laird, raising her eyebrows as she corrected Lucinda, 'simple and close to the truth. Junior official seconded from the Foreign Office to the Department for International Development. You will use your own name. Anyone looking you up will find a few references to you on the FCO and DfID websites, and if they look hard enough they might even find a paper you wrote for a conference on "Leveraging Synergies in the Humanitarian Community". It'll be buried deep on the DfID site by this afternoon. There's a copy on your desk, along with the IRs and a raft of other homework. Read and inwardly digest.'

'Yes, ma'am,' said Lucinda, getting up from the chair.

'One more thing, Spark,' continued Laird. 'All intelligence is to be sent by cable for my eyes only. My Eyes Only.'

Lucinda opened the door of Laird's office.

'And remember,' said Laird, shuffling some of the papers on her desk, 'this is good old-fashioned intelligence work. No gadgets, no toys.'

'Yes, ma'am.'

'Go and redeem yourself, Spark. This may be your last chance.'

CHAPTER SIX

The Rejectionists

Adnan's donkey lifted his nearside hind leg and swished his tail. A dozen geese shook the sleep from their heads and stretched their wings, greeting each other with soft honks as they prepared for their dawn patrol.

The village of Kanda Salam was an outpost in the badlands of Diyala, one of Iraq's northern provinces, where the territories were disputed and the ethno-sectarian fault lines had butted against each other for thousands of years, ingraining conflict and breeding extremism.

There was one road in, a seven-kilometre stretch of single lane tarmac that came from the east and stopped dead in the middle of the village. You didn't pass through Kanda Salam. There was nowhere to go.

A dry riverbed skirted the north end of the village before turning west and heading for a tributary of the Diyala River that in turn wound its way south-west to feed Lake Hamrin.

On all four sides, north, south, east and west, the sandstone ridges of the Hamrin mountain range encircled the village, protecting and suffocating it at the same time.

Eighteen single-storey buildings huddled together, random dots in a circle. The ugliness of the bare concrete breeze blocks complemented the unforgiving desert scrub. Only two of the buildings were plastered and painted. On the outer rim of the circle to the west, the house in two shades of pastel green belonged to the Mukhtar, the village elder. The mosque at the northern end of the village was two-tone brown.

A spider's web of cables bound the village together, connecting the houses to a yellow 100KVA generator, which was grateful for the night's rest.

A patchwork of fields, no more than twenty acres, kept the village alive. Just. The overworked soil struggled to provide sufficient nutrients for the stunted wheat and was dreading the melon season which followed hard on the heels of the harvest. A Ford 6000 tractor, flanked by a seed drill and cultivator, guarded the crops.

First light claimed the remains of the night sky, clearing a path for the sun. The inhabitants of Kanda Salam were asleep. They didn't see what Adnan's donkey saw.

A single column of twenty-five vehicles sped along the road towards the village. The lead vehicle was a Humvee with a .50 calibre, turret-mounted, Browning M2 heavy machine gun.

Five hundred metres out, ten vehicles peeled off from the middle of the column. Five right. Five left.

The first five – two Humvees and three Ford F-350 pickups, mounted with Soviet-designed 7.62mm belt-fed PKM machine guns – bore right to cut off the north and west exits from the village, making sure no one could slip across the river bed and disappear into the mountains.

The second five – also two Humvees and three F-350s – tore left through the wheat to cut off the escape routes south and west.

At three hundred metres, nine more vehicles broke rank from the main column, pulling out left and right to form a single line of attack. At two hundred metres, the commanding officer radioed from the lead vehicle ordering his part of the convoy to stop, which it did, a hundred and fifty metres out.

As the dust settled, Kanda Salam woke to find itself surrounded by twenty vehicles and a hundred men of the 42nd Brigade of Asaib al-Haq, one of the most lethal and battle-hardened Shia militias operating in Iraq.

Vehicles twenty-one to twenty-five, brand new black GMC Suburbans with blacked-out windows and two flags on either side of their bonnets, had stopped on the tarmac road five hundred metres out.

The commanding officer instructed his men to be patient and vigilant.

The turret gunners scanned their arc of fire.

Adnan's donkey swished his tail.

A single high-velocity round slammed into the side of the Commander's Humvee, but did not pierce the armour plating. The turret gunner ducked down an inch and opened fire with his Browning on the house to the left of the village entrance. The .50 calibre tracer rounds on fully-automatic ripped through the cancerous breeze blocks. Spent shell casings from the Browning danced through the air, glinting in the sunlight, before settling in a pile on the desert floor.

After five bursts, the gunner ceased fire. Puffs of concrete dust hung in the air and for a second an echo of fire bounced back from the mountains.

Silence.

From behind the house on the left, two pickup trucks emerged. The commanding officer couldn't tell what make and model they were because both trucks had metal plates welded to the front and sides encasing them in an armoured shell. Despite their extra weight, the trucks accelerated hard and headed straight towards the main Asaib al-Haq column.

The commanding officer didn't need to assess the situation. He knew both vehicles would be packed with explosives and that their drivers had one intention in mind. He barked orders over the radio.

The Humvee to his left was armed with a Mk19 40mm grenade launcher and the gunner fired two bursts of three rounds. One of the pickups exploded in a ball of flame. At the same time, to the right of the commander's vehicle, a soldier got out of one of the F-350s and aimed an RPG-7 shoulder-launched rocket-propelled grenade at the second pickup. The round sailed three feet past and exploded behind the pickup.

As the soldier grabbed another warhead, the Humvee gunner turned his grenade launcher on the suicide vehicle which was now less than eighty metres away. Rounds exploded left and right, but the vehicle kept coming.

Reloaded, the soldier fired the RPG again and this time his aim was true. The pickup stopped dead in its tracks, the front armour plate blown apart. The Humvee gunner put two grenades into the vehicle to be sure.

The commanding officer ordered his men to debus, proceed with caution, and clear the village house by house. He warned them to watch out for booby-trap improvised explosive devices, which could be hidden anywhere, buried under a tyre, connected to a door handle or stuffed inside the carcass of a dog. It was a standard MO of the Islamic State.

The men of 42nd Brigade entered from all four sides, clearing the houses one by one, working towards the centre of the village. They kicked down door after door. Crying women held babies in their arms, children held each other, tears of fear streaking down their dirty faces, and men lay prostrate, arms stretched out, fingers splayed, repeating they were not Islamic State, they were innocent farmers.

Two hours and one short firefight later, the men of 42nd

Brigade met at the yellow generator, job done. The sun had long since cleared the horizon and the men cast long shadows in the direction of the Diyala River.

The commanding officer phoned through a sitrep to one of the black Suburbans. The vehicle commander in the front passenger seat of the Suburban turned round and addressed the man in the back seat. 'Village is clear, General. Six enemy dead, three captured. No casualties on our side.'

'Take everyone to the mosque.'

The five black Suburbans cruised towards the village at forty miles an hour. By the time they had got to the end of the tarmac in the middle of the village, turned right, driven up the compacted dirt track and pulled up outside the mosque, seventy-three villagers and three Islamic State captives were under armed guard in the mosque courtyard.

The commanding officer opened the rear passenger door of the third Suburban and Major General Ali Hussein Hashemi got out.

General Hashemi was wearing a dark green military uniform. The black epaulettes which adorned his shoulders had two eight-sided stars below golden crossed swords, a golden wreath, and the word "Allah" written in gold in the shape of a tulip.

On his left upper arm there was a circular black and gold insignia. In the centre of the insignia was a rifle held in a clenched fist. Above the rifle were written the Arabic words, "Prepare whatever force you can", verse sixty from the Surah Al Anfal, chapter eight of the Koran. The date at the bottom of the insignia read 1357, the equivalent of 1978 in the Gregorian calendar. The final bit of writing on the insignia was in Farsi and it read, "Islamic Revolutionary Guards".

Major General Ali Hussein Hashemi was the commanding general of the Quds Force, the external arm of the Islamic Revolutionary Guard Corps, the IRGC, responsible for the extraterritorial military, espionage and sabotage operations of the Islamic Republic of Iran.

General Hashemi had a full head of dark grey hair, parted on the right, a neatly kept grey beard and thick black eyebrows. He was a handsome man.

Hashemi walked into the mosque courtyard. On his left, the three ISIS captives were on their knees, hands tied behind their backs with plastic zip ties.

'Execute these men.' Hashemi singled out the executioner with a look.

The young private soldier selected for the task stood to attention and saluted. He drew his sidearm and walked behind the captives. Without hesitating, he put the barrel of his pistol against the head of the first captive and pulled the trigger. The front of the man's head exploded and he fell forward, still on his knees, slumped, in a grotesque position, propped up with what was left of his face.

The private moved behind the second terrorist and pulled the trigger. The lifeless body fell forward and rested on its side. The third terrorist managed to shout 'Allahu Akbar' before the private's 9mm bullet punctured his skull, tore through his brain and exploded out of the front of his head in a pink spray.

'Who killed those geese?' asked Hashemi, looking at two of the birds which were tied together by their necks with a piece of string and lying just inside the entrance to the courtyard.

'I did, General,' replied a sergeant.

'Then you must pay for them. Also,' continued Hashemi, addressing the Asaib commanding officer, 'we must compensate the villagers for the damage to their crops.' Hashemi looked up at the mountains to the north, and squinted as the sun reflected off the red sandstone ridges. 'It is a hard and noble struggle to make a living from this desolate land. We must pay the exact amount the wheat would fetch at market.'

The commanding officer nodded assent.

'Who is the Mukhtar?'

An elderly man stepped forward from the crowd of villagers, head bowed. 'I am, Your Excellency.'

'My rank is General.'

'Yes, General.'

'Your family?'

Nobody moved.

'Your family?' repeated Hashemi.

'I have three daughters,' replied the Mukhtar, indicating behind him with an outstretched arm and open palm. 'I have no sons.'

Hashemi beckoned the three girls, who shuffled to join their father. The eldest, no more than seventeen, was pregnant.

'General,' the Mukhtar pleaded, 'these men came out of the mountains three days ago. They told us they would stay for a week and they would kill us if we did not give them food and shelter.'

'Do you know who Abdullah ibn Wahb was?' asked Hashemi.

'No, General,' replied the Mukhtar, hesitant, his brow furrowed.

'They called him the Scarred One. He was a soldier in the army of the fourth Caliph, Imam Ali.'

Hashemi bowed his head for a second. 'Imam Ali was the rightful leader of all Muslims after the death of the Prophet Muhammad, Peace Be Upon Him. Although Ali devoted his life to the path of peace, he was forced into a civil war with his Syrian rival Muawiya. They met in the year 657 at the battle of Siffin, a town known today as Raqqa. After three days of battle, Ali was on the brink of victory when the treacherous Muawiya, who knew the battle was lost, ordered his cavalry to advance with pages of the Koran pinned on the tips of their lances. As they approached Ali's troops, they followed this blasphemous act with the cry, "Let the Book of God be the judge between us".

'Ali's own men forced him to negotiate despite his protestations this was a trick typical of Muawiya. They would not listen and Ali had no choice but to call a truce and negotiate. On the long march back to Kufa, these same men became dispirited and turned their anger on Ali, blaming him for the truce upon which they had insisted.

'The leader of the dissenters was the Scarred One, Abdullah ibn Wahb. He split from the party of Ali and left Kufa with three thousand men to establish a fundamentalist order. They called themselves the Khariji, the Rejectionists.'

'General,' began the Mukhtar, but Hashemi closed his eyes, silencing the old man.

'The Khariji, the betrayers of Ali, were the most evil of all people, worse even than Muawiya. One day, they rode into a village to buy supplies. There they met a farmer who happened to be the son of one of the Prophet's earliest companions. They subjected him to an inquisition. An inquisition the farmer knew would end in his death. The farmer was a noble man, he refused to yield, he refused to pledge allegiance to the Khariji, he refused to betray everything he believed in. The farmer looked Abdullah ibn Wahb in the eye and said, "Ali knows far more of God than you do".

'The Khariji punished the farmer. The punishment involved the first recorded beheading of one Muslim by another Muslim. You, Mukhtar, have given succour to these Rejectionists. We will visit on you the same punishment.'

General Hashemi gave a curt nod to the Asaib al-Haq commanding officer.

Two men pushed the Mukhtar to his knees. One of the men stood behind the Mukhtar, pulling his head back by his hair and holding a knife with a six-inch blade to his neck.

A third soldier grabbed the Mukhtar's pregnant daughter by the arms and threw her to the ground.

'Please,' begged the old man, 'spare my daughter.'

'Who is the father?' asked the General.

'He died fighting these men in the war.'

'Do not lie to me. These men,' said Hashemi, looking at the three bodies, 'have been here before. She is carrying the bastard child of the Khariji.'

Hashemi nodded, and one of the soldiers hauled the girl to her knees. He held her arms behind her back. The sergeant stepped in, pulled his sheath knife and plunged it into the girl's side under the last rib on her left side. She screamed in agony as the sergeant forced the knife down and across her swollen stomach, splitting her open. Blood poured onto the courtyard of the mosque as her screams echoed around the sunlit mountains.

With both hands, the sergeant ripped apart her flesh, reached into the pit of her stomach and pulled out her unborn child. He ran the baby through, still attached to the umbilical cord, pinning it to the ground of the mosque courtyard. The girl, her face drained white, looked at her baby, looked at her father, and died.

The Mukhtar, ravaged by shock, would see no more. The soldier holding the knife to the Mukhtar's neck cut deep from the left carotid artery across his throat, slicing open the jugular vein. The old man collapsed to the ground, bleeding out in under a minute.

General Hashemi turned to the Asaib commanding officer. 'Do not forget to pay for the wheat and the geese.'

'Where to, General?' asked the driver as Major General Ali Hussein Hashemi got into the back of his black Suburban.

'Halabja.'

CHAPTER SEVEN

Baghdad to Erbil

Turkish Airlines Flight 302 parked alongside gate five at Baghdad International Airport. Before the seatbelt signs had been turned off, over half the passengers were scrummaging at the front of the plane, breaking through the flimsy curtain into the business class section, whacking the old and frail with oversized suitcases and plastic bags full of duty-free liquor.

Lucinda Spark was in seat 21A, looking out of the window at the terminal building. She had no desire to join the melee. There was no hurry. Her security team would be waiting for her.

As the throng of passengers piling out of the plane reduced to a trickle, Lucinda took her case out of the overhead locker, put her laptop bag over her shoulder, and walked down the aisle to the exit. The temperature in the jetway must have been thirty-five degrees, a pre-heated rectangular oven getting hotter by the minute.

A brown and orange threadbare carpet led Lucinda to the visa booth, the first of two queues. No one had been able to tell her how much a six-month, multi-entry visa would cost – somewhere in the region of a couple of hundred dollars – but the advice was to make sure she had some small denomination bills. Lucinda handed over her invitation letter and waited ten minutes for the immigration official to read the single piece of paper and process her visa. It cost two hundred and eighty-two dollars.

After being stamped into Iraq, Lucinda went to collect her luggage. The rubber-belted carousel was motionless, the passengers desperate to be first out of the plane milling around, smoking cigarettes, adjusting to the slow reality of being back in Baghdad.

Thirty minutes later, Lucinda strolled into the arrivals hall and approached a sign with her name on it.

'Hi, that's me.'

'Good afternoon, ma'am. I'm Geordie and I'm your team leader for the day,' said a blonde-haired, six-feet-two-inch ape in a thick Newcastle accent. His khaki shirt was straining to contain his shoulder and arm muscles.

'Let me take your bag. The vehicle's just outside.'

The armoured Toyota Land Cruiser was a white 200 GXR with bull bars. It had seen better days. Geordie spread a map over the bonnet.

'This is the airport here, and we'll be travelling down the airport road, Route Irish, to the International Zone.' Geordie traced the route with his finger. He was wearing All Terrain Combat gloves. 'It's about twelve klicks and shouldn't take more than fifteen, twenty minutes. Used to be the most dangerous piece of tarmac in the world. But that was back in the day. Safe as houses now, ma'am. Reet, if you're ready, just put this body armour on, and we'll be off.'

Geordie helped Lucinda into the cumbersome jacket.

'Mind your head,' he said as he opened the rear door. Geordie shut Lucinda in and climbed into the front passenger seat.

'This is Gazza, my driver.'

'Ma'am,' said Gazza from behind wrap-around Oakley shades.

'Gazza's from Baghdad, so we're in good hands. Been with me

since '04, we've seen some things. Real name Abdullah, but he's a big fan of the Toon Army, ma'am, and he's got a big, goofy smile, like, ain't you, Gazza?'

Gazza beamed as they drove off.

'So, you're with DfID, ma'am?'

'Yes,' replied Lucinda. 'Just a short tour.'

'You'll find lots of trees to hug round here. No offence.'

Lucinda smiled and said nothing.

'Reet, ma'am,' said Geordie as the vehicle slowed. 'We're about to leave the secure airport perimeter and get on Irish. Here comes the safety announcement. We will be travelling in a two-vehicle packet. We're the Bravo vehicle, the Alpha vehicle is dead ahead. If there is an incident, do not break the seal and get down as low as you can. If we do need to debus and cross-deck you into the Alpha vehicle, follow my instructions. If both me and Gazza are killed or incapacitated, press this red button here. It activates the transponder alarm. We use VHF Motorola radios to communicate between vehicles. Push here to talk. Depress to listen. We both have SG 551 assault rifles and Glock 9mm pistols. Any questions, ma'am?'

'No,' replied Lucinda.

'Don't worry, it's a routine trip these days.'

Lucinda recognised the three-lane Route Irish highway, or at least an approximation of it, from the three or four movies she had seen about the war. *Route Irish* itself, *Green Zone*, *American Sniper*, *The Hurt Locker*.

Palm trees passed by on either side as Gazza took it easy, going a steady ninety kilometres an hour. A blue sedan flew past them.

'Fast mover on your six, Alpha, move left,' Geordie called over the radio.

'Used to be a butt-clenching ride this, ma'am. Rockets and mortars being lobbed over the T-WALLs left and right. And you see that mosque on the left? Snipers up there taking pot shots. Total lottery getting in and out of here. Can't tell you how many mates I lost over the years. But, like I say, Driving Miss Daisy now.'

The two-vehicle convoy swept up an overpass and bore left onto the Qadisiya Highway. Jersey barriers funnelled the traffic.

'Entering the International Zone, ma'am. All good. The checkpoint'll take us ten or so minutes, as long as they're not in a bad mood. This is the one part of the journey that still makes me a little nervy, ma'am.'

'Why's that?' asked Lucinda.

'Wrong place, wrong time, ma'am,' said Geordie. 'You see all those civilian vehicles and taxis in the left-hand lane? They go pretty much straight through, hardly a search at all. Private security details in this lane? Well, you'll see. They'll open all the doors, look in the back, put the dogs round. You tell me, who's more likely to be trying to bring explosives into the International Zone or blow themselves up at a checkpoint? A Western security team or a dude driving a taxi? Who knows what's in the boot of that car? Still, it's their country, I suppose. All in the name of progress.' Geordie paused. 'Don't mean to scare you, ma'am.'

'Don't worry,' replied Lucinda. 'Nobody's blowing me up today.'

As they drove out of the checkpoint, Lucinda saw the Baghdad Clock Tower on her left, the first of the capital's iconic landmarks. She saw the Crossed Swords built to commemorate the Iran-Iraq War. Two sets of giant forearms cast in bronze bursting out of the ground holding stainless steel swords that crossed at their tips forty metres off the ground. The arms and hands were modelled from plaster casts of Saddam Hussein. The helmets of dead Iranian soldiers littered the base of the memorial.

They passed the Monument to the Unknown Soldier, a sprawling, sweeping cenotaph. Its centrepiece was a concrete, cantilevered dome set at an angle, like an alien spacecraft left behind from a visit to the Babylonian empire millennia ago.

Seven minutes later, the team pulled up in front of the main building in the British Embassy compound. Standing by the entrance was a diminutive woman with a pinched face, plain hair, dressed in jeans and a T-shirt.

'Hello, I'm Alison Worth, head of the DfID mission.'

'Hi, Lucinda Spark. Nice to meet you.'

'Look, I'm sorry,' said Alison in a soft Edinburgh accent. 'This is most irregular. I had no warning you were coming. Nothing from head office at all. Typical. And I have a meeting. Put your stuff in your room and go get something to eat. We can talk later this afternoon.'

Alison Worth jumped into another vehicle and disappeared.

'Don't worry, ma'am,' said Geordie. 'Gazza will take your stuff to your room and I'll show you where the dining facility is. They'll still be serving lunch.'

Lucinda was hungry, and the food looked good. She sat down at an empty table with a tray of lentil soup, roast chicken and rice, and a Caesar salad.

'May I?' said a voice appearing from behind her left shoulder.

'Alan Hollister, Head of Station. Good trip in?'

'Fine, no dramas. Isn't it a little obvious you sitting down with me the moment I arrive? I'm supposed to be working for DfID.'

'Absolutely not. I have a carefully crafted image as a Casanova. The office lothario. Watch this.' Hollister laughed and put his hand on Lucinda's forearm.

'Check out your eleven o'clock.'

Sure enough, two women at a corner table were looking over, whispering to each other. Lucinda could hear their eyebrows rising from across the room.

'Your reputation precedes you,' said Hollister.

Lucinda sat back in her chair. 'Tunis, I suppose.'

'Bugger Tunis, I'm talking about Fort Monckton. The training exercise where they drop you in town and you have to go to a local boozer and extract the name, address and passport number from some unsuspecting individual.'

'Ah, that,' smiled Lucinda.

'Yes, that,' replied Hollister. 'One of the most original techniques in the history of the exercise. Not very PC, though. But that will have to wait, we don't have much time.'

'Why not?'

'Because you're on the five o'clock flight to Erbil. We need you up there as soon as possible.'

'What about Alison?'

'Don't worry about Alison. Totally ineffective. Chocolate teapot. And when she tells you she's off to a meeting, what she really means is she's off to polish off a couple bottles of Chardonnay with a fellow soak from the United Nations refugee agency, UNHCR. I'll deal with her. You want some coffee?'

'Yes, please.'

Hollister returned with two cups. Lucinda smelt the coffee and regretted her decision.

'I know, not great,' said Hollister. 'What's your brief?'

'Threefold. One, Kurdish politics; two, Iranian influence; three, ISIS renaissance.'

'Forget one and three.' Hollister took a sip of his coffee. 'I've got those covered. I'll send you something every now and again, and you can cable Laird with the information. Knowing her, she'll then send it back to me with some facetious remark about being surprised I didn't know this, or hadn't reported that. All part of the game. You, Spark, focus on the Iranian angle. There have been some developments while you were in the air.'

'What developments?' Lucinda pushed her coffee to one side, untouched.

'I'm going to leave those to Elliot to explain.' Hollister nodded, agreeing with himself.

'Elliot?' asked Lucinda.

'Elliot… well, Elliot is Elliot. He's the GCHQ officer up there running the listening station.'

'Out of the Consulate?'

'No, and I suggest you stay well away from the Consulate. They are based in the Rotana Hotel and travel everywhere in armoured cars. You need to be a lot more mobile and travel when and where you want. You will stay with Elliot and Dave.'

'Dave?'

'There are two guys based up there. Elliot from Q, and Dave Harding from the Metropolitan Police. He rotates with a Security Service officer. Their job is liaison with local police, keeping an eye on Kurds going back and forth to the UK.'

'And what and where is there?'

'Fair question. It's the British Reconstruction and Implementation Team. Yes, I know, BRIT. Fatuous obsession with acronyms. I've emailed you a map. Take a taxi from the airport to Two Sides Road in Ainkawa, that's the Christian part of town. Tell the driver to stop outside the Vinery, an alcohol shop, quite good by the way. Walk down the street opposite, sixth house on the right. They're expecting you.'

'Thank you, Alan. Anything else?'

'Yes. Here's an ID to get you on the American base. Every morning at oh-nine-hundred they have an unclassified briefing with the humanitarian community. You know the sort of thing. Update on the security situation, information sharing, deconflicting the battlespace. Humanitarians and the military make for uneasy bedfellows to say the least, but quite a few turn up. The UN are pretty good. World Food Programme, UNHCR, UNICEF. So are some of the more hardcore NGOs like Samaritan's Purse and New York Medics. Others wouldn't be seen dead talking to the US. Médicins Sans Frontières, to name but one. Anyway, the briefing will give you a good start to build up a network. And that is about that, Spark. Any questions?' Hollister drummed the table with his hands.

'All good,' said Spark. 'I'll check in with you once a day. SMS. I'll try to make it every night at nineteen-hundred, but if I'm late, don't worry.'

'I won't panic unless you go dark for forty-eight hours. Deal?'

'Deal,' said Lucinda, getting up from the table.

'Good luck.'

Lucinda walked back outside where Geordie was waiting, her luggage already loaded in the back of the wagon.

'Well, that was short and sweet, ma'am. Something we said?'

Just before seven o'clock in the evening, Lucinda told the Kurdish soldier in the guard hut outside the house in Ainkawa that she was here to see Elliot. While she waited, she texted Hollister.

'Come in, come in, come in.'

Elliot Jones was exactly how Lucinda had imagined. He had shoulder-length, lanky black hair, parted in the middle and pinned back behind his ears. His skin was pale with an oily sheen, a constellation of acne dancing across his forehead. He wore a faded black Jimi Hendrix Experience T-shirt, denim shorts with a key ring attached to a belt loop, and flip flops.

Lucinda followed Elliot into the house.

It stank.

The first smell to assault Lucinda's nose was two-day old pepperoni pizza. Then came fried egg submerged in water from the pan perched on top of a mountain of washing up. The stale bubbles from soft drinks hung in the air, mixing with mouldy bread and mature cheddar cheese.

'You should pay your cleaner more,' said Lucinda.

'We don't have a cleaner. This is a classified facility.'

'Exactly.'

'I want to show you something. Dave's down police headquarters, which is good because he's not cleared to see this.'

'See what?' asked Lucinda.

Elliot walked into the sitting room where there was a table littered with papers, all with classified markings. Most were kept in place by empty cans of Red Bull. Elliot fired up his laptop, pointed at a fifty-five-inch monitor mounted on the wall and said, 'That.'

Lucinda stared at an incomprehensible mess. Hundreds of names, lines, circles, icons, numbers, interconnected, linked together, with no beginning, no end.

'It looks like I2 Notebook,' said Lucinda.

'Well, it isn't. This is far more sophisticated. It's a bespoke, unique piece of proprietary, number recognition analysis software designed by me. The problem being the firm think it's proprietary to them, not me. I should have made millions out of this. Pisses me off, which is why I call it Incandescent Rage.'

Elliot scratched his head and finished a half-empty can of Red Bull. 'Anyway, anyway, anyway, that's not the point right now. What do you see?'

'You tell me, Elliot, what do I see?'

'OK, OK, it's too complex for you, I know, I know, you can't see the patterns. But if I apply some filters…' Elliot's fingers flew over the keyboard.

Four highlighted names jumped out of the monitor. On the left-hand side, Musa Ali Abubakr and George Oluwale. In the middle of the screen, Hakim Nasri, and below his name at the bottom, Abu Issa.

'Let's filter out Abubakr and all his associated calls and numbers.' The information in the top left disappeared and the screen reset.

'Now, Oluwale,' said Elliot, pulling his chair closer to the table. 'He was a talker. There's a mine of intel to be got from that guy's phone, but let's filter him out for now.'

Oluwale disappeared. Lucinda started to make sense of what was left, but it was still a smorgasbord.

'Now for Hakim Nasri. Let's kill all the North African contacts, that'll clear things up a lot.'

'Stop,' ordered Lucinda.

Hakim Nasri's number now appeared on the left side of the screen, with Abu Issa's number still beneath. There was no direct connection between the two. The middle and right-hand side of the screen were still riddled with names and numbers.

'What's that number?' asked Lucinda, pointing to the right of the screen.

'That,' replied Elliot, 'is the key. It is the Iranian-registered number Nasri called after your meeting. We have never had that number on cover, I don't know why because it's hot. I pulled the metadata for the last six months. That phone is most definitely mobile. Tehran, Baghdad, Damascus, Beirut. It has also taken calls from all those places.'

'The last six months. How long did that take you?' asked Lucinda.

'All night. The Red Bull helps. I ran all the associated numbers through one of my algorithms and came up with hundreds of calls to Syria. Seemed random, but I then checked how the data packets from Abu Issa's calls to Oluwale were sent and asked the software to match that against the Syrian numbers. I got six matches over two of the satellite hops. Now, it's not an exact science and there's a bit of forensic guesswork. Also, I can't geo-locate the originating signals anywhere near as precisely as I would like...'

'Elliot, get to the point.'

'OK, OK, OK, I followed the packets back and by my reckoning all the numbers originate within fifty kilometres of Deir ez-Zor, eastern Syria. You want my opinion?' asked Elliot, and continued without waiting for Lucinda to reply. 'Either those six numbers all belong to Abu Issa or they belong to someone he lives with.'

'Impressive, a connection between Hakim Nasri and Abu Issa,' said Lucinda, 'and you did all this from here in Erbil?'

'Mostly. Had a little help from my NSA friend Helen at Fort Meade, Maryland. Special relationship and all that. You want the coup de grace?'

Lucinda looked at Elliot from under her eyebrows.

'Listen to this.' Elliot opened another window on the laptop and hit enter. 'It's in Arabic, but you can read the subtitles.'

Lucinda listened to the Arabic voice.

'Just had a meeting with a British woman… Ann Edmunds… says she represents a British crime group that want to partner… something not right about it… what do you want me to do? OK.'

'Took us a while to retrieve the voice, it's a bit scratchy and we only got one side of the conversation, but I believe that's your name in lights.'

'Yeah, and I know what they suggested,' said Lucinda.

'Oh, and I forgot to tell you. The Iranian number,' Elliot tucked his loose hair behind his ears, maximised Incandescent Rage, and punched a couple of keys. 'It belongs to a Colonel Rahimi. He's a serving officer in the Quds Force of the Iranian Islamic Revolutionary Guard Corps.'

CHAPTER EIGHT

The Ahl al-Bayt

Nine men in military dress uniform sat to attention at a giant V-shaped table. There was no chatter. No small talk.

The table was carved from two pieces of live edged cypress, felled from the Yazd province of Iran. Each piece was over a thousand years old. They were dovetailed together so that the apex of the V was four feet wide.

The table was the centrepiece of a magnificent meeting room measuring twenty metres by ten metres. Three of the four walls were panelled in oak. The two longer sides had open fires with ornate marble mantlepieces. Above one of the fireplaces hung a picture depicting a brilliant white horse, head bowed yet defiant, arrows sticking out of its neck, withers and rump. Above the other, in a glass display case, hung a curved sword with a forked tip like a serpent's tongue.

Walnut parquet flooring was partially covered by a twelve by six, hand-woven, silk Persian rug. The table, which had nestled into the rug over time, faced down the room, the legs of the V spreading before floor to ceiling windows which looked out on the shores of Lake Darbandikhan, fifteen kilometres west of Halabja.

Twelve places were set at the table. Each place had a black and white circular table mat with individual names written in Arabic calligraphy. The head of the table was at the apex of the V. It was empty. So too was the first seat on the right. All the other seats were occupied by the nine men in military dress uniform, with the exception of the final seat on the left at the top of the V. That seat was always left empty.

The door opened and Major General Hashemi strode in, followed by his staff officer, Colonel Khorasani. All nine men stood to attention and saluted.

'Good morning, gentlemen,' said Hashemi, returning the salute. 'Please, be seated.'

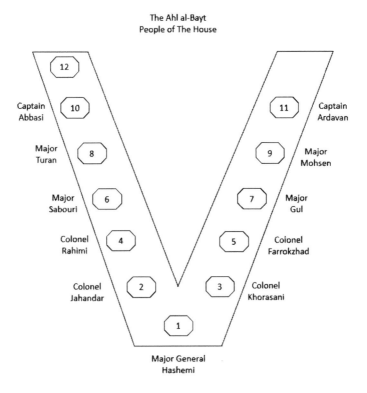

The Ahl al-Bayt
People of The House

Hashemi sat bolt upright, his hands clasped together resting on the table. 'Gentlemen,' he began, 'fourteen hundred years ago, two Muslim armies faced each other on the flat, interminable plains of Basra. Our Father, Imam Ali, known by the Prophet as Assad Allah, the Lion of God, had led his army from Medina to face the forces of Aisha and her brothers-in-law, Talha and Zubayr.

'As he did all his life, Imam Ali sought the path of peace. "Spare me the killing of Muslims," he begged of Allah. And even as the armies were camped on the field of battle, so close they could hear the opposing forces preparing the evening meal and breaking bread, he fought to avoid the shedding of Muslim blood with every breath in his noble body.

'For three days he negotiated with Talha and Zubayr, riding out again and again to meet them in the unforgiving heat of no-man's land, the necks of their horses intertwined as they searched for peace.

'But it was not to be. And the battle, one of the bloodiest of battles, the Battle of the Camel, marked the start of the Muslim civil war. Our community was torn apart and we entered the fitna, the terrible, soul-destroying split that has wrenched us apart for fourteen centuries.

'Remember, my friends, the words of Abu Musa,' continued Hashemi, glancing at the painting of the horse, 'a companion of the Prophet, who on the eve of the battle said, 'Fitna rips the community apart like an ulcer. The winds fan it, from the north and the south, from the east and the west. And it will be endless. It is blind and deaf, trampling its halter. It has come at you from a place where you were safe, and leaves the wise man as bewildered as the most inexperienced. He who sleeps through it is better off than he who is awake in it; he who is awake in it is better off than he who stands in it; he who stands in it is better off than he who rides into it.'

'The fitna has indeed been endless. But the time is approaching, gentlemen, when the community will return to being brothers, when we reunite in the first principles of Islam, when we embrace again the message taught us by the Prophet and his rightful descendants. The privilege has fallen on us, the Ahl al-Bayt, The People of the House, to lead this revolution.'

Hashemi paused, then looked at the officer second on his left and said, 'Colonel Rahimi, a review of our most recent operations, please.'

'General, the suicide operation in London was successful. Fifty-seven dead with responsibility claimed by the Islamic State.' Colonel Rahimi scratched the stubble on his cheek. 'We know the British authorities recovered a telephone from the van used by Oluwale in Oxford Street, and therefore they will have a name and number for Abu Issa. We don't believe this will lead to a compromise and we see no reason to stop using Issa. He is one of our most experienced assets with an excellent track record.'

'I concur,' said Hashemi, 'but let's put him out to pasture for a couple of weeks. Radio silence. And we need to develop a larger pool of cyber coaches. That is your action, Colonel. Progress report when next we convene.'

'Of course, General. We do have one concern, sir. Both operatives in the suicide bombing were smuggled to the UK through our north African network run by Hakim Nasri. As you know, General, Nasri was recently approached by a British woman claiming to be the lawyer of a well-known crime family. Nasri failed in his attempt to neutralise her. We have good reason to believe she is a British agent.'

'Do we have her real name?'

'No,' replied Rahimi, picking up a piece of paper. 'We do though have a passport photo taken from the hotel where she was staying in Tunis, but the quality is not good.' Rahimi passed a grainy black and white photocopy to the man on his right, who in turn passed it to Hashemi.

'Find and eliminate this girl, Colonel. And now let us turn our attention to Operation Hidayah.' General Hashemi gestured to the man sitting next to Colonel Khorasani.

He was a Rottweiler with paws so enormous he couldn't straighten his fingers. A flat forehead and large protuberance of skin at the back of his neck were incestuous evidence that both his mother and grandmother had been married off to their first cousins.

Colonel Farrokzhad had made his way up the ranks of the Quds Force not by guile but by brawn. From those early days at the academy where he had fought and scrapped his way through basic training, Colonel Farrokzhad had always been prepared to do whatever it took. No matter how hard, no matter how brutal.

Some in the room secretly considered it an error to select Farrokzhad to lead the practical planning for Operation Hidayah. He was not known for his subtlety, and his intellectual touch could not be described as deft. But of all the men in the room, General Hashemi knew that Farrokzhad would be the last one standing, defending the general to the dying breath in his body. His loyalty was unswerving. And besides, Hashemi's dependable staff officer, Colonel Khorasani, was with Farrokzhad every step of the way.

'Operation Hidayah progress is satisfactory, General sir,' said Farrokzhad in his quiet baritone. 'The bomb factory in Spain is operational and will have produced five hundred kilograms of explosive materiel in advance of D-Day. The suicide teams across the UK have been selected and training is underway. We have not yet sourced the automatic weapons for the attack in London, but I should have news on that soon. That is all, General.'

General Hashemi congratulated Colonel Farrokzhad on his progress, and for a split second the tiniest of smiles creased the colonel's muzzle as he basked in the approval of his master. A pat on the head for retrieving a dead bird.

Looking beyond Farrokzhad to the men sitting third and fourth on the right, General Hashemi said, 'Major Gul, Major Mohsen, today we will not discuss the operations of our Shia militias in Iraq, nor their progress against the Islamic State in Syria. Nor will we touch upon our tactical relationship with Russia on the ground. Have you completed your written reports?'

'Yes, General,' replied Major Gul, speaking for himself and Major Mohsen.

'You will submit them to those assembled here at the conclusion of our meeting.'

'Now,' said Hashemi, turning to his left, 'Major Sabouri, I look forward to your update. Please, proceed.'

Major Sabouri pointed a remote control in the direction of the windows and a white screen descended from the ceiling, edging out the morning light and turning the oak panels darker still. The major stood up and walked to the screen. He patted his stomach, conscious, as he had been for the last six months, that if he didn't do something about it now his slight paunch would soon be beyond redemption.

'Gentlemen,' began Sabouri, the red light from his laser pointer darting across the screen, 'The Road to Damascus.'

The screen was filled with a map of the Middle East. The right side of the map was bounded by Tehran, the left by Cyprus. Southern Turkey covered the top, and Israel and Jordan were visible on the bottom. Across the map, emanating from Tehran, was a path marked with a thick black line.

It was the Shia road, the grand plan to give Iran permanent, unfettered access to the Mediterranean. A tactical road that would allow Tehran to take and hold ground in Iraq and Syria. An operational road that would serve as a supply route supporting Iranian troops and their proxy forces across the region. A strategic road, more than that a strategic vision, that would enable Tehran to control the heart of the Middle East and not just confront the Saudis and the Americans but conquer them.

It was also a road that furthered the secretive ambitions of the Ahl al-Bayt, this cabal of Quds Force officers led by Major General Ali Hussein Hashemi.

Section One of the road went from Tehran to the Iran-Iraq border at Khanaqin. From Khanaqin, Section Two turned south west to the town of Baquba, seventy kilometres north of Baghdad. Section Three headed north, along the old Route One all the way to Tal Afar to the west of Mosul. From Tal Afar, Section Four of the road crossed the border into Syria and passed through the towns of Mayadin and Deir ez-Zor. Section Five drove a path to Damascus, and from Damascus the final section of the road, Section Six, went via Homs to Latakia on the coast of the Mediterranean. A spur on this section led straight to Beirut.

Major Sabouri drove the route with his pointer. 'General, Sections One to Three are existing roads, although some upgrades have been needed in places to make it all two-lane highway. These sections are complete and secure, and we have near total freedom of movement. There are some Daesh pockets of resistance in Khanaqin and Baquba, but we have a heavy militia presence.'

Sabouri used the derogatory Arabic language acronym for the Islamic State, Daesh.

'Section Four from Tal Afar into Syria has been more problematic. We have pushed Daesh out of all the main towns and villages along the route to the border, but our construction teams remain susceptible to attacks from Daesh fighters who have reverted to a more traditional guerilla warfare insurgency.

'The route across the border is a new road and has not been completed. Daesh still has a significant presence in that region, and there are multiple sleeper cells in the area around Deir ez-Zor.' Major Sabouri drove his laser up the Euphrates River and drew circles around the town in eastern Syria.

'We have no choice but to go this way as the Americans, despite media reporting to the contrary, and the Turks, have too strong a presence in northern Syria. I estimate this will delay completion of the road by a year, General.'

Sabouri patted his stomach. 'The good news is we now have complete control of the terrain from Palmyra to Damascus, and Section Six to the Mediterranean is complete.'

'This is excellent news,' replied General Hashemi. 'See to it we deploy additional militia to protect construction teams, and,' said Hashemi, turning to Colonel Khorasani, 'send a Quds brigade to Deir ez-Zor. We need to rid that area of Daesh in the next six months. Captains Abbasi and Ardavan,' Hashemi addressed the two youngest men of the group sitting at either end of the table, 'you will embed yourselves with this brigade and report back. Understood?'

'Yes, General,' the captains replied in unison.

'Good. Moving on and to conclude, the financial report please, Colonel Jahandar.' Hashemi turned to the officer immediately on his left, who passed copies of a bound document to his fellow officers.

General Hashemi opened the document. The first page was a contents page with eight headings.

1. Executive Summary
2. People Trafficking
3. Black Market Oil Sales
4. Narcotics
5. IRGC
6. Real Estate
7. Ancillary Activities
8. Non-Bookable

Ahl al-Bayt net operating profit for the first quarter of the year was $417,868,752, a nine percent decrease on the same period the previous year. General Hashemi underlined the figure.

One immediately obvious reason for the drop in profits was the people-smuggling figures, which were down seven percent. A total of 75,000 migrants had been smuggled into Europe via north Africa and Turkey, generating a combined gross income of $385,000,000. It was a high-margin business with the profit just under fifty percent at $187,000,000, but political backlashes in Europe had led to a drop in the numbers of people being smuggled. It would pick up, thought the General. The flow may be stemmed temporarily, but this was one-way traffic with unstoppable momentum.

Black market sales from oil smuggled out of the oil-rich Iraqi town of Kirkuk into Iran had performed better than expected due to a sharp spike in the price of oil. The operation was run by a faction of the Kurdish political party, the PUK, crooked to the core. They took all the risk and for that privilege they paid twenty-five percent to what they thought was the IRGC but was in fact General Hashemi's Ahl al-Bayt.

The oil was bought by Iran at a ten-dollar discount from the Brent Crude benchmark, and for the first quarter that figure had been averaged out at fifty-two dollars a barrel. Sixty thousand barrels trucked over the border per day translated into a Q1 profit of $70,200,000 for the Ahl al-Bayt.

General Hashemi was pleased to see the steady growth in narcotics revenue. This sector of the business concentrated on amphetamines, with Captagon by far the biggest seller. The chemical base for Captagon was fenethylline. It was manufactured by Hezbollah in their Lebanese drug laboratories and sold across the Middle East. The spur of the Shia Road from Damascus to Beirut was there for more than one reason.

Captagon was sold to fighters on all sides of the conflict in Syria. Government forces, Daesh and other Islamic groups, factions associated with the Free Syrian Army, the Syrian Democratic Forces, anyone who wanted to feel invincible in battle and lose all sense of compassion. No one side had the monopoly on that.

Hashemi smiled when he saw the Captagon numbers for Saudi Arabia. It was becoming an epidemic with over a quarter of a million habitual users.

In Syria the drug was cheap, retailing at three dollars, but the greedy, hooked Saudis would pay up to twenty dollars a pill. The accounts averaged out the price per pill at eight dollars, which on sales of 200,000 pills a day generated $1,600,000. After production and distribution costs, Captagon alone brought in $108,000,000 for the quarter.

One part of the business which still made General Hashemi a little uneasy was the money skimmed from the Quds Force share of the IRGC budget. By appropriating five percent of the allocated spending, Ahl al-Bayt added $50,000,000 to its coffers.

Real estate had taken a big hit in the first quarter and registered an operating loss of $16,500,000. General Hashemi circled the figure.

The ancillary activities – extortion, bribery, kidnap and ransom – brought in a useful $8,000,000.

General Hashemi allowed himself a smirk when he read the non-bookable section of the financial report. It was a one-off amount of $400,000,000, just shy of the Q1 total for all the rest of the group's activities combined.

If a party of Qatari royals were stupid enough to take their prized falcons on a hunting trip to the western deserts of Iraq in search of the much sought-after game bird the houbara bustard, then they got everything they deserved. Which in this case was over a year in captivity and a ransom of a billion dollars, a sizeable portion of which went to the Ahl al-Bayt for mediating their release.

General Hashemi closed the report.

'If I may anticipate your questions, General,' said Colonel Jahandar.

'By all means, Colonel.'

Colonel Jahandar perched a pair of grey, rectangular framed spectacles on the end of his nose and flicked through the financial report.

'First, the number of migrants crossing to Europe has dropped significantly in the past six to twelve months. We view this as temporary and expect an uptick by the end of the year. Secondly, our real estate portfolio went deep into the red this quarter because we had a significant capital outlay on new properties in Mayfair and Manhattan. This sector will return to profitability in Q2. We should also remember that our real estate is primarily a capital rather than an income generating asset, a hedge against our other activities. Finally, I would note that I have not booked the Qatari ransom money in our main accounts as this was a rather fortuitous one-off.'

'You anticipate my thoughts well, Colonel. A most satisfactory performance. Indeed,' continued General Hashemi, 'our plans progress well. Let it never be forgotten, my friends, that we are The People of The House and our cause is righteous. In the Hadith al-Kisa, the Hadith of the Cloak, Prophet Muhammad's daughter Fatima tells of a day when the Messenger of God entered her house. The Prophet, Peace Be Upon Him, felt a weakness in his body and asked Fatima to cover him with a Yemeni cloak. Soon after, Hasan, Fatima's elder son, entered the house and asked to sit with his grandfather under the cloak. Muhammad granted Hasan's request.

'After a while, Fatima's younger son, Hussein, entered the house and sought permission to join his brother under the cloak. Muhammad granted Hussein's request.

'Then Imam Ali entered the house and was greeted by his wife Fatima with the words, 'Peace be upon you, Oh father of

Hasan and Commander of the Faithful.' Ali approached the cloak and asked permission to enter. And the Prophet replied, 'Peace be upon you my brother, my legatee, my successor, and my standard bearer, you may enter.'

'Finally, Fatima asked permission to join her family under the cloak.'

General Hashemi closed his eyes, inhaled and said, 'Muhammad then raised his right hand and prayed, 'These are The People of My House, the Ahl al-Bayt. They are my confidants and my supporters. Their flesh is my flesh and their blood is my blood.'

'There can be no doubt, gentlemen,' continued Hashemi, 'that from the Hadith of the Cloak, The People of The House flow. The true family of the Prophet is enumerated in this Hadith, and Imam Ali is designated by Muhammad as his successor.'

General Hashemi stood up, followed by all the officers of the Ahl al-Bayt.

'I am from Ali and Ali is from me. We are today's guardians of the believers.'

CHAPTER NINE

We're the CIA

'You have a nice day now, ma'am.'

'Thank you,' replied Lucinda, walking through the access control point and into the US Military Air Base located next to Erbil International Airport.

Like most military bases, the US base in Erbil had started small with no grand ambitions. In the summer of 2014, operational necessity had taken precedence over strategic design. The Islamic State had launched a blitzkrieg series of attacks and large swathes of Iraq and Syria had fallen under its control. In January, they overran the western deserts of Iraq, sweeping through the province of Anbar and occupying the cities of Fallujah, Ramadi and Hit. Facing little to no resistance, they turned north, and by June 2014 they had captured the city of Mosul, proclaiming it the capital of the new Islamic Caliphate. The world, let alone the Middle East, had been taken completely by surprise.

After a short operational pause to catch their breath and consolidate their gains, ISIS attacked again, seizing large tracts of northern and central Iraq and advancing to within twenty kilometres of the Kurdish capital. The Iraqi Army melted away, deserting in huge numbers, four hundred thousand troops disappearing overnight, leaving all their equipment on the roadside. Hundreds of US-supplied M1 Abrams main battle tanks abandoned, thousands of Humvees and artillery pieces left idle, automatic weapons in their tens of thousands, even uniforms and boots littered the roads, leaving behind a giant, fully-armed *Marie Celeste* for the Islamic State to board.

The thin green line of Kurdish Peshmerga troops fared little better. They kept what little equipment they had, but they retreated in force, unable to stem the Islamic State tide.

The US scrambled fast air from Incirlik Air Base in Turkey and from naval assets in the Mediterranean to stop the ISIS advance in its tracks. Baghdad and Erbil could not be allowed to fall. Not after eight years of occupation. Not now, not ever.

And so began the war against ISIS. In Erbil, that meant a large hangar housing a handful of Apache attack and Black Hawk utility helicopters surrounded by office and accommodation tents for a small US military detachment.

By the time Lucinda walked onto the base, it had changed beyond all recognition. Temporary tents had become trailers which had become permanent buildings, spreading incrementally to occupy most of a square kilometre. The US had been joined by all the usual Coalition suspects. The British, the Dutch, the Italians, the Canadians and a host of others.

Lucinda went through the directions given her by the corporal at the access control point. Go straight down the main drag, that's Anderson. Turn left on Kozlowski, then second right into Dorsey Square. Cross the square and take Stoneman. Continue down Stoneman until you see the chapel on your left. The Joint Operations Command Center is right opposite. It has the letters J O C C written in large capital letters on the outside. Can't miss it.

Lucinda admired the US tradition of naming streets on their

bases after service personnel killed in action. It was one of many ways they honoured their dead.

As she walked down Anderson, Lucinda absorbed the hum of a military base in a conflict zone. There was nothing else quite like it. A couple hundred yards to her left, a pair of CH-47 Chinook helicopters were coming in to land, the distinctive, comforting whirr of their tandem rotors providing a soundtrack to the activity below.

Generators growled and puffed black smoke into the air. Everything was on the move. Uniformed soldiers were driving up and down the roads in olive green Alligators, the base utility vehicle of the US military. Others were walking to the gym wearing the ubiquitous grey T-shirt with the word ARMY printed across the chest, M4 assault rifles slung over their shoulders.

It wasn't pure testosterone, but it was power.

Lucinda turned into Dorsey Square, the main recreation area of the base. A basketball court in the middle was surrounded on three sides by shops. One entire side housed the PX, the US military postal exchange shopping outlet, where it was possible to buy just about anything. Tactical clothing, laptops, barbecues and picnic chairs were among the more conventional items on sale. Vacuum cleaners, irons and protein shakes also filled the isles. As did liquorice cigars, biltong, and Islamic prayer mats embroidered with US military insignia. Not exactly a nod to cultural sensitivity, more a gimmicky souvenir to take home.

Food and drink dominated the rest of Dorsey Square. Popeye's Chicken, Papa John's Pizza, Cinnabon, Green Beans coffee shop.

No one gave Lucinda a second glance. She was part of the military machine. She was wearing a black polo top, dark blue jeans and desert boots. Her access badge was attached to a lanyard round her neck. No make-up, no jewellery, hair held in a ponytail with a dark green scrunchie.

She was tempted to try a Green Beans espresso and drink it in the seating area on the fourth side of the square, but there wasn't time. Instead, she walked down Stoneman as far as the chapel and found the JOCC. The corporal was right. You couldn't miss it.

Lucinda flashed her badge and entered a building with two sets of concrete walls three feet thick. The inside of the building must have been a hundred metres by sixty, the size of a football pitch. A five-metre-wide corridor led down the middle of the first half of the building with offices off to the sides, plywood constructions with laminated sheets of A4 on the doors announcing the occupants and purpose of each office.

The second half of the building was an open-plan operations room. On the left, a vast suite of monitors filled the entire wall with interactive maps and live-feed drone footage. On the right, a bank of desks seating a hubbub of at least a hundred operators.

The final door on the right before the operations room was the meeting room. Lucinda entered.

She walked straight to a table at the back of the room, heading for the coffee and donut station.

'Interesting aroma,' said a voice joining her at the table.

'Yes,' Lucinda smiled. 'You Americans seem to think this black filtered muck stewed for hours passes for coffee.'

'I wasn't talking about the coffee, sweetheart. I can smell British Intelligence a mile away.'

Lucinda looked up. 'I guess it takes a spook to smell a spook.'

'Ha! Name's D'Souza. Jake D'Souza. Resident Langley spook. And unless we get hitched, babe, you ain't never gonna know if that's my real name.'

'Lucinda Spark, and that is my real name, whether we get hitched or not. So, what have we got here?'

Jake D'Souza was six feet tall. He had light brown hair with streaks of blonde, courtesy of a long tour in the Middle East. His hair was short, but long enough to be swept back off his forehead. Deep blue eyes trapped Lucinda in the corner of the room. She put him in his mid-thirties. He had a wispy goatee beard, which he stroked when he said, 'Nada. Let's get through this crock and then I'll take you where the real action is.'

They took a seat at a horseshoe table. Three American NCOs occupied the top of the table although two spaces were left in the middle. Sitting on the same side as Lucinda and Jake were two women, dressed like them in civilian clothes. Opposite them was an Iraqi Army captain, a Kurdish Peshmerga major and sandwiched between them a third man in civilian dress. He looked uncomfortable in the presence of military uniforms.

Colonel Sanchez walked into the room, commanding the space in an instant. 'At ease,' she said to no one in particular.

Jake tipped his chair on its back legs and leant over to Lucinda.

'Wow, we are honored,' he said. 'See that tub of shit with the Colonel? He is the Deputy Minister of the Kurdish Ministry for Refugees and Internally Displaced Persons. They love a snappy title.'

Whoever he was, the colonel made him look bad. Colonel Sanchez's uniform was immaculate, her military bearing and cropped hair screamed no-nonsense professionalism. Despite her command, the NCOs had jumped to attention and saluted.

Mind you, thought Lucinda, *the Kurdish deputy minister would look bad next to Jabba the Hutt.*

'He's the kind of guy,' said Jake, 'that could get into your room even when the door's closed. A primordial slime that would ooze under the gap at the bottom and metamorphose back into the human shape you see before you. Very rarely comes to these things, must have something else to do on base.'

'What's his role?'

Jake didn't have time to answer as Sanchez called the meeting to order.

Jake was right, as was Hollister, up to a point. The meeting was of no discernible benefit to anyone. One of the NCOs gave a brief security update, but the main point of discussion was access for the humanitarian community. It was one of the most challenging issues facing the UN and non-governmental organisations in any conflict environment.

Aid, whether food, water, shelter, medicine, always needed to be delivered quickly, but when military forces occupied the same space that meant getting permission. And in the Middle East, permission meant a stack of letters, signed, counter-signed, dated and stamped. A time-consuming process at the best of times. Even worse when signatory authority was vested in a few, senior individuals. Delegation was not a strong point in the region.

The deputy minister, Lucinda learnt, was the access gate-keeper, but all he wanted to do was rant and rail about the disrespect and inefficiency of the aid community.

'What did I tell you?' said Jake as they walked out of the JOCC an hour and fifteen pointless minutes later.

'Who is that guy?'

'Akram Rasul. Fat, corrupt, and a bag collector for the minister, but you can't get access to the camps without his say-so. He's come a long way. Worked at Stockholm airport before he came back to Kurdistan. Rumor has it he was the guy who brought your lost luggage to the hotel. Anyway, enough of him, we got more important things to do.'

'Like what?' asked Lucinda.

'A little something I'm running. It's classified NOFORN, US personnel only. But what the hell, come along for the ride. Just don't open your Limey mouth. Think you can do that?'

Spark and D'Souza headed towards the landing zone. The two CH-47s had long since cleared the LZ and were parked up in a bay surrounded by T-WALLs with another six Chinooks for company. Additional bays housed an assortment of Apaches and Black Hawks. Lucinda noted two Osprey V-22s, the tiltrotor vertical takeoff and landing aircraft.

'I like the connection between Hakim Nasri and Abu Issa, by the way. Good work. I've been trying to get the Agency to focus more on the Iranian angle for some time, but I've been barking up a lone tree.'

'How do you know…'

'We're the CIA. We know things about pigeons, Lilly.'

'Excuse me?'

'Spend any time with me and you'll figure it out, girl. You're a bright spark. C'mon, let's hustle.'

D'Souza led Lucinda into a desert-brown Alaska XP military shelter. A tent. Rapidly deployable, with a portable generator, the Alaska XP was used by the US military the world over.

'Nice of you to join us, D'Souza.'

Lieutenant Colonel Bosman was perched on a white plastic table. Sitting at another plastic table on the other side of the twelve-feet wide tent was Master Sergeant O'Neill, all six-four of him, complete with thick red beard that covered half his face. His Heckler & Koch 416 carbine rested on the table.

'And who's this?' asked Bosman.

'Paige Turner, over from Langley on a short visit.'

Bosman raised his eyebrows.

'Paige, this is Lieutenant Colonel Bosman, Delta Force squadron commander. And this is Delta assault team leader Master Sergeant O'Neill.' D'Souza pulled out a chair for Lucinda and took a seat himself.

'So, how'd it go?' he asked.

'Complete bust. Nothing there.' O'Neill flipped open the lid of a laptop and gave a commentary to the pictures on the screen.

'Building was empty. Three mattresses on the floor and ash from a fire in the middle of the room. Only other sign of life was goat shit. Given how isolated the building is, I would say local ISIS teams use it as an overnight stop, maybe when on the move or maybe just to get out of the caves and sleep under a real roof once in a while. Nothing to recover from the site. No papers, no documents, no nothing.' O'Neill shut the laptop.

'Sorry fellas,' said D'Souza. 'Can't win 'em all.'

'All part of the game, D'Souza. I suggest you have a word with your source, though. Nice to meet you, Miss Turner,' said Bosman as he and O'Neill got up and left.

'Paige Turner, really?' Lucinda smiled at D'Souza.

'Hey, spur of the moment deal. I like it. Kinda catchy.'

'Oh, please.'

'You wanna a ride? I've gotta go into town and squeeze the dude who gave me this heap of shit information.'

Lucinda was tired. It had been a long first day. She was sitting with a cold beer in an Armenian restaurant just off Two Sides Road in Ainkawa. She ordered the manti, a wonton dough stuffed with spiced lamb meat, baked in the oven for half an hour and served with tomato sauce and garlic yoghurt.

After dinner she stopped at the Vinery alcohol shop and took a bottle of Calvet Chablis out of the chiller. It was far from her favourite French wine and the bottle set her back twenty-five bucks, but it would do.

Back at the house, Lucinda could hear music coming from Elliot's room, but there was still no sign of the elusive Dave. She grabbed a glass and a corkscrew and went upstairs.

Lucinda kicked off her desert boots, took off her clothes and jumped in the shower. The pressure was just enough for it to be functional rather than enjoyable, but she still stood under the shower head for a full five minutes, the water running down the back of her neck, her hands pressed up against the tiles.

Once dry, she wrapped a knee-length lungi round her waist and threw on a T-shirt. She poured a glass of wine and sat down at her laptop. Elliot had hooked her up to the secure VSAT network that afternoon.

Lucinda opened the first of two unread emails. It was a draft cable from Hollister on the political situation in Kurdistan. 'Not much substance to it, I'm afraid,' Hollister had written, 'but it'll give you something to send Lady Laird. H.'

Lucinda dragged the text of the cable into a new email and changed some of the wording to make it more her style. A few comments made by Deputy Minister Rasul at the morning JOCC meeting helped Lucinda add a little flavour of her own.

'Spark,' said the second email, 'would be nice to know if you made it to Erbil. Send first report. And remember the brief. Laird.'

Lucinda wasn't going to reply to that. She re-read the text of her cable and hit send. That's all you get for now.

Lucinda shut the laptop, poured a second glass of wine and went out onto the balcony. She sat on the dusty tiles, her back and head resting against the glass of the sliding door, her bare feet pressed up against the railings.

Thoughts and images floated through her mind as she stared up at a blood-red moon. Lucinda gave them free rein, allowing her subconscious to determine when they came and went, in what order, and how long they lingered. She saw the Crossed Swords in Baghdad, Hollister smiling in the canteen. She thought of Firas, wondering what his last moments must have been like. Did he even have time to think? She was in Sir Philip's office, she was having dinner with Miles. She thought of Kim and touched the small indentation on her right temple. A tear came to her eye.

She thought of Jake D'Souza. He was brash, arrogant, a typical cocksure American. Worse than that, he was charming and attractive. Very attractive.

Lucinda thumped the back of her head against the glass door, finished her wine, and went to bed.

CHAPTER TEN

Abu Issa

On the corner of Anderson and Kozlowski a car horn made Lucinda jump. A boat of a vehicle pulled up beside her.

'What the hell is that?' asked Lucinda.

'Mornin' beautiful,' replied Jake. 'She's a 1979 burgundy Lincoln Continental Town Car. And she's armored, probably the only one in the world. Six liter, V8, rear-wheel drive. Naught to sixty in fourteen warp speed seconds, though I've never got her over forty-five. Must weigh damn nearly four tons with the armor plating.'

Jake had one hand on the steering wheel, an elbow poking out of the driver's side window, and a large grin on his face.

'Armored glass windows, but the motor's broken so they're permanently down. And the air con's shot. It's hot as balls in here.'

Lucinda put her hands on the roof of the Lincoln and leant in towards Jake. Her badge swung between them.

'The ad ain't wrong,' beamed Jake, 'full luxury, full comfort, full pleasure. She's got an eight-track cassette stereo with quadrophonic sound. Bench seats in deep red velour. I found her laid up in a junk yard in Baghdad and got her running again. She's my base runaround. One of a kind, and I love her. Jump in, girl. We got stuff to do.'

Lucinda walked round the front of the car, hauled open the passenger door and sank into the cushioned seat.

'I should warn you,' said Jake, 'the brakes are as soft as my Aunt Maisie's lemon meringue pie. So, you want the good news?' he continued, putting the Lincoln into gear. 'Looks like we found your boy Abu Issa.'

'What?' exclaimed Lucinda. 'When, where?'

'Syria. About fifteen klicks north of Deir ez-Zor. Intercepted a call last night from one of the numbers we have for Colonel Rahimi of the Quds Force.'

'One of the numbers?' questioned Lucinda.

'Hey, the relationship may be special, but we don't give everything away. Hang on, sweetheart.' Jake turned the steering wheel three hundred and sixty degrees to make a right into Jackson.

'Not great at cornering, part of her charm,' he smiled. 'These guys don't like to talk on the phone, but sometimes they have to. The good news is we have an exact location. Can't say one hundred percent it's Abu Issa, but we have some HUMINT corroboration that makes it very likely. And before you ask,' said Jake, straightening the Lincoln up, 'I really can't share any of that.'

'I don't need to know the intel, I just need to know it's Abu Issa. You sure, Jake?'

'If I was a betting man, Spark, which I am, I would lay a hundred bucks on it. You wanna go get him?'

Lucinda thought of Cristine Laird's parting words two days earlier. This is good old-fashioned intelligence work. No gadgets, no toys.

'Is your Aunt Maisie's lemon meringue pie soft?' she replied.

'Didn't think you could turn me down. OK, gotta start braking. We need to stop in about a half a mile.'

They pulled up outside the bay with the Chinooks, got out and walked towards the Alaska shelter. Lieutenant Colonel Bosman rounded the tent from the other side.

'Good morning, Miss Spark,' said the Colonel. 'D'Souza came clean. I didn't really think you were Paige Turner. Bit much even for the CIA. It's a pleasure to have the Brits with us.'

'Thank you, sir.'

'Shall we?' invited the Colonel.

A dozen of the hairiest, scariest men Lucinda had ever seen were sitting at the white plastic tables, chatting in groups of two or three. Relaxed, joking, they were all in civilian clothes and several had beards that gave Master Sergeant O'Neill's a run for its money. He was sitting on the right at the front.

'Who's the podium for?' asked Lucinda.

'You,' replied Jake. 'Don't worry, just follow my lead.'

'Gentlemen,' the Colonel began. 'We have intel on a high value target. Full brief will follow when you reach the forward operating base, but for now all you need to know is it's a night-time assault on a small compound in Syria. And you go tonight.'

Colonel Bosman hit the remote and a satellite image of a compound surrounded by date palms flashed up on the screen. There were two outbuildings among the trees and a two-storey concrete house inside the compound.

'This second image was taken this morning from a Predator unmanned aerial vehicle,' continued Bosman, pushing the remote control. 'There is just enough space to land two birds in the compound, but the pilots will need their A game. O'Neill will work up the initial assault plan and brief it once you get to the FOB. D'Souza, target information.'

Jake took the podium and asked the Colonel to go to the next slide.

'This is Abu Issa. Real name Omar al-Haddad. Jordanian citizen, mid to late thirties. Known associate and disciple of Abu al-Zaqarwi back in the day. He's a cyber coach for the Islamic State. He recruits online and once he has someone hooked, he guides and encourages them, all from the comfort of that compound. This fucker can be on the phone with a terrorist right to the very last minute. We believe Haddad is responsible for directing over a dozen suicide bombings and is actively engaged in planning future operations. We've been working closely with British Intelligence and together we've been able to connect the dots. Spark, you're up.'

Lucinda moved to the podium and looked around the room. Two of the guys in the front row whispered to each other.

'Fifty-seven people were murdered five days ago in the London attacks. Hundreds injured. Abu Issa – Omar al-Haddad – was on the phone with one of the terrorists, George Oluwale, minutes before he ran down innocent civilians in Oxford Street. Oluwale killed eighteen people, four of them American citizens. As D'Souza said, we believe Abu Issa runs an active network of terrorists preparing to conduct attacks. He has a lot of information in his head. We need him alive.'

Colonel Bosman looked at his watch.

'It's zero-nine-thirty. Go get something to eat, get some rest. Wheels up at thirteen-hundred.'

Jake opened the passenger door of the Lincoln. 'You need some clothes. Let's go shopping.'

They parked on Kozlowski and walked to Dorsey Square. A game of one-on-one basketball had drawn a crowd.

In the PX, Lucinda flicked through a rack of shirts.

'Make sure it's long-sleeved and fire retardant,' said Jake, picking out a pair of trousers.

Lucinda selected a maritime blue 5.11 Spitfire Shooting shirt. She looked at the sizes and held a couple of shirts against her body. She picked a small.

'Here,' said Jake, tossing a pair of black 5.11 Fast-Tac cargo pants at Lucinda. She checked the size. It was right.

'I'll go get a pair of gloves, you go check the shades.'

Five minutes and two hundred and fifteen dollars later, Lucinda was sitting with a Green Beans espresso in the seating area of Dorsey Square. She was wearing her brand-new Oakley Flak sunglasses in matt black. The basketball game was still on.

'Not bad,' she said, 'but not great. A proper espresso should be two sips, three at the most. You do go for volume, you Americans.'

'Quantity over quality every time, babe. So, tell me something about yourself, Spark.'

'OK,' hesitated Lucinda, not sure she wanted to play this game.

'For example, what's your favorite coffee?'

Lucinda laughed. 'Vergnano, since you ask, from just south of Turin. Not readily available in a PX.'

'Your turn,' said Jake.

'I'll meet you at the LZ at twelve-thirty. I've got a couple of errands to run.'

'That's not really a question, Spark. What we have here is a failure to…'

'See you later, D'Souza. And thank you.'

Back at the house, Lucinda opened her laptop. She clicked on "new email" and typed in Cristine Laird's address.

The cursor blinked at her.

She deleted the empty draft, opened a second new email, and typed in Alan Hollister's address.

The cursor blinked. Lucinda deleted the draft.

She grabbed her phone and looked up Hollister's number. 'All good,' she typed, 'will be busy tonight so don't expect a radio check.'

Lucinda scrolled through the list of names in her favourites. Mum. Dad. Louisa. She typed a quick message to Louisa.

After a ten-minute shower, Lucinda lay on the bed, wrapped in a towel, letting her body dry naturally. She couldn't sleep, it was the middle of the day, and a nervous excitement pulsed through her body. After half an hour she put on her new clothes, went downstairs and made herself an avocado and lettuce sandwich.

At exactly midday, Lucinda left the house and headed back to the base.

*

'Here, take this.'

Jake handed Lucinda a Glock, three magazines and a waistband holster. Lucinda checked the weapon was clear and inserted one of the magazines. It held seventeen nine-millimetre rounds.

Two Chinooks were fired up on the LZ, their rotor blades spinning, ready for takeoff. Twelve Special Force operators of Delta Assault Team 2, fully armed, clad in combat fatigues and carrying sixty-pound packs, emerged from the tent. Alongside one of the men trotted a Belgian Malinois K9 combat dog. Delta Force split into two teams of six and boarded the Chinooks.

Jake nodded to Lucinda. They moved to the second Chinook and walked up the ramp. Lucinda buckled herself into a canvas seat on the right side of the aircraft. Jake handed her a pair of ear defenders.

The deep thrust of the engines fought with a high-pitched whine as the Chinooks lifted off and banked right. They climbed up over the base and skirted the edge of Erbil before turning west.

The pilots kept the aircraft well inside their operating envelope, climbing at a steady eight hundred feet per minute and travelling at one hundred and forty knots. At that speed it would take an hour to cover the one hundred and sixty-eight miles to the forward operating base in Kurdish-controlled northern Syria.

Within fifteen minutes the Chinooks had reached the River

Tigris. Jake tapped Lucinda on the shoulder and pointed through the porthole behind them shouting the word, 'Mosul.'

The city was dissected down the middle by the Tigris. Lucinda was surprised to see the eastern part of the town didn't look too damaged, but she was shaken by the western half. It was more than a war zone. It was a cataclysm of biblical proportions. The old city was destroyed, hardly a building left standing. Lucinda wondered how many bodies were still buried beneath the concrete coffin. How many improvised explosive devices lay dormant waiting to explode, a final deadly gift from ISIS to families brave enough to return. She tried to look for the remains of the great mosque of al-Nuri, destroyed by ISIS in one of their crazed fits of vandalism, but she couldn't spot it and the Chinooks moved on.

For the next twenty minutes, they flew over the Nineveh plains, a patchwork of cultivated strips, small rural communities eking out a living.

About a hundred miles into the flight, Mount Sinjar rose out of the alluvial steppe, running east to west. A few years earlier, at the height of the Islamic State advance, forty thousand Yezidis had taken refuge on the mountain, desperate to avoid the ISIS genocide.

'Crossing the border into Syria,' shouted Jake over the noise of the engines. The Chinooks started their descent and ten minutes later they landed at the forward operating base, a Kurdish Syrian Defence Force facility. The political expedience of the American electoral cycle may have suggested the White House was pulling its troops out of Syria, but on-the-ground military reality meant US Special Forces used Kurdish bases when the need arose.

When they had cleared the noise and swirl of the rotors, Jake put his hand on Lucinda's shoulder. 'Briefing in the hangar.' Lucinda turned and nodded. She noticed two Black Hawk helicopters parked up on the edge of the LZ.

'Listen up, gentlemen,' said Master Sergeant O'Neill. He briefed every aspect of the mission from start to finish in minute detail. He briefed what the mission would look like if it went one hundred percent according to plan. He briefed what could go wrong. He briefed contingency plans to cover every eventuality.

O'Neill was matter of fact. No drama, no bravado, no nonsense. The men of Delta Force Assault Team 2, who Lucinda had seen so relaxed and at ease earlier in the day, bullshitting among themselves, were rapt in their attention. A steely concentration Lucinda had never witnessed before. Fighting men preparing to do what they were trained for, what they do best. A shiver went down her spine and the hairs on her neck stood up. This was where she was meant to be, and it excited her. Physically and mentally.

After the brief, Jake led Lucinda to a small row of tents behind the hangar.

'Home for the next few hours. You get this one all to yourself. Try to get some rest. I'll come by at seven and we'll grab something to eat. Don't sweat it, Spark, this is an easy gig, it's a midnight run.'

Lucinda lay down on a spartan army cot and clasped her hands behind her head. Her 5.11 shirt gripped her body. She replayed O'Neill's brief in her head, going over every detail. Not one extraneous thought interrupted her concentration.

Dinner was lamb chops and rice. It was OK, but Lucinda picked at her food. She sat opposite Sergeant Klein, the combat dog handler. She didn't learn much about Klein, but she did find out that Solomon was six years old and close to retirement. He had completed over fifty combat missions, including twenty-two parachute jumps. Klein knew Solomon had more than done his duty and deserved retirement as much as any Special Forces soldier, but Klein hated the idea of being separated, of going into combat without Solomon by his side.

At just after one in the morning, Lucinda walked back to the hangar from her tent. Go time was zero-two-hundred. Quiet, final preparations were underway. Minor adjustments to scopes and sights, uniforms being patted to check everything was in the right place, knee pads secure, boots tight and comfortable. Every member of the team was in his own zone.

D'Souza was sitting on the floor leaning against the hangar wall, his wrists resting on his knees, hands hanging loose. Lucinda took a seat next to him.

'What's your blood group?' he asked.

'A positive.'

Jake took a marker pen out of a pocket on the left sleeve of his shirt, picked up a helmet on his right and wrote 'A+' on the side.

'Ready?' he asked.

They stood up.

Lucinda put on her body armour and took her hair out of the ponytail. It fell free. She bent forward, back combed it for a second, then threw her head back. She ran her fingers through her hair and swept it back into the ponytail, tying it up in a double twist of the scrunchie. She grabbed the ponytail and pulled it tight.

She took the Glock from the holster and dropped out the magazine into her left hand. She double-checked the chamber was clear, clipped the magazine back and re-holstered her weapon. She took the helmet from Jake.

Jake exhaled. Lucinda had transformed a series of functional movements into an intoxicating ballet. Four Acts merged together in thirty sensual seconds.

'What?' asked Lucinda.

'Nothing, Spark.'

'Let's go get Abu Issa,' she said.

'Doing right ain't got no end,' said Jake in a husky accent.

Lucinda was beginning to figure him out.

Twelve degrees. Low humidity. A waning moon. Intermittent cloud cover. Good conditions, if not ideal.

The modified MH-60 Black Hawks flew fast and low, piloted by crew from the 160th Special Operations Aviation Regiment. They were flying through enemy territory and needed to avoid Russian air defence radar. In and out while Ivan was safely tucked up in bed. That was the plan.

The compound was seventy miles south-west, well within the Black Hawk's combat operating range. They would be on target in twenty-five minutes. Thirty minutes on the ground. Exfil. If all went well, they should be back on base by zero-three-thirty, complete with one extra passenger.

Spark and D'Souza were in the second Black Hawk, callsign Tango-2. The six Delta Force operators with them in Tango-2 were calmness personified; three of them appeared to be asleep.

Ten minutes out they started to conduct final checks and one of the aircrew opened the doors of the Black Hawk.

Time to target five minutes.

Lucinda's heart rate increased, beating in rhythm with the blades of the Black Hawk. She took a deep breath.

'We have visual.'

Tango-1 came to a sudden halt, hovering ten metres above the ground. Five operators fast-roped out of the helicopter. Two went to the back of the house, three to the front. The Black Hawk touched down inside the compound. Klein and Solomon jumped out.

Lucinda's senses went into overdrive. She suddenly became aware of the deafening noise of the helicopters as they broke the silence of the night. She could smell the clouds of dust as they flew up and out from the ground.

Tango-2 hovered outside the compound as six Delta operators fast-roped. Once they were free of the ropes, the Black Hawk glided sideways and touched down next to Tango-1. There was just enough room.

The compound was in darkness. There were no lights on in the house. Night vision goggles guided the assault team.

Weisz sledgehammered the door open. O'Neill was the first man in. He scanned his field of vision. Clear. He moved further into the house. Weisz and Cobb followed, weapons raised, scanning.

Three minutes on target.

They had assaulted a thousand buildings, but you never knew what to expect. Hostiles returning fire, a suicide bomber, the building rigged with explosive devices.

O'Neill moved into the room on his right. Clear. Klein entered the house and signalled Solomon to check the room. He trotted in, as calm as the rest of Delta Force, and covered the room in an anti-clockwise direction, staying close to the walls, sniffing left and right, up and down. He dwelt for a split second at a chair, his olfactory senses on high alert checking for trace elements.

Cobb patted O'Neill on the shoulder and took over point. The team moved as one, communicating without words, each knowing exactly the role of the other.

Five minutes on target.

Cobb entered the room to the left.

A muzzle flash blinded his night vision. Cobb returned fire. Two shots. Tap tap. A hostile went down.

Weisz tapped Cobb on the shoulder and entered the room. The hostile was a boy, fifteen at the most. Weisz kicked the AK-47 away and scanned the rest of the room. A woman in the far corner held a child in her arms. They didn't look to be armed, but Weisz couldn't take the risk. The woman could be wearing a vest. In three quick paces he was on them, lifting them up, searching their bodies, blocking the rest of the room with his body in case they detonated.

Clear.

Cobb entered the room, his weapon trained on the boy. Blood from two bullet holes in the boy's chest was seeping into his Barcelona football shirt.

Fuck.

Seven minutes on target.

Outside, Mathis and Cortez had cleared the outbuildings – nothing but a few chickens – and the Delta Force Tango-2 team had secured the perimeter. Their job was to isolate the compound and dissuade nosey neighbours from coming to take a look.

O'Neill was back on point, moving up the stairs. He could hear his breath in the grainy green of the phosphor screen of his NVGs. As his head was level with the top of the stairs, a second hostile opened fire. O'Neill crouched down, avoiding a hail of bullets which slammed into the wall, spitting out chunks of masonry.

He moved left, returned fire. Three bursts of two rounds. He moved to the top of the stairs. The hostile fired again from a doorway. O'Neill aimed two rounds at his right upper body. The hostile dropped.

Eight minutes on target.

O'Neill approached. He couldn't be sure, but it looked like Abu Issa. O'Neill kicked the weapon away and stepped through the doorway over the still breathing body. Flames gave the room a dim, flickering light. Clear.

Solomon went through the house methodically, ensuring there were no explosive devices.

Building secure.

'Medic,' called O'Neill over his radio.

Twelve minutes on target.

Spark and D'Souza leapt out of the Black Hawk and went straight upstairs. D'Souza stopped to identify the body. Spark moved on.

The flames danced higher from the pile of documents in the middle of the upstairs room. O'Neill was stamping them out with his right boot. Lucinda grabbed a blanket and threw it and herself over the flames, smacking down on the blanket trying to starve the fire of oxygen.

Fourteen minutes on target.

That left sixteen minutes to go through the house and strip it of all available intel.

O'Neill wanted it done quicker. 'Hurry up, people, wheels up in ten.'

Lucinda went through the pile of documents, saving what she could, extinguishing burning edges with her gloved hands, shoving them into a bag. She fished out over a dozen mobile phones and a laptop buried among the papers.

D'Souza was with the medic attending to Abu Issa.

Twenty-three minutes on target.

'Let's wrap it up, people. We're going, ma'am. Now.' O'Neill pulled Lucinda to her feet. Lucinda put the last of the documents she could save into the bag.

Tango-1 and Tango-2 lifted off.

Twenty-seven minutes on target.

One extra passenger.

Lucinda sat back in the Black Hawk, the bag of documents and phones between her legs. Abu Issa was opposite her, a cannula in his arm, being attended to by the medic. His hands were fastened in front of him with a plastic zip tie. He had taken two rounds to his right chest and shoulder. He was sweating, but stable.

Left behind in the compound, Abu Issa's wife held her daughter and wept by the lifeless body of her son. Three more nameless casualties in a never-ending war.

The adrenalin was coursing through Lucinda's body, her heart rate over a hundred and twenty. She wanted to interrogate Abu Issa and go through all the phones and documents now. She took a mini Maglite torch out of a sleeve pocket, held it between her teeth and rustled through the bag. She fished out an A4 notebook with a hard cover. The bottom corner had been burnt, but the book was intact.

Lucinda opened the book at random. It seemed to be back

to front. Of course it was, it was in Arabic. She skimmed over a couple of pages. Her heart skipped a beat. Oh my God. This was gold.

She looked up at Abu Issa, the torch still in her mouth. The light shone on his bearded face. His eyes were full of hate.

At zero-three-twenty-nine, callsigns Tango-1 and Tango-2 touched down at the forward operating base. Apart from some minor fragmentation wounds sustained by Cobb, the mission had been a complete success.

★

Jake led Abu Issa to the tent Lucinda had slept in for much of the day before the mission. He sat Abu Issa on the army cot. 'We don't have an interrogation room. This will have to do.'

They had gone straight from the Black Hawk to the tent, Jake waving the medic away, insisting on time alone with Abu Issa. He and Lucinda hadn't had the chance to talk and she had no idea what he planned to do.

D'Souza stood above Abu Issa and without warning punched down hard with his right fist. Abu Issa's nose cracked and his head swung hard to the right from the force of the punch. Abu Issa lifted his head and spat blood on the floor.

Jake walked to the other side of the cot so Abu Issa couldn't see him and winked at Lucinda.

'He knows we can't torture him,' said Jake, 'but there is one piece of good news.'

Jake walked back around and stood beside Lucinda. He lifted Abu Issa's chin with his index finger. 'Abu Issa here is Jordanian. And I have some friends in the Jordanian General Intelligence Directorate that would love to ask him some questions. You, my friend,' said Jake, leaning in face to face with Abu Issa, 'have a plane to catch.'

CHAPTER ELEVEN

e-Cable from Erbil

CX Report

Intelligence Grade: A

Source Reliability: 1

Executive Summary

- Significant cache of terrorist data retrieved
- Data belonged to Abu Issa, Islamic State recruiter and cyber coach
- At least five individuals are actively planning attacks on the UK mainland
- Attacks possibly codenamed Operation Hidayah
- Identity of the five individuals known
- Telephone numbers and biographical information of the individuals recovered
- Abu Issa's call history with Iranian handler recovered
- Other high-value intelligence recovered, including laptop, telephones, terrorist recruitment manual and historical records from the Islamic State Caliphate

Details

1. Abu Issa, real name Omar al-Haddad, the Islamic State cyber coach responsible for directing George Oluwale to conduct the terrorist attack in London on 17 April, is in the custody of Jordanian Intelligence following a CIA/US Special Forces operation.

2. A significant cache of high-value intelligence data was retrieved during the raid. This includes an "Operations Diary" which provides details of seventeen individuals involved in terrorist activities in the UK.

3. George Oluwale is one of those individuals. There are five pages of hand-written notes in the diary that detail his recruitment, journey to the UK, and handling once in the UK. Abu Issa takes notes of multiple conversations with Oluwale. At the end of the Oluwale entry are the words "file closed".

4. Eleven other individuals in the diary also have the words "file closed" at the end of their entries. Five individuals do not have these words in their entries. In each of the five "open files" the phrase Operation Hidayah is used. It is not used in any of the closed files.

Comment: In addition to Oluwale, at least seven of the other individuals whose files are closed by Abu Issa are known to have conducted terrorist attacks in the UK. It is probable further research will reveal all twelve individuals with closed files either conducted terrorist attacks in the UK or were arrested by the authorities.

Given the above, it is likely that the five individuals who do not have closed files are still at large and planning to conduct attacks in the UK.

Further, it is probable that the attacks are planned to be coordinated and have been given the codename Operation Hidayah. There is no information on the nature or timing of the potential attacks. End of Comment

5.   The names of the five individuals are:

    a.   Yousif Khan

    b.   Sadique Adeel

    c.   Akram Jabbar

    d.   Mustafa Tasifa

    e.   Ahmed Said

6.   The mobile telephone numbers, limited biographical information, and a summary of Abu Issa's notes on the five individuals are contained in Annex A to this report.

7.   Information on the twelve individuals who have closed files is included in Annex B to this report.

8.   Abu Issa kept a separate record of his contact with an individual referred to by Issa as "R". These contacts include text messages and telephone calls. It is clear from the exchange that "R" is Abu Issa's handler and is responsible for giving instructions on when and where terrorist attacks in the UK are to be carried out.

Comment: Given separate reporting, it is likely that call record analysis will show the individual referred to as "R" is Colonel Rahimi of the Quds Force. This is the first known intelligence which demonstrates the Iranian Quds Force is behind a concerted campaign of terrorist activity in the UK.

This is a significant development. The Shia Quds Force is using Sunni terrorist recruits to further its extraterritorial agenda. It is not clear if this terrorist campaign is sanctioned by Iran's Supreme Leader or if the Quds Force, or indeed an element within the Quds Force, is acting unilaterally. Colonel Rahimi reports to Major General Ali Hussein Hashemi, Commanding Officer of the Quds Force. End of Comment

9. Abu Issa kept a "recruitment manual" where he describes how and where he recruited individuals to his cause. This includes a wide range of internet chat rooms. Abu Issa was also handed recruits whom he was instructed to develop. According to Issa, these recruits came from a variety of backgrounds and places including, but not limited to: the Islamic State Caliphate while it existed, migrants from multiple countries looking to emigrate to the UK (and Europe), refugee and internally displaced persons (IDP) camps. According to Abu Issa, after the collapse of the Caliphate, IDP camps across Syria and Iraq became fruitful recruiting grounds. Issa names a number of camps in his manual.

10. A full list of the internet chat rooms detailed by Abu Issa is contained in Annex C to this report. Countries which feature in his manual are detailed in Annex D. Refugee and IDP camps mentioned by Issa are at Annex E.

11. Other documents recovered by the operation to capture Abu Issa include observations on life in the Caliphate. Abu Issa lived in Fallujah, Iraq, for much of 2014 and 2015, and moved to the Deir ez-Zor area in 2016.

12. It is clear from the documents that during the life of the Caliphate, Abu Issa, in addition to acting as an online cyber coach, worked in the information technology and propaganda departments of the Islamic State. The documents provide significant historical data on Islamic State propaganda.

Comment: The laptop and telephones recovered are in the custody of the CIA. Information detailing Abu Issa's observations of life in the Caliphate and his role in IT and propaganda will form the subjects of follow-on reports. End of Comment

Lucinda closed the lid of her laptop and took a large hit from her Jack Daniels and coke. It was a little sweet for her taste, but she had ignored Jake's advice to top it up with Jack.

D'Souza took a slug from his Jack and coke. He was sitting in an armchair in the corner of his trailer on the Erbil airbase surrounded by mounds of paper bundled together in neat piles on the floor.

'Now that was a good day at the office,' he said, getting up and stepping over bundles. He went to the fridge and dropped four ice cubes in his glass. He pulled out the bottle of Jack, a fresh can of coke, and mixed himself another drink.

'You want another, Spark?'

'Yes, D'Souza,' she said, draining her glass. 'A little less coke this time.'

After Abu Issa had been put on a C-130 Hercules to Amman, Jordan – the only passenger on the manifest – Spark and D'Souza had gone back to Jake's trailer with the bag of documents. Lucinda was still on a high from the raid and wasn't ready to sleep so they had a first run-through, sorting the documents in a priority order.

By 7 am Jake was asleep in his chair and Lucinda was hit by a sudden wave of tiredness. She contemplated taking the bed, but decided to head back to the house in Ainkawa. She left D'Souza a note saying she would be back in a few hours. Lucinda could hardly keep her eyes open on the way home and all she wanted was a shower and bed. But she never made it. She fell asleep fully clothed and woke at ten.

She showered, made herself one of the most delicious bacon sandwiches she could remember eating and went back to the base.

At 10.45 am she knocked on Jake's trailer and walked in. She was wearing light blue jeans and a dark green, long-sleeved T-shirt.

Jake had moved from the chair to the bed and was fast asleep. He slept on his side, one arm under the pillow, scrunching it up towards his face. A single bedsheet covered the lower half of his body. He looked peaceful, but there was a feline quality to D'Souza as he slept. Lucinda felt he could pounce at a moment's notice. He had a lean, muscled torso, and powerful shoulders.

His right calf and foot poked out from the bottom of the sheet.

'D'Souza, rise and shine,' said Lucinda, kicking the end of his bed.

As he turned over the sheet wrapped itself around his lower body, hugging and revealing his shape. He was beautiful.

'I'll rise, but I won't shine. Rustle us up some coffee, Spark. It ain't Vergnano, just ordinary Joe.' D'Souza nodded in the direction of a cupboard and headed to the shower cubicle holding the sheet round his waist, its folds dragging along the floor behind him like a wedding train.

They spent the whole day going through the cache of documents. In the beginning, they competed, racing through the documents as fast as possible, showing off their mutual prowess in Arabic, each trying to outdo the other. At some point, competition merged into cooperation and they worked together, doubling their output, swapping documents, helping each other out with translation, Lucinda rifling through Jake's well-thumbed dictionary.

Jake went out for food at around 3 pm and came back with two pepperoni pizzas and a dozen barbecue chicken wings. They didn't take a break. Lucinda ate three slices of pizza, feeding them into her mouth as she continued to work. She chucked the crusts back in the box.

From the moment they picked Abu Issa up they knew they had a wealth of intelligence, but by 7 pm that evening they had gone through all the documents and realised they were sitting on a gold mine.

They couldn't believe what they had. They tested each other, D'Souza forcing Lucinda to justify her conclusions, demonstrate the evidence. Lucinda took her turn as prosecutor, cross-examining D'Souza, trying to trip him up, tear holes in his story, destroy his credibility. She couldn't.

Elements of the Iranian Quds Force had an active terrorist campaign in the UK and they were using Sunni terrorists to do their dirty work, blowing themselves up in the name of Allah. It wasn't clear if this was part of a rogue Quds Force element with their own unknown agenda or whether this came from the Iranian Supreme Leader himself. It also wasn't clear what role the Islamic State played. The attacks were carried out in their name and they claimed responsibility. Were they being willingly duped, or did they just claim any attack, happy it served their cause irrespective of what the real motivation was? Or, worst of all, were radically opposed Sunni and Shia factions conspiring together to wage a war in the far abroad? In the Middle East, you could kill your friend and fight on the side of your enemy on the same day.

Jake went to the fridge and got out the bottle of Jack. It was eight-thirty in the evening. He poured two glasses.

'So, how are we going to play this?' D'Souza asked. 'I've already got Langley on my ass wanting to know what's in the documents. They want them shipped back pronto.'

'Well, it's fair to say the documents belong to the CIA. You deserve them after last night.'

'Yeah, but I don't see why you can't put them in a series of reports back to your folks. Gonna make a big splash, Spark.'

'And what do I say when they ask me where I got the information?'

'You tell the truth. Local liaison with CIA officer.'

'In that case,' said Lucinda, handing Jake her empty glass, 'it's lucky I brought my laptop with me.'

Fifteen minutes later Lucinda had drafted the e-cable and D'Souza had read it twice to fact and proof check. It was ready to go.

'I'll go back to the house and send it from there.'

'Why bother?' said Jake. 'I can hook you up to a Langley satellite and we can bounce it straight to your folks in London. Langley will see it, of course, but they're gonna get all the information anyway. And I need to send all this back tonight so the experts back home can squeeze every last bit of intel out of it. You want another, Spark?'

'Yes, D'Souza,' she said draining her glass. 'A little less coke this time.'

Lucinda opened her laptop back up. Jake got up from his chair and stepped over the semi-circle of paper bundles. He made the third round of Jack and cokes and put them on the table.

He leant over Lucinda and started to play with the settings on her laptop. His left arm brushed her shoulder, his breath ruffled her hair like a spring breeze catching a curtain through an open window.

'Right. Distribution,' said Lucinda. Then she muttered, 'For Your Eyes Only, my arse.'

'Excuse me?'

'Nothing,' she replied.

Lucinda stared at the cursor blinking back at her. In the "To" line she put Cristine Laird's address.

She paused.

In the "Cc" line she entered Head of Baghdad Station Alan Hollister's and SIS Chief of Staff Ramesh Varma's email addresses.

'This will make some waves,' she said as she hit send and watched the e-cable disappear into the ether.

'OK,' said Jake, finishing his third glass. 'Now, to the more important stuff. What next?'

'London are going to go into overdrive and will have a thousand questions. But they've got enough to keep them busy for a while. I'm going to go to one of the IDP camps mentioned by Abu Issa. Sniff around, get a feel for the place. That's a start, but what I really want to do,' Lucinda continued, 'is meet Major General Ali Hussein Hashemi.'

'Good luck with that, beautiful. Everybody talks about him and nobody can find him. He's the Scarlet Fucking Pimpernel.'

CHAPTER TWELVE

Dust and Thorns

The waters of Lake Darbandikhan were low. It would be another hard summer. The snowpack from the Zagros mountains had provided sufficient melt water, but Iranian engineers had diverted the River Sirwan for the construction of the Daryan dam. A vital project for the Islamic Republic, but it was starving Darbandikhan of its lifeblood.

Major General Ali Hussein Hashemi sighed as he looked out over the lake from the window of his private study. The sun was low in a cloudless sky, casting the surrounding hills and mountains in late afternoon shadow across the lake. It looked tired, as if it wanted to skip the next two hours, be done with the day, and slip below the horizon early.

'Come in,' said the General.

'The Ahl al-Bayt are gathered, sir.'

'Thank you, Colonel Khorasani.'

General Hashemi turned to the oak-panelled wall of his study and pressed a lever. A door concealed in the wood panelling popped open and he walked into the meeting room. Seven members of the Ahl al-Bayt were sitting at the V-shaped table.

Absent were Captains Abbasi and Ardavan, on their way to Deir ez-Zor with a Quds Force brigade.

'Gentlemen,' said Hashemi, taking his seat at the head of the table, 'when Prophet Muhammad, Peace Be Upon Him, first revealed he had received the words of God in a visitation, he asked his closest kinsmen, "Which of you will assist me in this cause?" None spoke but Ali, though he was the youngest of those present. "I, oh Prophet of God, will be your helper in this matter." Ali thus joined the Prophet and became the first follower of Islam.'

Hashemi pushed a button on the edge of the table in front of him.

'Years later, on the final pilgrimage and just three months before his death, the Prophet declared, "The time approaches when I shall be called away by God. I am leaving you with two precious things and, if you adhere to both of them, you will never go astray. They are the Koran, the Book of God, and my family, the Ahl al-Bayt. He of whom I am master, of him Ali is also the master".'

The door opened and a servant carrying a tray of drinks entered. He placed a glass of liquid syllabub sweetened with honey in front of each member of the Ahl al-Bayt. It was the General's favourite drink, which he took in times of joy and times of distress.

'Our Father, Imam Ali, was present at the beginning, he was present at the end. He is our Alpha and our Omega. And yet, he was denied three times.'

General Hashemi took a sip from his glass. The others followed.

'When the Prophet passed from this earthly prison, Ali shut himself in a chamber and prepared the Prophet for the grave. He mourned, he prayed, he washed the Prophet's body. And while he busied himself with this most holy of tasks, a Shura council was called. With the Prophet not yet in his final resting place, nay, with the breath barely gone from his body, the Medinans and the Meccans, the Helpers and the Emigrants, squabbled over the succession. Supporters begged Ali to attend the Shura, to lend his voice, but he would not leave his beloved Prophet's side.'

Hashemi paused and looked around the room, staring each man in the eye. 'Abu Bakr, father of the wicked Aisha and thereby father-in-law to the Prophet, was chosen to be the first Caliph, successor to the Prophet. And so began Imam Ali's twenty-five years of Dust and Thorns. They called him Abu Turab, Father of Dust, and our Father himself said during this time he lived with dust in his eyes and thorns in his mouth.

'Despite being denied, Ali, in the greater interests of Islam, swore allegiance to Abu Bakr. For Ali, humility and nobility paved the path to peace.

'Twice more he was denied. When Abu Bakr was on his death bed, he nominated the warrior Omar as his successor. What did Ali do? To keep the peace, he married Abu Bakr's youngest widow, Asma, and gave his own daughter, the Prophet's oldest granddaughter, to Omar in marriage.'

Hashemi took another sip from his glass. 'The years of Dust and Thorns had but barely begun. Omar was a just and strong ruler, extending the reach of Islam across foreign lands, but when he died, Ali was passed over again, Othman succeeding as Caliph.

'Othman,' General Hashemi spat the word, 'Othman the corrupt, the venal, Othman the Umayyad. This third denial was the most bitter of all. The Ahl al-Bayt were truly disinherited. The seeds of the fitna had been planted and now they had been watered.

'Othman had the temerity to call himself the Deputy of God, claiming divine sanction while stealing the wealth of the people to pay for his luxurious palaces. The property of Islam was embezzled, enriching his clan, the clan to whom he gave all the positions of power.

'And the worst of these was Walid, the governor of Kufa

and Othman's half-brother. When Walid appeared drunk in the mosque and vomited over the side of the pulpit, the people of Kufa demanded he be flogged. Othman refused them. For once Aisha was on the side of the Ali, the side of the righteous, and during Friday prayers at the mosque in Medina she raised a sandal and said, "See how this, the Prophet's own sandal, has not yet even fallen apart? This is how quickly you have forgotten the Sunna, the practices of the Prophet".

'Quiet calls for Othman to abdicate soon became a clamour, but he refused to step down. It was our Father, Imam Ali, who was asked to mediate. He abhorred the behavior of Othman, but he knew the law must be respected, that a chosen successor of the Prophet could not be forced to renounce his leadership, that the principles of Islam were sacred. For weeks he kept the peace seeking a solution, but dark forces undermined Ali at every turn and stirred the feelings of the mob, whose anger soon became impossible to control. One day they broke into Othman's palace and a small group found the Caliph in his chamber reading the Koran.

'Othman, the third Caliph, was assassinated by Muslims. The first cut from a dagger released their fury and the thirsty assassins fell upon the Caliph with their knives. Othman's blood spurted from his many wounds. It covered the walls, it covered the carpet. It covered the pages of his Koran, defiling the Book of God.'

General Hashemi drank the last of his syllabub and pushed the glass to one side. 'Gentlemen, the Ahl al-Bayt will not be denied again. Colonel Khorasani, an update, please.'

'We have suffered a severe setback,' began Khorasani. 'Our intelligence reports that Abu Issa was captured by the Americans last night.'

All heads turned to Khorasani. 'We believe he was flown to Jordan, but we do not have confirmation. We must assume that information on the British angle of Operation Hidayah has been compromised.'

The stunned silence was broken by Colonel Rahimi, who cried out and doubled up in pain.

'Colonel Rahimi,' said the General, 'you seem to be unwell.'

Beads of sweat dripped down the colonel's forehead. 'What you are feeling, Colonel, are the first symptoms of strychnine poisoning.'

Rahimi's fingers snapped shut in a fist and he let out another guttural cry. He looked in horror at General Hashemi.

'Derived from the fruit of the Strychnos nux-vomica, the strychnine tree. The poison works quickly, Colonel. At this very moment, the glycine receptors on your motor neurons are being blocked and this is causing a severe muscular tightness. It will get worse and considerably more painful. You will experience a series of convulsions, each one a gradation of pain. Within an hour, the spasms will be uncontrollable.'

Colonel Jahandar and Major Sabouri, sitting on either side of Rahimi, pushed their chairs back.

'Some victims have been known to break their own backs, so violent are the spasms. Death can take several hours. You failed me, Colonel.'

'General...'

'Save your energy, Colonel. The pain, as we can see, is already excruciating. Eventually your neural pathways will be paralysed, and you will die from asphyxiation. But despite your failure, I am willing to show you mercy.'

General Hashemi nodded at Colonel Farrokzhad. The loyal Rottweiler knew exactly what his master wanted. He got up, walked round the table and stood behind Rahimi. Farrokzhad put his enormous left arm around Rahimi's neck and started to squeeze. Rahimi struggled in vain, his arms trying to tear himself free from Farrokzhad's grip, his feet kicking against the underneath of the table, his body seized by convulsions.

Not flinching, Farrokzhad looked at his master, who nodded

again. Farrokzhad cupped Rahimi's jaw in the shovel of his right hand and ripped hard, snapping the Colonel's neck.

'Thank you, Colonel,' said Hashemi. 'Failure will not be tolerated, gentlemen. Major Gul, you are tasked with resurrecting the British part of Operation Hidayah and salvaging what you can. Time is not on your side. Colonel Farrokzhad will now focus on the attacks in Spain and here in Iraq.'

'General, sir,' said Major Turan, from the left side of the table. 'Surely the wisest course of action is to delay the operation. Let our intelligence network find out more. How compromised are we? We must not risk discovery.'

'You sound like a Kufan, Major Turan,' snapped the General. 'When Imam Ali called the Kufans to stand by his side in his hour of greatest need, they turned their backs. "You gurgle like slack-jawed camels," he told them, "slurping at their water. You fill my heart with pus and you line my breast with anger".'

Major General Hashemi stood up. 'Do not line my breast with anger, Major Turan. There will be no delay.'

CHAPTER THIRTEEN

The Camp

Andrew Simmonds looked at his watch and swore under his breath. Fucking Poms. Out of the goodness of his heart he does her a favour and she can't even be bothered to turn up on time. Still, she was hot, which is why he agreed to do the favour in the first place. He guessed he could forgive her. Bitch.

'Sorry I'm late, Andrew,' said Lucinda, a little out of breath.

'No worries and call me Simmo. Hop in, let's go.'

Lucinda had been running late all morning. Her CX report had sent the British intelligence machine into overdrive.

One of the individuals, Sadique Adeel, was known to the authorities, red-flagged six months ago, but he was not considered an active threat so was not under any form of surveillance. None of the other four appeared on any government department watch list.

The Security Service, the Home Office's Office for Security and Counter-Terrorism, and the Counter-Terrorism Command of the Metropolitan Police were frantically trying to locate all five individuals and were already arguing over whether to apprehend or surveil them.

GCHQ had their heads buried in Cheltenham as usual. Not in the sand, but in the numbers. New telephone numbers were being put on Priority One cover, old numbers were being checked, and one of the largest ever network mapping exercises had been launched.

The possibility of missing a lone wolf terrorist or even a sleeper cell always existed, but a massive investment in intelligence and police counter-terrorism resources had yielded significant results over the past two decades. The homeland was safer.

Not anymore. The tired cliché was that a terrorist only had to be lucky once, the authorities had to succeed every time. Spark's report showed the odds had shifted even more firmly in favour of the terrorist.

Lucinda had hauled herself out of bed at 6 am and opened her laptop. A rash of emails littered her inbox. She downed a pint of water to launch the counterattack against the effects of last night's Jack and coke and headed for the shower. Twenty minutes later she was back at the laptop with her first coffee of the day.

She started with the two emails from Cristine Laird. The first was titled "Report" and read, "Spark, important information, good report. We need to discuss. Call me. Laird." The second had "Call me" in the subject line and one word in the body of the text, "NOW". Lucinda checked her phone. Three missed calls from Laird.

She clicked on the email from Ramesh Varma. "Spark, this is an excellent, if deeply troubling, report. The information has been forwarded to all the relevant agencies and we are doing everything we can to locate the individuals. Great work and keep it coming. Stay close to the CIA. Varma."

Baghdad Station Head Alan Hollister was a little more succinct, typing simply "Well Done" in the subject line.

Lucinda clicked on a mail from Ben Williams, a colleague who had been on the same SIS intake. 'Spark, that is one big f**king cat you just threw among the pigeons. You should see the commotion your report has created. And I'm not just talking Vauxhall. Half of Whitehall is chasing its tail. Good work. If there's anything you need from this side, let me know. Ben.'

She ought to call the office, but Lucinda convinced herself that not even Laird would be in yet and it was too early to disturb her at home. She didn't want to deal with headquarters right now. They had more than enough to get on with. Instead, she hit "reply" to one of Laird's emails and typed, "Long day yesterday, sorry I didn't get in touch. Have follow-up meeting with CIA this morning, then heading out to Jeddah IDP camp. Will be out of comms. Spark."

Nothing wrong with that. After all, she was the agent in the field. HQ should fit around her schedule, not the other way round. Lucinda closed the laptop and headed to the base.

'Safe to say we've woken up half the western world. I was on with Langley till 4 am.' Jake took a bite of his Cinnabon Stix twisted pastry, holding it between thumb and forefinger, waggling it at Lucinda between bites. They were sitting in the early morning sun by the side of the basketball court on Dorsey Square.

'I'm taking a slightly different approach,' said Lucinda. 'Am ignoring HQ. Told them I'm out all day. What's your plan, D'Souza?'

'I'm outta here, babe. Done. Wheels up in half an hour. Debrief the Station Chief in Baghdad, then back to Langley.'

A wave of disappointment surged through Lucinda. 'You don't deserve that, Jake. How can they pull you back now?'

'Deserves ain't got nothing to do with it,' D'Souza replied with a smile. 'And don't sweat it, Spark, I'll be back a week Thursday. Sweet of you to care though.'

Embarrassment replaced disappointment. Stupid girl.

'You're an arse, D'Souza.'

Jake took a pen out of his pocket and gave it to Lucinda.

'Take this. It's got a transmitter in it. Nothing fancy, but it'll do the job. I know you have one in your phone, but it's always good to have insurance. Right, I gotta split.'

A round wooden table made from pallets separated them. So too, as they stood up, did a sudden awkwardness. They didn't know whether to shake hands or kiss. They fumbled through both. Lucinda's hair fell forward and brushed Jake's face as they kissed on the cheek.

'You're a betting man, D'Souza,' said Lucinda. 'You see those two pigeons on the roof of the PX? I'll bet you the brown pigeon flies off before the grey one.'

D'Souza laughed. 'You obviously know things about pigeons, Lilly. I said you were a bright spark.'

Jake put his left hand on Lucinda's shoulder and kissed her again. Once, on the lips.

'Stay safe, beautiful.'

Lucinda watched him leave.

Her phone beeped a reminder. Bugger. She was late.

Andrew Simmonds – Simmo – was a forty-something Australian with thinning hair, blotchy skin, and a black shirt that was one size too small for his bowling ball stomach. He worked for a small NGO called Melbourne Medics.

Lucinda had met him at the JOCC meeting on the airbase. He had been sandwiched between the Iraqi captain and the Kurdish major. At the end of the meeting, he made a beeline for Lucinda, introduced himself and handed her his business card. He didn't seem to notice D'Souza.

He had mentioned he was a planning a trip to the Jeddah IDP camp, south of Mosul, in the next few days. Lucinda called him on the Monday night and asked if she could tag along. He waffled a bit about the inconvenience of changing the access request, but he didn't take much persuading.

Fifteen minutes into the journey Lucinda knew that Simmo had worked in a host of conflict and disaster zones. 'The circuit' as he called it. Yemen, South Sudan, Bangladesh, Papua New Guinea, the Philippines. 'Same bloody lot everywhere you go. Nice to see a new face.'

Lucinda was surprised he noticed her face at all, as he spent most of the time staring at her breasts, thinking he was being surreptitious, when he may as well have announced his intentions over a loudspeaker and run a flag up a pole. He had that irritating ability of making a woman conscious of what she was wearing.

The fitted white Hawes & Curtis poplin shirt with single cuff left open at the wrist did, Lucinda had to admit, show off her figure well. The starched white collar emerged from behind her loose hair culminating in sharp triangular tips. Her pronounced collarbone was visible under the open neck, the top two buttons undone. The tailored cotton cut highlighted the curves and swell of her breasts. Tucked into her blue jeans, the shirt pulled tight against her flat stomach and tapered waist. Lucinda had been thinking of someone else when she dressed that morning.

After the fifth mental undressing of the journey, Lucinda made a point of looking at the pale white circle of skin on Simmo's ring finger and said, 'Married or divorced?'

Unembarrassed, Simmo explained that he was MBA, Married But Available, and proceeded to justify his compartmented existence. It was difficult to sustain a relationship when you worked away for such long periods of time. Casual sex was, well, casual. A lot of people did it. 'We don't all wear sandals and bark at the moon,' he said.

'That's the problem with this world,' said Lucinda. 'Too many TLAs.'

'TLAs?' asked Simmo.

'Three Letter Acronyms,' replied Lucinda. She made a display of digging some documents out of her bag. Simmo got the hint and started to play with his phone. Frigid bitch, he thought to himself.

They reached the edge of the Kurdish-controlled area, near a town called Makhmour, and had a five-minute drive through no-man's land to the first Federal Iraqi checkpoint. As soon as they reached it, Lucinda noticed a difference in attitude. Less friendly and much more thorough with the paperwork. Mahir, their driver, was struggling to convince the Iraqi private that everything was in order and all the right permissions had been obtained. Not according to the private, they hadn't. The exchange followed a familiar pattern and soon exploded into an argument, voices raised, hands gesticulating.

'Fucking typical,' said Simmo. 'Happens all the time.'

The soldier peered in through the driver's window and motioned for Lucinda and Simmo to get out of the vehicle.

'Whatever you do, don't get out. Looks like we'll have to turn around and abort for the day.'

Lucinda threw a lightweight scarf over her hair, opened the door and got out.

'Fuck,' said Simmo, staying in the vehicle. 'What the fuck is she doing?'

At first, the soldier was shocked a woman was talking to him, but shock soon gave way to anger and he started shouting again. Mahir tried to intercede, but succeeded only in pouring fuel onto a fire that was beginning to get out of control. Lucinda told him to get back in the vehicle.

Five heated minutes later, Lucinda jumped back in and they were allowed through the checkpoint.

'So, you speak Arabic. What the fuck did you say to him?'

Lucinda had explained they were humanitarians and had been invited to Iraq by the Iraqi government. That they were guests in the country and guests should be treated with respect. She also suggested calling the private's superior officer and if that didn't work, why didn't she call the Minister of Defence. She considered him a close, personal friend.

'I've insulted his honour, threatened his masculinity, and I doubt I'll be on his Christmas, or Eid Mubarak, list, but I don't have time to fuck about. Thanks for your support, by the way.'

Not waiting for Simmo to reply, Lucinda opened a report on the Jeddah IDP camp. It made for tough reading.

Jeddah was in fact a series of camps established in late 2016, early 2017, to cope with the humanitarian consequences of the offensive to retake northern Iraq from the Islamic State. The report was a microcosm of the international humanitarian effort across Iraq. Indeed, Lucinda thought, it was representative of conflicts throughout the Middle East. Maybe every disaster zone the world over.

The United Nations was behind the curve from the start. They always were. Galvanising the international community and extracting funds from donors ahead of a human catastrophe was always a challenge, no matter how inevitable the catastrophe. Governments and their people were reactive, needing the news networks to beam horrifying images of women and children ravaged by war into their living rooms before conscience translated into hard cash.

The stories were harrowing. Jeddah housed IDPs from Mosul, Qayyarah, Hawija, and a thousand other towns and villages across northern Iraq. They had fled in their hundreds of thousands, desperate to escape the fundamentalist clutches of the Islamic State. They had taken their cars if possible, but most escaped on foot, walking by day and sleeping in the open air at night or, if they were lucky, in the empty guts of bombed-out buildings.

Trying to escape the Caliphate was a punishable offence, and as they got to the front line the risks increased exponentially.

Snipers picked off targets at random, improvised explosive devices lurked, primed to detonate, minefields threatened an indiscriminate death.

The lasting trauma of life under ISIS and the conditions in the IDP camps were such that the relief felt from reaching safety was short-lived.

None of the camps was ready in time and the aid agencies were overrun by the swarm of displaced. After losing so many male family members to ISIS, families faced a further separation once they got to the Jeddah camp. All men over the age of twelve were segregated and held in pens so the authorities could verify their identity and ensure no Islamic State terrorists had infiltrated their numbers. Many had lost identity papers, thereby facing an interminable wait, kept apart from their loved ones.

The women and children fared little better. Insufficient numbers of camp personnel meant that registration could take days. And once they were registered, a lack of accommodation meant many were forced to sleep outside. Those lucky enough to get a tent still faced critical shortages. Mattresses were scarce, so too were food, potable water, cooking gas, and basic kitchen utensils.

Sanitation was a problem. Lucinda read that one part of Jeddah had eleven functioning latrines for over ten thousand people. They were shared between the sexes, stripping women of what little dignity they had left. 'It is not unusual to see signs of human defecation in the areas surrounding the latrines,' the report noted. That cold, clinical phrase did not begin to do justice to the plight suffered by the displaced, nor the image it created in Lucinda's mind.

Disease was the obvious corollary, exacerbated by the lack of available or appropriate medicine. The United Nations struggled to play catch-up, capable only of applying a thin strip of plaster to a gaping wound.

To make matters worse, unidentified armed actors were often seen patrolling the camp, controlling food distribution. Women suffered routine abuse, dragged out of their tents to be raped or forced into prostitution rackets. Traumatised children ran terrified into the tents at the sight or sound of a helicopter overhead.

The report made the early days of Jeddah sound like a favela run by gangster thugs. The poor, the dispossessed, were always the victims. And just when they thought they had nothing left to lose, that was when they lost everything. Their dignity, their children, their lives.

Lucinda rested the report on her lap and looked out of the window. They passed towns and villages with barely a building left standing. Roofs caved in, walls missing, layers of concrete flattened like collapsed wedding cakes. The war was over, but the mental and physical remnants would take years to clear, let alone rebuild.

'Shit,' said Simmo, 'looks like some bigwig is visiting. Much more security than usual.'

A handful of Humvees and a dozen pick-up trucks lined the approach to the camp. A snap checkpoint had been established. Mahir negotiated access.

'They look like Badr Corps, one of the many Shia militias. Not overly friendly, but better than Asaib al-Haq or Kataib Hezbollah.'

The camp resembled a fortress, surrounded by a two-metre, chain-link perimeter fence, supported by Y-shaped metal poles that glinted in the sunlight. Razor wire stretched along the top of the fence, with rolls of barbed wire on the ground both sides of the fence. Maybe to keep people in, maybe to keep people out. Maybe both, thought Lucinda.

'How long do you need?' she asked Simmo.

'I've got a meeting with one of my local medics and two interviews to do. Hour and a half. Two, tops. That enough for you?'

'Should be,' said Lucinda.

Mahir parked the car in an open area to the right of the entrance and they made their way to the main access building, a beaten-up, prefabricated, white plastic trailer with the door hanging off its hinges.

It was chaos inside. Twenty people milling around, with nothing to do except play on their phones and get in the way.

'Right,' said Simmo, once they were back outside. 'Me and Mahir are headed over to the medical facility. It's right in the middle of the camp. I for one don't think you should be walking around on your own, but that's your lookout. Let me give you two pieces of advice. Keep that headscarf on and don't go near the mosque.'

'Why not?' asked Lucinda.

'Out of bounds. There's stuff goes on there we don't want to know about, recruitment to militias and God knows what else. We turn a blind eye. It's called the framework of consent.'

'Sounds like a nebulous term for bullshit to me. See you back here in a couple of hours.'

Simmo turned on his heels and stomped off in the direction of the medical facility, regretting his favour more with every passing second.

Lucinda put on an olive-green jacket cropped at the waist and tucked the tails of her headscarf under the collar to ensure it would stay in place.

The scale of the camp was as impressive as it was depressing. Lucinda recalled the numbers from the report. At its height, the camp housed over one hundred and forty thousand people. Today that number was eighty-seven thousand, of which twenty-five thousand were women, thirteen thousand men, twenty-six thousand girls, and twenty-three thousand boys.

The key facilities were located in the heart of the camp, the administration building, medical facility, a handful of shops and the mosque. They were surrounded by hundreds of regimented, square plots. Each plot had two rows of eight containerised housing units – CHUs in TLA parlance. At an average of just under five people per household that was in the region of eighty people per plot.

Lucinda did a quick calculation, counting the plots like floors on a horizontal tower block. It was back of a cigarette packet stuff and from her vantage point at ground level she couldn't get a full view, but she reckoned on a grid square of twenty-five by twenty-five plots. That was fifty thousand people.

That meant another thirty thousand plus were still in the tents which hugged the main body of the camp, shanty town extensions built on the hoof to cater for the constant stream of displaced humanity.

Most of the families were matriarchies out of necessity. Thousands of men that hadn't been dragged off and locked up on suspicion of being linked to the Islamic State were force-conscripted to the Iraqi Army with the vague promise of a few hundred dollars a month.

With the Caliphate defeated, over fifty thousand IDPs had somehow managed to return home, but the vast majority was still stuck in the permanent limbo of camp life. They had no homes to return to, the infrastructure was nonexistent, no water, no electric, no nothing. Small pockets of Islamic State insurgents had begun to reform in the sectarian badlands filling the security vacuum. Talk of jobs and investment was for the rarified, corrupt politics of Baghdad. On the ground, there was nothing.

Lucinda walked through the endless plots on the grid, trying to imagine the pain and misery these people had to endure, conflicted by the banal thought about how privileged she was.

A thick film of dust covered every surface. A haze of sand hung in a dirty yellow sky. Lucinda could feel the microscopic particles in her teeth, in her nose, settling on her clothes as she walked. It was twenty-six degrees, but in the open, arid camp packed with people and waste plastic it felt more like thirty. The summer months would be unbearable, temperatures hitting fifty and sandstorms turning the dirty yellow into a filthy orange brown.

Lucinda gathered a growing gaggle of children, laughing, smiling, wanting their pictures taken. The boys touched her hands and ran away, a one-way game of tag. The girls tugged at her jacket, mesmerised by Lucinda's foreign femininity, strange clothes, and auburn hair imprisoned under her semi-transparent headscarf.

Three black GMC Suburbans parked on the corner of the main square outside the mosque diverted Lucinda's attention.

The gaggle melted away as she headed towards the mosque, a few of the girls dragging Lucinda back by the hands, imploring her with their actions not to go any further.

She got within thirty metres before they noticed her. Three of the guards turned to each other and nodded in Lucinda's direction. She kept walking. The lead guard dropped his cigarette on the ground and adjusted the shoulder sling of his AK-47.

At twenty metres, the guards started to close the gap and motioned Lucinda to stop. She complied and made a conciliatory, non-threatening hand gesture. She had got what she needed. Twenty metres was close enough to identify the flags on the bonnets of the Suburbans. One was the national flag of the Islamic Republic of Iran. The other was the black and gold insignia of the Islamic Revolutionary Guard Corps.

It was worth a chance.

Lucinda backed away and headed towards the main shopping area of the square. She turned right and walked three blocks north, then right again and two blocks east. From there, she had a good view of the mosque compound.

Five of Lucinda's gaggle, all girls, were handing sweets to the guards. As she walked unnoticed across the road to the back of the mosque compound, one of the girls looked in her direction.

The compound was enclosed by a rickety, sheet metal fence. Lucinda was up and over it in two seconds. She squatted on her haunches with one hand on the ground and checked right and left. She stood up and walked to the back of the mosque.

Built from concrete and painted white, it was the only permanent building in the camp. The facilities in the main square were carved out of ISO shipping containers and the CHUs were prefabricated plastic units.

Lucinda leant against the wall of the mosque and studied the only other structure in the compound. It was an ornate Arabic tent. A pointed canopy sat atop a four-sided patchwork of red and gold heavy cloth. Guy ropes at a forty-five-degree angle pulled at the wooden tent poles, stretching the canopy tight.

Two guards stood outside, their backs to Lucinda, smoking.

Lucinda adjusted her scarf and walked towards them. Oblivious to her presence, she said, 'As-Salaam-Alaikum, Peace be upon you.' They turned and raised their weapons. Lucinda continued towards the tent entrance.

Both guards blocked access to the tent. Lucinda feigned surprise and tried to walk around them. One of the guards put the barrel of his rifle between Lucinda's breasts, pushing her back, shouting at her to leave the compound.

Lucinda stood her ground, the AK-47 jabbing into her breastbone. The guard whipped the rifle round with his right hand, the butt smacking Lucinda square in the shoulder. Hard. She fell to the ground.

The guards took a step forward and trained their weapons on Lucinda's prone body, screaming unintelligible orders.

A gentle voice brought control. 'What seems to be the problem?'

Lucinda looked up and saw Major General Ali Hussein Hashemi.

Hashemi stared at Lucinda, transfixed, for a second. He turned to the guards and berated them in rapid-fire Farsi, too quick for Lucinda to catch anything except the gist of a stern reprimand.

The General proffered Lucinda his left hand. 'Please, my dear.'

Lucinda patted down her jacket and brushed the thighs of her trousers. She pulled the scarf back over her hair.

'Thank you,' she said.

'Forgive me. These are my men and I am responsible for their intolerable behaviour. Come inside and have some tea. I insist.'

Lucinda followed the General into the tent.

'My aides, Colonel Khorasani and Major Turan. This is Sarbaz Anwar, the camp manager. I am Major General Ali Hussein Hashemi.'

Khorasani and Turan stood up and nodded, but they did not offer Lucinda their hands. Sarbaz Anwar seemed too intimidated to notice Lucinda and remained seated.

'Lucinda Spark. A pleasure to meet you, General. Gentlemen.'

'And to what, may I ask, do we owe the pleasure, Miss Spark?'

'I work for the British government,' replied Lucinda.

General Hashemi raised an inquisitive eyebrow and poured a glass of tea. 'A British spy, perhaps.'

'Nothing so glamorous, General. I'm a humanitarian with the Department for International Development. We are conducting a review of government aid spending. I am here to do an assessment of the British contribution to the Jeddah camp.'

'Ah,' said the General, handing Lucinda the tea and offering her a seat, 'the great British conscience to help you sleep better at night. I find you have a rather unbalanced stick and carrot approach. First, you drop thousand-pound bombs from the sky, then you buy blankets for those you make homeless.'

'I wouldn't put it quite like that, sir. The—'

General Hashemi held up his hand.

'Again, forgive me, my dear.' Hashemi lingered on the "e" and rolled the "r", making three syllables out of the word "dear".

'I have a tendency to lecture. It is a weakness of mine. But what I really meant,' continued the General, 'is what are you doing here at the mosque? You are not Muslim?'

Lucinda took a moment to drink some tea. By sheer chance she had found herself in the lion's den. She might never get this opportunity again.

'I am Christian, General, but we all seek guidance from God. I believe the Arabic term is Hidayah.'

A thin smile played on General Hashemi's lips.

'Indeed. And what does God guide you to do, my dear?'

'General, I cannot claim to know the will of God, but my faith tells me to help the poor and dispossessed.'

General Hashemi took a business card out of his wallet and a Montblanc pen from the breast pocket of his shirt. 'Your faith serves you well.'

He scribbled on the card and handed it to Lucinda. 'I would like to hear more about the British aid programme. My personal number, Miss Spark.'

Lucinda looked at the card. Above the number General Hashemi had written, "Humayra, I look forward to your call".

'General,' interrupted Major Turan, 'let me check on the men.'

'Of course, Major,' General Hashemi replied, waving Turan away.

As he left the tent, Lucinda caught Major Turan's eye.

She had seen that look before.

She looked at the briefcase on the table.

She had seen that look before.

Major Turan hurried from the tent.

'Bomb,' Lucinda screamed and launched herself at the General, tackling him to the ground and smothering his body. Colonel Khorasani reacted just as quickly, throwing himself on the table just as the bomb in the briefcase exploded.

Khorasani took the main impact, blown apart by the force of the blast. The tent was ripped to shreds by shrapnel that tore through everything in its path.

Lucinda lay on the inert body of the General, her senses deadened, consciousness fading. She saw her sister Louisa. They were children. Louisa was locked outside the house, crying, tapping on a windowpane. Tap tap tap. Lucinda tried to get up to let her sister in, but her legs wouldn't move. Louisa cried. Tap tap tap.

PART TWO

CHAPTER FOURTEEN

Halabja, 1988

18th Esfand

They have sent me children. A battalion of brainwashed children, some as young as you, my child. They wear black headbands inscribed with the word "Karbala" and ask excitedly how far it is to the holy cities. Somehow, I must integrate these boys into the brigade, protect them from themselves as best I can, but there is no time.

I received word this morning to prepare for the assault on Halabja. We await the final command from Grand Ayatollah Khomeini himself, but we are to launch in the next few days. We will start with the outlying villages, bombarding them with artillery before a ground assault. I pray to Allah the civilians have left or can find sufficient shelter.

We must find a way to break the stalemate in this Godforsaken war.

20th Esfand

Excitement among the boy recruits is reaching fever pitch. They are hungry for battle, eager to serve their Supreme Leader and their God. My senior officers and I have seen too much bloodshed to share their enthusiasm, but the old can never influence the young in such matters. They think our days are done, foolish old men that we are! I seek to encourage and to temper.

I am wary of the days ahead. Our intelligence agents intercepted a copy of a directive from Ali al-Majid, Iraqi commander of the north. It is old, but it talks about bombardments day and night to kill the largest number of Kurds possible. In the prohibited zones to the north, the directive orders Iraqi troops to execute every Kurd they find between the ages of 15 and 70.

We know chemical weapons were used to clear the Jafayati valley last month, but that was a military target. Surely even Saddam Hussein would not use chemical weapons against his fellow Iraqi citizens in a town as a big as Halabja?

22nd Esfand

We have cleared the surrounding villages with little resistance and mercifully few casualties. The Iraqi Army chose to withdraw, not to fight. Tomorrow we launch the main thrust of Operation Zafar 7, the attack on Halabja. Our artillery has been bombarding Iraqi Army facilities all day. The objective then is to move north to capture Sulaymaniyah and west to Lake Darbandikhan.

25th Esfand

We have taken Halabja. The Iraqi Army retreated, putting up no resistance. I do not understand why. We now have a clear run to Lake Darbandikhan, an important water source for Baghdad. Halabja was well garrisoned. Why would they choose to retreat? We must expect a response.

I am writing from the Istikhbarat Iraqi Army intelligence building which we have made our temporary headquarters. It is now close to ten o'clock at night. My foolish young lions are celebrating in the street, firing shots into the air. They believe they will be in Karbala and Najaf within the week. Who am I to disabuse them of this notion?

When I look into their eyes, I see you, my child. Joy, hope, the belief that anything is possible. I wish I could hold you in that state of innocence forever, that you never have to see the things I have seen.

I feel a great unease. This is not over.

26th Esfand

My pen has hovered over this blank page for hours. My hands are shaking. It is cold, and my heart is sick.

It was a beautiful spring morning. The sun was bright in the sky, bathing the city in warmth, not a cloud overhead.

At exactly eleven o'clock, a terrible thunder ripped through the air. I knew from the sound this was not just conventional artillery. The Iraqi Army was using napalm. We ran into the streets telling the people to get into their shelters, get underground. Huge explosions of fire rocked the city, balls of orange flame shooting into the sky, swallowed by thick, black smoke. I ran back to the Istikhbarat building and went down into the shelter.

For four hours they bombarded the city, hundreds upon hundreds of shells landing indiscriminately. My officers and I sat in silence, listening to the incessant thunder, knowing how close the shells landed not just by the sound, but also by the amount of dust that shuddered to the floor with every explosion.

At 3 pm it stopped.

We emerged from the shelter, as did the inhabitants of Halabja. An eerie silence had fallen over the town. Dust hung in the air.

I do not remember whether I heard or saw them first. Six Su-20 bombers flew past us overhead, fast and low. They dropped their payload in the north of the city. Six MiG-23s followed straight behind them.

I heard the distant thud of their bombs and saw smoke clouds rise from the ground. White clouds, black, yellow. Chemical weapons. Dropped in the north, not the centre of the city because of the prevailing wind. The smoke clouds mushroomed and drifted towards us. Another sortie of six planes flew in from the west.

I wasn't wearing my suit, but I did have my mask. I screamed and waved like a madman, running up and down the main streets, shouting at people to get back inside. Birds and dogs were already lying dead in the street. I saw people stumble, rubbing their eyes, coughing, collapsing to the ground. My skin was itching, hot with pain. I ran to the shelter, doused myself with water and put on my suit.

We sat there for three hours as the attack continued. Three hours. Wave after wave after wave, the scream of the jets followed by constant thunder. We sealed the door as best we could with wet rags, terrified of what was happening outside.

They told me later, on the walk, they could smell apples, garlic, pepper, rotten eggs. A kaleidoscope of chemicals.

I can barely bring myself, my child, to describe the horror of what confronted us when we emerged a second time from our shelter.

Bodies lay everywhere. Men, women, children. A grotesque apocalypse. Faces were swollen, eyes looked like they had popped out of their sockets, blood streamed from their noses. I saw a truck, the driver slumped over the wheel, bodies piled up in the back. I couldn't count the bodies, there were too many limbs poking up from under the dead bodies on top of them. Cars and trucks full of the dead, frozen in their desperate attempts to escape. I saw a man with his face covered, lying on the ground by the steps of a house, clutching the body of a baby. The empty face of the child looked heavenward.

And still they died. Survivors were wandering the streets, blinded, bleeding from their mouths, their noses, tearing at their clothes, limbs blistered, screaming in agony, and laughing, the

140

most horrible sight of all, laughing hysterically and then collapsing and dying before my eyes. I know what madness is.

We had pitifully few masks, but we handed out those we had. We drenched people in water. And we walked. We walked out of Halabja. A poisoned column of people with the most pathetic of military escorts.

We walked towards the border. It was raining heavily in the hills, and the ground became thick with a cloying, clagging mud. Allah had truly abandoned us in hell.

And still they died. One by one overcome by the effects of the gases, exhausted. Children dying in mothers' arms, fathers handing their children to a friend, a neighbour, before lying down to die.

I do not know how many we managed to airlift back to Iran, but we saved some.

I will sleep here tonight, in this mountain village, listening to the rain, weeping for the dead.

27th Esfand

I can never leave Halabja. Please forgive me, my child. My place is here with the dead, with my young lions who will never see manhood, my young lions who have been so betrayed by our leaders.

The rain did not fall in Halabja last night, and the breathless air is still thick with gas. It hangs over the city like a mountain fog. I cannot smell the apples. I smell only the rotten odour of death.

I shall bury as many of my boys as I can, before I join them.

Goodbye my child. My precious, beautiful child, I pray that Allah protects you from this madness.

Your loving father.

Major General Hashemi ran his fingers over his father's final words, closed the diary, and put it back in the top drawer of his desk.

CHAPTER FIFTEEN

The Affair of the Necklace

Shafts of light fought their way into the room, breaking through chinks in the curtains. A sheet of dust particles danced on a screen of two-dimensional light.

Lucinda opened her eyes and stretched her legs. Either the bed had been moved or the window was in the wrong place. She sat bolt upright, threw back the covers, and swung her legs over the side of the bed. She was wearing blue cotton pyjamas. She checked she still had her underwear on. She did.

The bedside table had a lamp and a half-empty glass of water sitting on a coaster. No phone. Lucinda got up and walked to an armchair by the window. Her clothes had been washed and pressed. She rifled through her bag. No phone. She tipped the contents on the bed. Still no phone, but the pen Jake had given her was there. So too was General Hashemi's business card. "Humayra," he had written, "I look forward to your call."

She remembered the tent. A Major. Toran, was that his name? She remembered the look in his eyes. She remembered the briefcase bomb and throwing herself at Hashemi, but nothing after that.

Lucinda pulled back the curtains and was blinded by the morning light. As her eyes adjusted, she could have been in a clinic in the Swiss Alps. The sun reflected off a brilliant blue lake. Rolling hills covered in grass and dotted with trees and shrubs were surrounded by jagged mountains that pierced the blue sky above.

Lucinda turned back to the room. There was a key in the inside lock of the door. She tried the handle and sure enough the door opened. She poked her head out.

No guards. No one. Just a long landing with a green carpet and four identical doors on either side, spaced at exact intervals.

So, she wasn't a prisoner. Not in the conventional sense, at least.

Lucinda locked herself in. The room had an en-suite bathroom and she undressed and stepped into the shower. Luxurious vials of shower gel, shampoo and conditioner continued the Swiss clinic motif. The hot water beat against Lucinda's body as she scrubbed herself back to humanity.

Fifteen minutes later, Lucinda was dressed in her blue jeans and white poplin shirt. She put on her desert boots, which felt clunky, out of place. She walked out of the room, turned left along the landing and descended three flights of stairs, running her hands along smooth, hardwood bannisters that reminded her of her childhood home.

At first, the house gave her no clues. No smells. No sounds. No signs of life. But as she stepped off the final stair and stood looking at an enormous entrance hall with a marble floor and twin chandeliers so hideous in their brashness she couldn't help but stare, Lucinda smelled breakfast.

She turned left and walked through a door that revealed a small dining room. One place was laid at the head of the table, surrounded by a semicircle of food.

Two metal dishes were laden with sliced cucumbers, tomatoes and olives. A square of soft, white cheese sat invitingly on a plate.

Lucinda sniffed it. It was sheep's cheese. There was a butter dish, and a jar of jam. Cherry. She could smell eggs, but there were none on the table. Lucinda salted and ate two pieces of tomato, bypassing the plate in front of her. She spread a thick slice of cheese on a piece of cucumber and wolfed it down.

As she reached for an olive, a swing door on the other side of the room opened and a short, fat woman dressed in chef's whites entered, bottom first. She was carrying a glass of tea on a saucer in one hand and two plates in the other.

'Hello,' said Lucinda. The woman smiled, her lips disappearing into the mountainous folds of her cheeks. She put the tea on the table in front of Lucinda, along with an omelette and a plate piled high with leavened, taftoon bread.

If Lucinda had been starving before, the smell of eggs and warm bread made her ravenous.

'Thank you. Where am I?' asked Lucinda, tearing off a hunk of bread and dipping it in the omelette.

'Yesss,' the woman giggled in reply and left.

There was nothing Lucinda could find out right now and the mantra was never miss an opportunity to eat or sleep. You never knew when the chance would come again.

The omelette was made with tomatoes and spiced with turmeric. There was also a hint of garlic, sweated in oil. Lucinda tore off another strip of bread and smothered it in butter and jam. She took a sip of tea. It was hot, sweet and delicious.

Lucinda looked up as the door swung open again, expecting to see the chubby maid bringing another plate of food. Instead, she saw Major General Hashemi. He was carrying two cups of tea, but it was his clothes that grabbed Lucinda's attention. He was dressed in black polo neck top, brown jodhpurs and knee-length black riding boots.

'I am glad you have found your appetite, my dear. And I am very glad to see you. How did you like the omelette?'

Hashemi took a seat next to Lucinda and popped an olive in his mouth. He didn't look to have a care in the world.

'It was delicious. I would never have thought to put turmeric in an omelette.'

'It is a classic Persian dish. So simple, yet so many ways of doing it. This is my mother's recipe. Now, tell me, how do you feel?'

'Fine, I think, General. But where am I? What happened? How long have I been out?'

'You will have a lot of questions, my dear, but do not worry about them now. All that matters is that you are alive and that you are my guest here at my house on the shores of Lake Darbandikhan. The doctor has passed you fit and well, no injuries, just a slight concussion. But he has advised complete rest and relaxation. This is the perfect place to be.'

'General, what happened? I remember Major Toran, a bomb. What happened to the other man?'

'I see we must ignore doctor's orders, temporarily at least. Very well. We had a spy in our midst. But you need not concern yourself, Major Turan has been dealt with. Very sadly, my aide, Colonel Khorasani, was killed. We had been together more years than I care to remember. He gave his life to protect me. And you, my dear, also saved my life. I owe you a debt of gratitude beyond words. But I am curious to know how you knew there was a bomb in the case.'

'The eyes, General. It's a long story from a long time ago, but I could see it in his eyes.'

'Perhaps I could enjoin you to share your story with me over dinner this evening?'

'Perhaps, General, though it is very personal, and I have never shared it with anyone.' Lucinda didn't want to give anything away, least of all to the man who must surely be her enemy. 'General, forgive me, but do you have my phone? I should let the Embassy and my boss at the Department for International Development know where I am, that I'm OK. They will need to come and get me.'

'Do you ride?' asked Hashemi.

'Excuse me?'

'Do you ride? Horses.'

So, she was a prisoner. She was in Major General Ali Hussein Hashemi's house on the shores of Lake Darbandikhan. The head of Iran's external military and espionage apparatus. A man feared and feted in equal measure across the region. The man who was quite probably planning a major terrorist attack on London, and God knows what else. And here she was, Lucinda Spark, British secret agent, eating an omelette and being asked if she could ride.

'Not for a while, but yes, I can,' Lucinda replied.

'It is the perfect way to get some fresh air. Exactly what the doctor ordered. Those boots won't do, but we can find a more suitable pair that might fit you.'

'General—'

'My dear, you saved my life. You are my guest. Now come with me.'

They walked through the swing door down a short corridor and into a kitchen which had the facilities to cook on an industrial scale. Stainless steel work tops filled two sides of the room. Along another wall, half a dozen fridges and chest freezers were lined up in height order. The chubby maid had her hands in one of the sinks, suds up to her elbows. She didn't look up as the General and Lucinda walked straight past and out through a door at the far end.

An avenue of mature beech trees stretched ahead to a single-storey stone building almost a hundred metres away. Lucinda turned to look back at the house. If she had woken up in a Swiss alpine clinic, she had now been transported to the Loire valley. The house wasn't of the grandeur or scale of the great chateaux of

146

Chenonceau or Villandry, but it would have made a more than respectable country seat for a seventeenth-century French finance minister. The slate roof was steeply pitched and adorned with finials. Dormer windows jutted out at symmetric intervals. The only thing missing was a tower with a conical roof.

'From my time in France,' said Hashemi. 'I fell in love with the architecture and have tried to replicate it in my own humble fashion. This house, this lake, is my retreat. Where I come when I need to get away from the troubles of the modern world.'

Halfway down the treelined avenue, Lucinda stopped dead in her tracks.

'You have leopards?' she asked.

In a large, fenced area through the avenue on her right, two leopards lay stretched out in a tree, the tips of their tails twitching.

'Persian leopards. Panthera pardus saxicolor. A mating pair, at least I hope they are a mating pair. They are native to this area, but almost extinct. One has not been seen in the wild for five years. I brought this pair over from Iran and hope to breed from them and release their cubs into the wild. They have not been too cooperative thus far, have you, my beauties? Look over there.'

Hashemi pointed to a second fenced area as they kept walking. 'Capra aegagrus. A wild goat native to this area. Or rather, an ibex. Also endangered.'

A small herd of six ibex were busy munching their morning hay. Lucinda found them even more striking than the leopards. They had black heads and a single black stripe down their backs. White sides, black underbellies and legs with black and white striped socks for feet. Long, curved horns gave them a magnificent, magisterial air. Several kids frolicked among them, pleasantly surprised by their ability to spring off all four feet.

'I have a small safari park. Several species like the leopard and ibex are part of my programme to reintroduce, or at least maintain, native species in the wild. But I have zebra from Africa

147

and you may be interested in the red deer from Scotland. We will take a tour later, but now, here we are.'

They had reached the stone building at the end of the tree-lined avenue. It was the stable block and it smelled of straw, horse pee, and manure. Eight stables ran the length of the back wall, and as soon as Hashemi entered, three horses put their heads out over their stable doors.

A groom emerged from one of the tack rooms and handed Hashemi half a dozen carrots. The General went straight to one of the centre stables.

'Ah, Lahik, how are you, my prince?' The horse nuzzled Hashemi's shoulder and searched for the carrot in his hand. Hashemi unbolted the door to Lahik's stable and the beast trotted out.

'Do not worry, my dear, he is harmless. At least when I am here.'

The General held out the palm of his hand and Lahik stood still. 'Watch this,' said Hashemi, as he walked six steps backwards, Lahik not moving, staring at his master, ears pricked.

General Hashemi nodded his head once and Lahik followed suit, bowing until his neck arched and his nostrils touched the ground.

'There's a good boy,' continued Hashemi, issuing the instruction that was Lahik's cue to come forward for another carrot. Heads were now poking out of all the other seven stable doors, watching the display with jealousy.

'This is my prince, Lahik, the Pursuer, named after Imam Hussein's horse killed at the battle of Karbala. You like my Arabs?'

'They are magnificent, General,' Lucinda replied, in genuine awe at the sight of eight purebred Arabs. All white, and all with the tapered, dish-like nose and high tail distinct to the breed.

General Hashemi started work on Lahik with a stiff brush and a curry comb. He spoke in Farsi to the groom. 'I have told him to prepare Alima for you. Go and get yourself acquainted. She is the Wise One. Arabs form a closer bond with humans than any other breed of horse. But be warned, if you have anything to hide, Alima will find you out straight away. She is too clever by half that one. Here, take her a carrot.'

Lucinda followed the groom into a stable. Alima clopped towards her and Lucinda held out her hand, the carrot flat on her palm. Alima snaffled the carrot as Lucinda stroked her neck and the back of her ears. She had a slight star, no more than speckles of black on her forehead. Her facial features were so delicate she could have been made of china. But she was fourteen hands and had a muscle structure that was anything but china. It was sheer, equine power.

'You see, she likes you.' Hashemi threw a tan leather saddle with a high pommel onto Lahik's back and reached down to fetch the swinging girth from under the horse's belly. 'We'll mount outside. You can use the stone to help you get on.'

Lucinda ignored the large, rectangular slab of stone sitting by the side of the stable block. Instead, she put her left foot in the stirrup, gripped the pommel, bounced a couple of times on her right leg and swung herself into the saddle. Not quite like riding a bike, but not far off.

'It will take you a while to get used to her, but Alima is quiet and understanding. She has an easy, affable gait. We will go up into the hills above the lake. It is beautiful at this time of year. I am sure you will love it, my dear.'

The leather of the saddle was soft and fitted Lucinda's shape well. The ankle-length riding boots the groom had found gave her much more control than her desert boots would have done. Right, Lucinda thought to herself, toes up, heels down, knees tight against the stirrup leather, straight back.

From the back of a horse, the size of the estate quickly became obvious. They walked past the red deer enclosure which was behind the ibex. Lucinda looked for the zebra but couldn't see them. A mile or two in the distance, down by the shore of the lake, she saw a small village surrounded by fields.

'There isn't really a limit to the property,' said Hashemi, reading Lucinda's thoughts. 'We take a slightly different view of land than you do, my dear. Those fields below belong to the villagers. Wheat and barley mostly. Everything up until them is effectively part of this estate. So too are the hills behind the house. But we never really own anything, do we?'

It was a glorious day and the sun wrapped Lucinda in a blanket of warmth. She had no need of a jacket. The sun, a clear blue sky, water rippling on the gilded surface of a lake, farmland, rolling hills and mountains. It was as if Lucinda had been transported to an idyllic day in a make-believe childhood. Complete with an Arab mare, every little girl's dream.

Except it wasn't a dream. She was the General's captive. How much did he know? Did he suspect anything? Maybe she could get away. Lucinda considered escaping on horseback. But that was ridiculous. Even if she did manage to make a break for it, the thought of turning up on the back of Alima outside the British Consulate in Erbil took the ridiculous deep into the realms of the sublime.

No, she was an agent of the British Government. She had uncovered a terrorist plot and here she was with the probable mastermind. Her job was to get to know him, to find out whatever she could and somehow get that information to London.

'General, I am curious,' said Lucinda, addressing the General's back. Alima had fallen obediently into line behind Lahik as they walked on in single file. 'The card you gave me. I know the word "humayra" means red in Arabic, but what's the significance? It can't just be my hair, which by the way I wouldn't describe as red.'

'The moment I saw you, lying on the ground, covered in dust and your headscarf loose, you reminded me of her. Of Aisha.'

'Aisha?'

'See what happens if you try to ride alongside.'

Lucinda kicked Alima with her heels and the mare broke into a trot. As she came alongside, Lahik threw his head left and nipped Alima, who fell back a couple of steps. Lucinda kicked again. Lahik nipped Alima back into place. It was a game they had played before.

'Alima is Lahik's favourite, and he indulges her, but he will not let any of the mares pass him,' said Hashemi with a large grin on his face. He was happy, relaxed.

Hashemi turned, his left hand resting on the cantle at the back of the saddle. He rode on the buckle. 'If you are to understand the politics and the conflicts of this region, my dear, you must understand the history and the culture of Islam. And if you are to understand the history and culture of Islam, you must know the story of Aisha, the one the Prophet called "Humayra".'

'Aisha,' continued the General, 'was the daughter of Abu Bakr, one of Prophet Muhammad's closest companions and the man who became Caliph on the death of the Prophet. In addition to being Abu Bakr's daughter, Aisha was also a wife of the Prophet.

'Sunni Muslims claim that Aisha was Muhammad's favourite wife, but this is not so. This is demonstrably not so. Khadija, the Prophet's first wife, was his favourite. She was, as you would say, the love of his life. Muhammad and Khadija were married for twenty-five years. Khadija was there when Muhammad was nothing more than a poor trader. Khadija was there when he had his first revelation, when he became the Messenger of God. She supported and sustained him. Muhammad was monogamous until Khadija died. Only after her death did he marry again.

'And he took ten wives after Khadija's death. Ten. Why? This was the beginning of a new era, unions needed to be made, tribes and clans needed to be brought together, wounds healed. These were political, diplomatic marriages for the future of Islam. I admit, of those ten, Aisha was clearly the Prophet's favourite, and he enjoyed her more than all the others. He indulged her. She was perhaps his weakness.'

The General seemed to be arguing with an unseen adversary, trying to prove a point that evaded Lucinda.

'Aisha herself says she was six years old when they got engaged and that the marriage was consummated when she was nine. But she was prone to exaggeration, little Humayra, and it is more likely she was twelve, but that is not the point. The point is she was a little girl, a silly, capricious, little girl.

'And she was jealous. Jealous of the nine other wives, but jealous most of all of Khadija, over whom, of course, she had no control. What use is it to be jealous of the dead? And why was she jealous of Khadija?'

The General answered his own rhetorical questions. 'Because Khadija gave the prophet children. Not one of Muhammad's other wives bore him children. Not one of them ever became pregnant. Perhaps this was the price of revelation, the necessary sacrifice of becoming the Messenger.

'Before the first revelation, Khadija had given the Prophet six children. Two boys who died in infancy and four girls. Imam Ali, the rightful heir to the Prophet, the chosen successor who was denied, married the Prophet's daughter Fatima, and they had two sons, Hasan and Hussein. A direct male line to the Prophet.

'Aisha was jealous of Fatima, jealous of Ali, jealous of their male heirs, jealous of what the Prophet called the Ahl al-Bayt, the People of the House. The Sunni call Aisha the Mother of the Faithful, yet she was barren.'

'General—' began Lucinda, but she didn't finish her sentence. Both Alima and Lahik had picked up their feet and were pulling.

'We usually canter along this strip. It is all uphill. Are you OK with a little canter?' General Hashemi gathered up Lahik's reins.

Before Lucinda could answer, she saw Lahik's muscular rear

push down into the ground as the Arab stallion launched into a graceful canter. She kicked Alima who needed no encouragement to follow.

Lucinda wasn't sure if it was the uphill slope or whether Alima was sensitive to the novice on board. Maybe a bit of both, but Lucinda enjoyed a controlled canter, her bottom deep in the seat of the saddle, pushing in sync with Alima's stride. It was exhilarating, and after just a few seconds Lucinda didn't need to concentrate on Alima or where she was going. Alima was doing everything for her and Lucinda had time to enjoy the surroundings.

As they climbed, Lucinda revelled in the spring green covering the hills. The oleander was already in bloom, violent pinks, reds and purples flashing across the carpeted canvas. There were mulberries, hawthorns, and a host of trees and shrubs she didn't recognise.

Unannounced, Alima broke back into a trot. Lucinda rose in the stirrups, leant forward and patted her on the neck. They had come out on the crest of a hill with one of the most spectacular views Lucinda could remember. They were high above the lake and could see the village and farmland below.

General Hashemi's entire estate was laid bare. Lucinda could see the front of the house, which had a stone, imperial staircase and a circular drive with a fountain in the middle. To the left of the house was a formal garden. Even at this distance the scale was impressive.

Lahik and Alima stood together, each playfully nipping the other. Neither was blowing hard and they didn't even seem to have broken a sweat.

'This is my favourite place in the world,' said Hashemi, looking down to the lake. His reins were loose. His left hand rested on his left thigh.

'Let me tell you the story of the Affair of the Necklace. It is where it all began. The fitna, the split that has plagued Islam for fourteen centuries.'

General Hashemi clicked his tongue and kicked with his heels. They walked on.

'In the early years, the Prophet launched many military campaigns across Arabia to unite the tribes under the banner of Islam. The campaigns could last several months and it was not unusual for the Prophet to take one of his wives with him. More often than not, he took Aisha. As I said, he enjoyed her more than the others. And as a child, Aisha not surprisingly loved the adventure and the romance of the desert. I believe, too, she loved the battle, the feats of valour, and perhaps even the violence. It is recorded by the first Islamic historians how she would urge men on in the heat of battle, shrieking out rallying cries to the faithful.

'At the conclusion of one campaign, Muhammad and his men camped at an oasis no more than a day's ride from Medina. As was the custom, they struck camp an hour before dawn. Aisha wandered off a short distance to find some privacy to prepare herself for the final leg of the journey. She returned to the main body of men and was helped by one of her servants into the covered howdah on top of her camel. That was how the wives of the Prophet travelled.

'As Aisha waited for the caravan to move off, she realised her necklace was missing. It had been a gift from the Prophet on their wedding day. She searched the inside of the howdah to no avail. Where could it be? She knew she had it when she woke that morning. It must have fallen off when she went to the bushes. Perhaps it snagged on a branch.

'Aisha did what any girl would do. She slipped out of the howdah unseen and retraced her steps. Aisha searched bush after bush, scouring the sand with her hands in the half-light, getting more and more frantic with each failed attempt. Eventually, to her great relief, she found the necklace and managed to recover every single bead.'

Lahik and Alima were listless, plodding on with their heads

bowed, paying no attention to the story. General Hashemi continued. 'Aisha smiled as she walked back to the caravan, happy that such a precious gift was safe and relieved that the Prophet would never know she had almost lost the necklace.

'But it must have taken her longer than she thought to find, because when she emerged from the bushes the caravan had gone. It was not even in sight, but it couldn't be that far away, surely? Perhaps she could run after it, catch up, after all the tracks were easy to follow. But that, thought Aisha, is not what a wife of the Prophet would do. Particularly his favourite wife. It would be unseemly to be seen running behind the caravan, shouting out for it to stop. No, better to stay where she was. They would soon notice that she was missing, and Muhammad would send a detachment back for her. He would probably come himself.

'Aisha herself said of the incident, "I wrapped myself in my smock and then lay down where I was, knowing that when I was missed they would come back for me".

'Except she wasn't missed. And they didn't come back for her. Not during the journey and not even after they arrived in Medina. No one saw her dismount from her camel at the end of the journey, they just assumed she had. Aisha was Aisha. She was willful and did not stand on ceremony. She had probably slipped away to see her mother to regale her with stories of the men's exploits.

'My dear, let us stop for a cup of tea,' said Hashemi. They had continued walking along the ridge of hills with the lake on their right. Up ahead, Lucinda saw the groom standing at the open tailgate of a Toyota Land Cruiser.

General Hashemi lifted his right leg over Lahik's neck and slid off. Lucinda made a more traditional dismount.

'Do not worry about tying her up.'

Lucinda let the reins go and Alima bent her head and started harvesting mouthfuls of grass.

155

'Here,' said Hashemi, pouring a cup of steaming tea from a flask. 'And have a cookie. These are made with walnut and these are koloocheh with cardamom, cinnamon and saffron. Are you enjoying the story?'

'Yes, General, I am. I must confess I know little of Islamic history, and nothing of the human story at its core. It's fascinating.'

'I think it is high time you called me Ali, my dear,' continued Hashemi. 'Now, where were we? Ah yes, Aisha alone in the oasis. Enter Safwan, a young warrior in Muhammad's army. Safwan had been delayed on the journey back to Medina and was riding alone during the heat of the day. He was grateful to reach the oasis where he could stop, drink, and rest a while before embarking on the final twenty miles.

'Of course, he recognised Aisha immediately. He helped her onto his camel and led her back the whole way. They reached Medina just before nightfall. Safwan had done a good deed, but the people of Medina did not see a chivalrous knight rescuing the abandoned wife of their Prophet. What they saw was a young, precocious woman, a wife of the Prophet no less, sitting tall on a camel being led into Medina by a handsome warrior.

'The gossip began even before she dismounted. A young, childless girl married to a fifty-year-old man. What can you expect? She spent the entire day in the oasis alone with a virile fighter, half her husband's age? And all she can think of as an excuse is that she lost her necklace. Does she take us for fools?

'The poets got to work and Aisha's reputation soon lay in tatters. The truth matters not. And you must remember, my dear, these were the early days of Islam. Among the faithful, the Prophet Muhammad's standing was absolute, but there were plenty of dissenters, searching, as dissenters always do, to cast doubt, to undermine, to sow the seeds of discord. As Aisha's reputation suffered, so too did that of the Prophet.'

The General finished his tea, gave Lahik the rest of a cookie and gathered up his reins. 'Let us ride on. Check your girth and tighten it a notch.'

'General, Ali,' said Lucinda, mounting Alima, 'what happened? That's not the end of the story.'

'Oh, my dear, we haven't changed. Petty rivalries require but a spark to set the world ablaze. The Prophet at first ignored the gossip, knowing it to be salacious, untrue. He was, of course, above such idle scandal, but scandal, as they say, is its own reward.

'Soon Muhammad could afford to ignore it no longer, but what was he to do? If he divorced Aisha, might not this be seen as an admission of guilt? And if he forgave her, might not this be seen as the actions of a foolish, indulgent old man? It may seem trivial to your western sensibilities, my dear, but it is no exaggeration to say the future of Islam hung in the balance. And all because of a young slip of a girl.'

'Ali,' protested Lucinda, 'you cannot blame—'

'Patience, my dear. Reserve your judgement until the end of the story. The Prophet sent Aisha home to her father, Abu Bakr, and turned to Ali for advice. Ali was renowned for his use of language, his poetry, but the advice he gave Muhammad was strangely terse. Maybe this is because the main account we have is from Aisha herself.

'Ali advised the Prophet to divorce Aisha. "There are many women like her," he said. "God has freed you from constraints. She is easily replaced".'

General Hashemi looked at Lucinda and let the words hang in the air.

'Is that it?' said Lucinda. 'That's no resolution.'

'Calm yourself, my dear. The Prophet paid a visit to Abu Bakr's house to confront Aisha, maybe to divorce her, we will never know. While there, he fell into a trance and was visited by God. God declared Aisha's innocence and Muhammad proclaimed this in public. The revelation is contained in the Koran.

'Muhammad had already received a revelation instructing the Prophet's wives to wear a veil to protect their dignity when they went into the fields to relieve themselves, but a few weeks after the Affair of the Necklace, the Prophet had another revelation known as the Revelation of the Curtain. God instructed the Prophet's wives be protected in their homes by a thin muslin curtain to keep them from the prying eyes of any man not their kin. They were now protected both inside and outside the house. The veil was only meant for the wives of the Prophet, but over time it was adopted by Muslim women far and wide.

'And that, my dear, is the story of the Affair of the Necklace. Ali and Aisha became adversaries. She would never forgive him the advice he gave the Prophet. Much of the split in Islam can be traced back to the relationship between Ali and Aisha and her foolish actions.'

General Hashemi turned in his saddle. 'Now tell me, what do you think?'

Lucinda reminded herself her task was to befriend the General, but that didn't mean she had to act like a lamb. 'It strikes me, Ali, that, like all religious texts and stories, it is a matter of interpretation. I am no Islamic scholar and my understanding of the Sunni Shia schism is rudimentary. But if I take anything from this story, it is this. A young girl, a child, excited by adventure, made an innocent mistake that was turned and twisted by a savage bunch of society gossips to humiliate her. You said so yourself. At the risk of offending you, I would go so far as to say this is typical misogyny. Always blame the woman for the faults of man.'

'Your view,' sighed the General, 'merely confirms that women have no place in politics.'

'You don't seriously believe that, General?'

'The point is not whether Aisha slept with Safwan or not. Whether this was a planned assignation, which I do not believe it was, or whether it was purely an innocent act of fate. The point, my little Humayra, is that none of this would have happened if Aisha had remained at home. Yes, I do believe it. War and the affairs of state are the business of men, not women.'

Lucinda caught her breath, stunned at the ignorance of such an erudite man. Damn befriending him, she was going to give him both barrels.

But she didn't have time.

Alima pricked her ears and started to pull.

CHAPTER SIXTEEN

The Battle of the Camel

They had reached the edge of an oak forest. It forged a natural barrier in the contours of the land. Below, the gentle hills stretched out sedate and serene. Above, the hills were grassless, wilder, turning themselves into mountains.

General Hashemi fought to hold Lahik, who was straining at the bit. 'There is a lovely gallop through this forest. I am going to let Lahik loose. But don't worry, you can take your time, my dear. The path is easy to follow and it's about two miles long. There are a couple of obstacles, which you can go around. Arabs are not known for their jumping, but these two will be fine. I'll meet you at the other end.'

General Hashemi gathered his reins and dug his heels into Lahik. They were off.

Fuck you, thought Lucinda. She kicked Alima hard and set off in pursuit.

As soon as she entered the forest, the temperature dropped five degrees, the canopy of oak leaves denying the sun all but sporadic access. The ground was soft and Lahik's hooves threw up mud at Lucinda and Alima.

They had given Hashemi a six-length head start, but he was not pulling away. Lucinda checked to see she was in control. Well, as in control as she could be. Style went out of the window. This was a race, pure and simple. Her toes pointed down to the ground. The stirrup irons felt secure tucked up into the heels of her riding boots. Thank God for the boots. Lucinda's legs gripped hard. She stood in the saddle, leaning forward, hunching her upper body to reduce wind resistance. Her hands, tight on the reins, grabbed Alima's withers.

General Hashemi looked back, surprise registering for a second on his face. He smiled and nodded in approval.

Lucinda pulled back the mare's left ear. 'Right, Alima, let's see what the girls can do.'

Sensing the challenge, Alima quickened her pace. The track was straight and about two metres wide. The oakleaf canopy hemmed them in and loose branches stuck out at random. Lucinda was slapped by one on the arm.

The gap was down to three lengths.

There was a righthand bend up ahead. Lucinda couldn't tell how sharp it was, but she moved Alima over to the right and kicked on. As they approached the corner, Alima's head was level with Lahik's rump. Seeing the gap, Alima quickened again and got the inside track. General Hashemi had to pull Lahik back to stop the stallion from losing his feet round the bend and Alima emerged neck and neck with Lahik from the corner.

Lahik stared at Alima, fire in his eyes. He threw his head right and bucked, jolting the General in the saddle. Alima refused to yield as the two horses galloped flat out side by side.

Lucinda saw a tree trunk lying across the path fifty yards ahead. Two feet high, should be fine. Before she could even think whether she should slow down, try to count strides, both horses leapt the obstacle, flying through the air, landing in unison.

Alima kept pace with Lahik, going no more than a neck

behind. Lucinda was enveloped by the breathing of the horses, the pounding of their feet as they thundered through the forest. The General's leg bashed against Lucinda's as they fought for the lead.

There was another corner ahead. A lefthander. The General had the inside, but he moved over to the right, forcing Lucinda into the tree line. A loose branch smacked across her face. She pulled hard on the reins, just making it back onto the track and round the corner. They had lost five lengths.

'C'mon, Alima. Ha!' Lucinda kicked again and Alima found another gear. She was so powerful, so strong. Lucinda felt she had at least one more gear, maybe two. Alima had been given her head, allowed for once to fight, and she repaid Lucinda with everything she had. They were just two lengths behind, eating the mud thrown up by Lahik.

Another righthander and the track had started to turn downhill. Lucinda and Alima repeated their first move, barging in on the right, taking the inside line. Alima moved left, forcing Lahik and the General wide.

They came out of the corner ahead. Lucinda had to look back to see where the General was. Two lengths. Maybe three. 'Good girl,' she said, patting Alima. 'Now kick on.'

Lucinda felt alive, exhilarated, at one with the beautiful animal beneath her. She could feel every muscle of the mare straining, pushing, forcing them on. The adrenalin rushed through her body as it had the night they raided Abu Issa's compound. It was about being right on the edge, in total control of yourself and your surroundings, yet knowing such control was an illusion, it was fleeting, you could lose everything in a second. It was beautiful. It was liberating. It was like the best sex in the world.

'Shit,' Lucinda shouted. Rushing up to meet her was a giant oak trunk blocking the path in front. It must have been all of four feet high.

The General was within a neck, almost alongside. Lahik

looked as though he had plenty left in the tank. There's no going back now. *Let's go for it*, thought Lucinda.

But it was too late. Alima had sensed Lucinda's hesitation and she put in an extra stride before the jump. She wrapped the trunk with her front feet, forcing both herself and Lucinda off balance. They landed hard on the other side, Alima stumbling and going down onto her knees, sliding through the mud. Lucinda held on for dear life, completely out of the saddle, clinging to the mare's neck. Somehow this incredible animal managed to stay on her feet and she dragged herself forward with a mighty stride.

They were ten lengths behind and Lucinda had lost her right stirrup, but she wasn't going to give up. They galloped on, Lucinda desperately feeling for the stirrup iron which was banging against the saddle and smashing into her leg.

By the time she had both feet back in the stirrups and was ready to rejoin the race, they were twenty lengths behind and Lucinda could see a clearing up ahead. The path was leading them out of the forest. The race was over.

Lucinda sat back and pulled on the reins. 'Whoa, Alima, whoa! There's a good girl.' Alima slowed, dropping to a canter, then a fast trot. Lucinda stood in the stirrups. Pools of lathered sweat splashed off the mare as Lucinda patted her on the neck. Alima was blowing hard, jets of steam-like breath bursting from her flared nostrils. 'What a good girl.'

General Hashemi was waiting for them in the sunlight. Lahik was also blowing hard, snorting, glistening with sweat.

'You are an excellent horsewoman, my dear, a natural. You and Alima make a great team. I have never seen her race so hard. I must be careful never to underestimate you. But you are injured. We have not followed doctor's orders.'

Lucinda wiped her cheek where she had been struck by the branch. She saw blood on the back of her hand.

'It's nothing.'

Hashemi slipped off Lahik and held the stallion's head in his hands, kissing his steaming forehead. 'A proper race for you today. You did well, my prince.' He moved to Lahik's side, undid the girth and took off the saddle. Without looking at Lucinda, he said, 'Give Alima to the groom. He will take care of her.'

Lucinda jumped off Alima. Her knees buckled as she hit the ground. Her legs were like jelly, wobbling uncontrollably, and she had to fight to stay on her feet. Her shoulders and arms were on fire. Lucinda undid the girth and hauled the saddle off Alima's back. The groom took the saddle.

'Sit, my dear, have a drink. You can wash your face.' Only now did Lucinda notice a trestle table with a white tablecloth and two wooden chairs. She picked up a bottle of water from the table, leant forward and tipped it over the back of her head and down her neck. It was ice cold and gloriously refreshing. The water ran down her face, which she washed with her hands.

Lucinda exaggerated a stretch, extending her arms out to the side then raising them up and clasping her hands behind her head. She looked up at the blue sky above and held the pose.

'How do you feel?' asked Hashemi.

'I think I may be a little stiff in the morning. I'm pretty fit, but I'm not used to this type of exercise.'

Lucinda sat, grateful to take the weight off her aching legs, and poured herself a tall glass of the ice-cold water. She was still out of breath, still exhilarated.

The table sat in the shade of an oak on the edge of the forest and was laid for two. Green and black olives, tomatoes, cucumbers, a mixed salad chopped fine, feta cheese and a plate of herbs – basil, tarragon, coriander – covered the table. And bread, a mound of bread.

Lucinda could see the heat haze emanating from a homemade barbecue sitting on two columns of red bricks. She poured herself another glass of water and sat back. Her white poplin shirt would need washing again. It was covered in mud.

General Hashemi's house and the village were no longer visible, hidden behind one of the hills below. Not a single man-made structure was in sight and the view of the lake and surrounding mountains was stunning.

Hashemi and the groom were washing Lahik and Alima down. 'There,' said the General, 'go and rest a while, my darlings.' Alima turned to Lahik, who ignored her and trotted off.

'I think his nose is a little out of joint,' smiled the General, walking to the back of the pickup. 'Forgive my manners, my dear, but the horses must come first.'

'Of course, Ali.' Lucinda decided to keep using the General's first name. If she was going to elicit some useful information, she needed his trust. 'Alima deserves the attention more than me. She gave me quite a ride. I thought we had you at one point.'

'I must confess you did have me a little worried. Now, what would you like? There is beer or wine. I don't drink, but I believe the wine is quite good.'

'I would love a glass of white if you have it, Ali. Thank you.'

General Hashemi returned to the table with a bottle of 2015 Christian Moreau Grand Cru Les Clos. Lucinda didn't know the wine, but it had the enticing pale gold colour typical of Chablis. As the General poured her a glass, Lucinda could smell almonds and peach.

'To you, my dear,' said the General, raising his glass of water. 'And thank you.'

'And thank you, Ali, for your hospitality,' replied Lucinda. 'It is a little surreal to be sitting here with you, an Iranian General, high up in the hills of Kurdistan. But it is beautiful, and I am very happy to be here.'

'What would our masters say?' joked Hashemi.

'I think I have rather more than you, and I don't think they would be best pleased.'

'Then, just for now, let us pretend there is no one else in the world. Sit, enjoy your wine, enjoy the view, and let us talk while I cook.'

Hashemi fished two paper packets from the back of the pickup. 'Barbecue kebabs for lunch. Two types. One, ground lamb with garlic, parsley and sumac – the key – and the other, whole pieces of lamb.' Hashemi put several skewers of meat on the barbecue with separate skewers of tomatoes and onions. The lamb sizzled and spat.

'They look delicious. Tell me,' said Lucinda, holding her wine and admiring the view, 'what happened to Aisha in the end?'

'I told you that Aisha was the daughter of Abu Bakr and that Abu Bakr became Caliph after the death of the Prophet. Well, as wife of the Prophet and now daughter of the First Caliph, Aisha's position was secure. She used her status as widow, together with the power and patronage of her father, to build her own power base. The manipulative little girl grew into a powerful political figure in her own right.

'And all the while she harboured her hatred of Ali. The bitterness grew inside her like a cancer, spreading through her being, seeping into every pore. By the time Ali became Caliph, twenty-four long years after the death of the Prophet, the two were barely on speaking terms. Worse, Aisha now felt threatened, fearing Ali would reduce her influence, take her estates away.

'Ali was blamed for the murder of Othman, his predecessor as Caliph. He had, in fact, tried to intercede between the disparate factions that threatened to tear the Caliphate apart. Ali always sought the path of peace. But to no avail, and as soon as he became Caliph, Aisha started plotting his downfall. She stoked the fires of opposition, striving to undermine his right to be Caliph from the start.'

The General turned the skewers and wafted the smoke away from his face. He joined Lucinda at the table.

'Ali was proclaimed Caliph in the city of Medina, and when

the news arrived in Mecca, Aisha went straight to the great mosque. There she stood, by the black stone of the Kaaba. She knew exactly what she was doing. Do you know what the Kaaba is, my dear?'

'It's the building in the middle of the mosque, the one around which pilgrims still walk today during the Hajj,' replied Lucinda.

'Yes, it is. The Kaaba is the holiest site in Islam, it is the very house of God and it is to the Kaaba Muslims face when they pray. There is a black stone in the eastern wall of the Kaaba. It was a gift bestowed by Allah on Adam and Eve, and they used the stone in the altar they built. The very first altar on which our parents gave thanks to the Creator.

'And there, on that very spot, Aisha stood and proclaimed, "Seek revenge for the blood of Othman and you will strengthen Islam".'

General Hashemi shook his head and sighed. 'Aisha rallied the people of Mecca behind her. Two of her brothers-in-law, Talha and Zubayr, joined her cause, each coveting the Caliphate for himself.

'They could not face Ali in Medina, he was too strong. So they planned to march to Basra and then north up the Euphrates to Kufa, strengthening their army and creating a force that could not be matched. Iraq, as it still is today, was the key. He who controls Iraq, my dear, controls the Middle East.

'But they did not reach Kufa. When Ali got word that Aisha was marching to Basra with an army of Meccans, he set out with his own army from Medina. It was October in the year 656. The two armies faced each other on the flat plains of Basra, evenly matched with ten thousand troops on each side.

'Ali was desperate to avoid bloodshed and he negotiated with Talha and Zubayr for three days, riding out again and again to meet them in the unforgiving heat of no-man's land. But it was not to be. And the battle, the Battle of the Camel, marked the start of the Muslim civil war. Our community was torn apart and we entered the fitna, the terrible, soul-destroying split that has wrenched us apart for over a thousand years.'

General Hashemi finished his glass of water and walked back to the barbecue to turn the skewers.

'Aisha herself rode at the head of her army, the first Muslim woman to lead troops into battle. Not even the infamous Liver Eater had done this.'

'The Liver Eater?' asked Lucinda.

'You have a lot of Islamic history to read, my dear,' smiled Hashemi. 'Lunch is almost ready. Her name was Hind. At the Battle of Badr in 624, the first major battle between the Meccans and the Medinans at the very beginning of Islam, Hind's father was killed by Muhammad's uncle, Hamza. One year later at the Battle of Uhud, the tide turned the Meccans' way and Hamza was slain by a mighty Abyssinian slave warrior. When battle was done Hind scoured the field, searching for Hamza's corpse. She found it.

'She cried out in victory, unsheathed her knife and plunged it into Hamza's body, ripping it apart. She cut out his liver, held it high above her head and tore it apart with her teeth, the blood dripping down her chin. Hind spat out the pieces and ground them into the dirt. Her name was well deserved, but, as I say, she did not lead an army into battle. That first was Aisha's privilege and destiny.

'The howdah of Aisha's camel was draped not with muslin but with chain mail covered in red silk. She sat tall above the horse cavalry, the leader, the rallying point. She screamed out battle cries learnt on those early campaigns with the Prophet, urging on her men. "Show your valour, sons of mine. You are heroes, you are mountains," she cried, "death to the killers of Othman".'

Hashemi put the kebabs, onions and tomatoes on two plates and brought them over to the table. 'Would you like a glass of red wine to go with your kebabs, my dear?'

Lucinda prided herself on her ability to retain complete control after a few glasses of wine, but this was not the time to test her pride. She needed to stay sharp, not give any advantage to the General. 'Thank you, no,' she replied. 'I will finish the glass of white and have water with my lunch. I wouldn't want to be under the influence and in charge of an Arab mare. Bon appetit, Ali.'

'Bon appetit, my dear. I hope you enjoy the kebabs.' General Hashemi picked up a piece of bread the size of a dinner plate and tore off a hunk. He wrapped some of the kebab, onion and tomato in the bread.

'Reports from eye-witness survivors describe one of the bloodiest battles ever known. The fighting lasted from early morning to mid afternoon. Thousands of men were slaughtered.'

General Hashemi paused. 'Not perhaps the most appropriate of lunch conversations.'

'Possibly not,' replied Lucinda, 'but, please, go on. It's fascinating.'

Hashemi picked up a skewer and stripped off a piece of lamb with his teeth.

'One story tells of a soldier whose leg was severed and he picked it up to use as a weapon. Can you imagine the carnage of hand-to-hand combat on the field of battle, my dear? Not like the remote warfare of today, drones flown by pilots thousands of miles away, dropping bombs on towns and villages they will never know. This was men at close quarters, giving no quarter, limbs being hacked off, bodies decapitated, guts spilling onto the battlefield, turning the desert sands red with blood. Men related to each other on opposing sides. Tribes, clans, families, cousins, fathers, sons, killing one another, splitting Islam apart, cutting the heart out of the Prophet's message.

'By noon both Talha and Zubayr lay dead. The battle was swinging decisively in Ali's favour, but Aisha would not retreat, she would not yield. Still she urged her fighters on.

'As the day wore on, most of those that had not been killed laid down their arms. Only a few hundred of Aisha's most loyal troops remained to protect her. And at the head of those troops was the standard bearer. Holding the reins of Aisha's camel in one hand and her banner in the other, he was defenceless. When the first was cut down, a second took his place, only to face the same fate. One by one the standard bearers were slaughtered, seventy men all told. The dwindling remnant of Aisha's troops begged her to surrender, but still she refused, screaming them on, berating them for their defeatism and extolling them for their bravery in equal measure.

'After the battle the poets would ask, "Oh Mother of ours, the most uncaring Mother we know, did you not see how many a brave man was struck down, his hand and wrist made lonely?" Another wrote, "Our Mother brought us to drink at the pool of death. We did not leave until our thirst was quenched. When we obeyed her, we lost our senses. When we supported her, we gained nothing but pain."

'Finally, Ali managed to end the madness. He shouted an order to hamstring the camel and one of his men managed to slash the animal's tendons. They say there was never a sound louder than the bellowing of that camel, the camel after which the battle was named. It drowned the voices of the warriors in death and collapsed to the ground with Aisha still inside the howdah.

'Aisha was wounded. She had an arrow in her upper arm, but it was only a flesh wound. Ali approached and at last she conceded victory. "Oh Mother," Ali said to Aisha, "may God forgive you."

'After the battle, Aisha was escorted back to Basra by Ali's men. Ali himself wandered the battlefield alone, praying over every single corpse. "Oh God," he prayed, "had I but died two decades before this day."

'Perhaps he should have tried and executed Aisha. Some of Ali's advisers suggested just this course of action, but Ali, as ever, chose peace, mercy, reconciliation. "She is the wife of your Prophet now and forever," he said, striving for unity over revenge. Aisha was taken back under full military escort to Medina. She was not a prisoner, and to show his respect, Ali rode the first few miles alongside her. Once back in Medina, Aisha retired from public life.'

General Hashemi pushed his plate away. 'How were the kebabs, my dear?'

'Very good, Ali. Thank you. It sounds like Aisha remains a divisive figure to this day.'

'Yes,' replied Hashemi. 'To the Sunni, Aisha is the Mother of the Faithful. She is known by them as Al-Mubra'a, the Exonerated. To the Shia, the true believers, Aisha is Al-Fahisha, the Whore.'

Lucinda poured herself half a glass of wine. 'Then I'm not sure I should be flattered by you calling me Humayra, Ali.'

'My dear, fear not, it was merely your youth and beauty that reminded me of Aisha. But I think often of the early days and what we have become. Conflict in the Middle East is a dark, meandering river that can trace its source back through fourteen hundred years of history.'

'I would like to know more, Ali,' said Lucinda, finishing her wine.

'I think perhaps that is enough for one day,' said Hashemi. He was distracted, almost maudlin. 'And I think we should be making our way back.'

The groom had tacked up Lahik and Alima. Lucinda stood up. Her body hurt. Muscles she didn't know she had were aching, but she wasn't going to show any weakness. She grabbed the reins, put her left foot in the stirrup, bounced on her right leg a couple of times and threw herself into the saddle.

General Hashemi stood next to Lahik, his hands on the reins, his foot in the stirrup. He paused and looked at Lucinda.

'Let us not be adversaries, my little Humayra. That would be unfortunate.'

General Hashemi mounted Lahik and they started the ride back to the house.

CHAPTER SEVENTEEN

Cue Gardens

Sir Philip Colville-Browne stared out of his office window overlooking the Thames. It was a miserable, unrelenting day. Sheets of rain lashed the window. London buses and black taxicabs splashed across Vauxhall Bridge in the early morning gloom.

'It is a little embarrassing,' said Sir Philip, 'to be told the whereabouts of one of our agents by the CIA.'

Ramesh Varma and Cristine Laird were sitting at the round meeting table. Occupying one of the two chairs in front of C's enormous empire desk was Miles Cavendish.

Sir Philip returned to the desk and picked up a satellite image sitting on top of a pile of papers in a brown, manila folder. 'And another thing. Would anyone care to tell me what Lucinda Spark is doing riding a horse, which looks very much like an Arab mare to me, with the commanding officer of the Iranian Quds Force? Anyone?'

Sir Philip flicked the picture back towards the file, but it overshot and slid across the desk, gathering speed on the polished leather. Miles stapled it to the surface with the palm of his hand before it could escape.

'Cristine, facts.' Sir Philip remained standing, his fists planted on the desk, his tie perpendicular.

'Three days ago, Spark went to the Jeddah IDP camp south of Mosul. We know this from the CIA and the man she travelled with, an Australian called Andrew Simmonds. He works for a medical NGO. We can dismiss much of his statement as self-serving. Simmonds is clearly keen to inflate the importance of his role. All we know for certain is that Spark was there and so too was Major General Hashemi. Somehow, Spark managed to meet him in the mosque compound and a low-yield device exploded inside the tent where they both were. We have no intelligence on who was behind the explosion, but both Spark and General Hashemi survived. From the imagery we have and the intercepts of Iranian military traffic, we believe there were at least two fatalities.'

'I don't care about the fatalities. I care about the health, whereabouts and safety of my agent.' Sir Philip snatched the receiver of one of the phones on his desk. 'Daisy, sorry to be a pain, but you could bring us some coffee?'

Sir Philip cradled the handset. 'At least we know where she is, and if she's riding Arab mares in the mountains of Kurdistan, we can assume she's healthy enough. Options?'

'Three, as I see them, sir. One, do nothing and assume Spark's legend is intact. She is undercover with the prime suspect in a planned terrorist attack on UK soil. She is doing her job. We work out ways to support her, then extract her in due course if needs be, but we leave her where she is.'

'Two?'

'Two,' continued Laird, before pausing as the door opened and Daisy Thorn, the Chief's personal assistant, entered with a tray of coffee.

'Thank you, Daisy,' said Sir Philip. 'Carry on, Cristine. No need to stop.'

'Two, we initiate diplomatic contact immediately. Our

Ambassador meets the Iranian Ambassador in Baghdad. We believe one of your generals has an aid worker of ours. Jolly kind and all that, but we'd quite like her back. Options one and two are not mutually exclusive and if we bring this to the attention of the Iranian government, it might afford Spark some protection.'

Daisy closed the door behind her.

'Would you mind, Ramesh?'

'Certainly, sir.'

'And three,' continued Laird, 'assume Spark's legend is blown, she is being kept hostage against her will, riding horses or not, and we try to negotiate her out or send in a team to get her.'

'Ramesh, is the drone in the air?'

'Yes, sir.' Varma handed Sir Philip a coffee. 'It took off from Erbil at zero-eight-hundred local. We took control in mid-flight at zero-nine-hundred. All systems operational and the drone has been on target for forty-five minutes.'

'Good. Make sure they don't crash it. It's our most expensive toy.' Sir Philip closed the file on his desk and sat down with a sigh. 'What about the five individuals in Spark's report, Ramesh?'

'Three have now been located and are under surveillance. Two are in the London area, Brent and Croydon. No connection between the two has yet been found. The third is in the Manchester area, Gorton. As for the other two, neither the police nor the Security Service have unearthed anything. They are ghosts.'

'I want to know how the three we know about got here, when, and any and all connections, past or present, with the outside world. If they've made any calls, sent letters, written a bloody postcard, I want to know about it. And the same goes for the other two as soon as they're identified.'

Miles Cavendish crossed his legs. 'Anything from the Jordanians?'

'Not a word. Three days they've had Abu Issa in custody. God knows if he's even still alive. You know how robust the Jordanians can be.'

'Sir, we have movement on target,' interrupted Varma, picking up a remote control.

All eyes turned to the far wall. A 250cm by 150cm reproduction of Sir George Hayter's painting *The House of Commons, 1833*, disappeared vertically behind the gilt frame to reveal a monitor. 'That,' said Varma, 'is General Hashemi's house on Lake Darbandikhan.'

Circling twenty-thousand feet in the skies above the lake, the RQ-3S Predator unmanned aerial vehicle was beaming live pictures of General Hashemi's house via the Ku band satellite data link. For the last hour it had been remotely piloted by a team in a windowless operations room six floors below C's office in the basement of the MI6 building.

The Predator drone had an impressive array of sensors, including synthetic aperture radar and forward-looking infrared, but it was images from the prototype Daedalus system on which all eyes in C's office were focused.

The Daedalus camera system was born from collaboration between the US Defense Advanced Research Projects Agency – DARPA, the creator of the internet – and the UK's Defence Science and Technology Laboratory. The resulting hi-tech baby they created had one hundred and eighty-four five-megapixel sensors melded together to produce a one billion gigapixel camera capable of recording twelve frames per second. Daedalus had the capability to survey an area of five square miles, but today it was focused on half a square mile with General Hashemi's house slap bang in the middle.

Three black GMC Suburbans swept round the fountain in the middle of the circular drive and parked in front of the house.

'Six-inch resolution, sir,' said Varma. 'We can't read the number plates, but we can tell the make and model.'

'That's him,' said Laird.

Sir Philip watched General Hashemi walk down the steps towards the open rear door of the middle Surburban. Hashemi paused and looked up.

'He can't hear it, can he?'

'No, sir,' replied Varma. 'Even on a clear day, you can't hear anything with the drone at twenty thousand feet. And with the new sound suppression technology, he definitely has no idea we are watching.'

General Hashemi got into the Suburban and the three vehicles drove off round the fountain and down the long driveway.

'Do you want us to follow him, sir?' asked Varma.

'Wait!' exclaimed Miles. 'That's Spark.'

To the left of the screen, Lucinda emerged from a side entrance and walked down a short flight of stone steps into the garden.

'Pan left. Centre Spark,' ordered Sir Philip.

Varma typed an Instant Message on his phone and five seconds later the image on the monitor moved and centred on Lucinda.

'Zoom.'

Lucinda grew on the screen. She was standing at the entrance to the garden. She stretched her arms out sideways and brought them above her head in a slow, exaggerated movement. She clasped her hands together, held the back of her head, and stood motionless for sixty seconds.

'Good girl,' said Miles, 'that's one of the safe signals.'

'So, now we know where she is, how she is, and that she does not feel under threat or in imminent danger. Ramesh, how long can the drone stay in the air?'

'Forty hours, sir, but we limit it to thirty-six. That includes flight time back to base.'

'Stay on Spark. Anything in the vicinity of that house moves, I want to know about it. And let me know when Hashemi returns.'

'Yes, sir.'

'Ramesh, Cristine, thank you. That's all for now.'

Varma and Laird left the room.

'You know Spark better than anyone, Miles. What do you think?'

'Cristine's right,' said Miles, getting up and walking over to the window. 'Options one and two are not mutually exclusive. We should engage the Iranians immediately. Lucinda is young and inexperienced, but she is strong, driven, and brilliant at thinking on her feet. I haven't seen a recruit like her for a long time. I would leave her in place for now, but we do need a contingency plan.'

Sir Philip stared at the screen, silent for over a minute.

'If you didn't know otherwise, you would say she was taking her morning constitutional without a care in the world. I agree, Miles. Our Ambassador is at the Iranian Embassy in Baghdad as we speak, passing on pretty much exactly the message Cristine suggested.'

'And the contingency?' asked Miles.

The rain was getting worse, the London sky darkening by the second.

'Seeing as it's one of your legacies, Miles, I will tell you. I spoke to the PM last night. An eight-man team from The Unit deployed to Erbil first thing this morning. By mid afternoon they will be on one hour's notice to move.'

'That's the right decision, Philip.'

'Maybe, but as to when or if I send them in to get her, God knows.'

Miles nodded. 'That's why you're sitting in that chair, not me.'

'Hah!' retorted Sir Philip. 'Fat chance, but if this bloody weather clears up do you fancy lunch at the Club?'

'Yes,' replied Miles. 'And let's break open a bottle of the '96 Musar.'

Alone on the monitor, Lucinda went back into the house.

CHAPTER EIGHTEEN

Twelver

Dress, Givenchy. Black, halter-neck, backless, midi, belted at the waist, made of silk. Shoes, Louboutin. Patent leather, crystal-studded sandals with four-inch stiletto heels and ankle strap. Bag, Bottega Veneta. Black, crocodile clutch. Earrings, Persian silver, drop, with emerald inset, matching her eyes.

Lucinda Spark looked at her reflection in the mirror. Waves of auburn hair caressed her bare shoulders. The silk of the dress was smooth and sensual against her body, the material just covering the curves of her breasts, an erotic suggestion of her nudity beneath.

She turned and looked at her bare back, the semi-circular cut of the dress hugging her lower spine, just above her buttocks. She lifted her right foot, spinning it on the point of the stiletto. She must have been wearing five thousand pounds' worth of clothes and accessories. It was a little over the top, but Hashemi had good taste, Lucinda had to give him that.

A side table was laden with makeup products. Foundation, blusher, mascara, eye shadow, eye liner. Lucinda ignored them all, applying only the cherry red lipstick.

She had no idea how the evening would pan out, but breakfast seemed an eternity ago, and after the day's events Lucinda was not optimistic.

'Good morning, my dear. I hope you don't mind omelette again for breakfast.'

General Hashemi spatula'd the eggs onto Lucinda's plate and placed the saucepan on a cork mat on the table. He was wearing an apron over his military uniform, the black and gold IRGC insignia standing proud against the sharply pressed dark green of his shirt.

'I don't mind at all, Ali. Good morning. You look as if you are going out?'

Hashemi sighed as he helped himself to a slice of omelette. 'Duty calls, I'm afraid, my dear. I was hoping we might go riding again today, but I will be out most of the day.'

'Well, I think perhaps I should call the Embassy, Ali. Let them know where I am, that all's well. I really should be leaving.'

'Oh, my dear, let's not burst this delightful little bubble just yet. We will call them tomorrow. And then we can return to our normal lives. Now, enjoy your breakfast.'

Two mobile phones next to Hashemi's eggs vibrated, dancing around each other in a silent game of chess. 'Is there no peace?' asked Hashemi, drinking his tea.

Lucinda got up from the table with the General and walked through the brash entrance hall. For a moment, she pictured handing Hashemi his briefcase, complete with newspaper and packed lunch, and giving him a farewell peck on the cheek with wifely wishes for a good day at the office. She didn't know which was more absurd; the image of domestic bliss or the reality of the situation in which she found herself.

Lucinda watched Hashemi descend the imperial staircase and climb into one of the waiting black GMC Suburbans. She turned back through the entrance hall and went out through a pair of French windows.

The first part of the garden was formal. A shin-high maze of perfectly trimmed box hedge. All equilateral triangles, squares and rectangles, filled with rose beds and separated by gravel pathways. A carved, wooden pergola towered in the middle of the maze, draped in a climbing plant. A vine maybe. On the far side, the box and rose gave way to a lawn edged with beds full of various shrubs and flowers, difficult to determine at this distance. At the end of the lawn, a stone wall with parkland beyond, rolling its way down to the shores of Lake Darbandikhan.

Maybe that's where the zebra were. It was tempting to find out, but Hashemi's absence had given Lucinda an opportunity she dare not waste.

Time to regain the initiative.

First things first, a safe signal. The rose garden was still in shadow, the side of the house blocking the rising sun, but the thin lattice of early morning cloud was wisping away and it was clear enough.

Lucinda stretched her arms out sideways and brought them above her head in a slow, exaggerated movement. She clasped her hands together, held the back of her head, and stood motionless for sixty seconds. She looked up, hoping to God someone was watching her from up there.

She looked left. The dust cloud had settled on the drive, confirming the General's convoy had gone. Lucinda waited another minute to be sure and then walked back up the stone steps into the house.

Apart from Hashemi, the only other person Lucinda had seen in the house was the chubby maid. She made her way through the dining room and down the corridor to the kitchen, where the maid was busy with her hands in the sink. She didn't seem to wander far from this corner of the house.

Lucinda decided to start from the top and she took the stairs to the third floor two at a time. She checked every one of the seven other rooms on her floor. She didn't expect to find anything of interest and her expectations were not disappointed. All the rooms were identical. All spare bedrooms, all made up, but with no signs of life. Lucinda was the only guest.

The second floor was where Lucinda expected to find some promise. A wide, carpeted landing offered two doors on the right.

Lucinda tried the first. It was open.

The room, which must have been twenty metres long by ten metres wide, was dominated by an enormous V-shaped table. The table was made from two pieces of live edged wood. Not mahogany, not oak. Lucinda wasn't sure what it was.

Twelve places were set at the table. One at the apex, five on the right and six on the left. Each setting had a black and white table mat with different Arabic calligraphy on each mat. There were no papers on the table and no drawers to search. Nothing of interest.

The V of the table led down the room, the ends opening up before a floor-to-ceiling window. The walls on either side were oak-panelled and had open fires with marble mantlepieces.

Lucinda looked at the picture above the fireplace on the right. It was a stylised painting of a white horse, an Arab stallion, presumably on the field of battle, with arrows sticking out of its neck, withers and rump. The horse's head was bowed.

Above the fireplace on the left was a sword with a forked tip in a glass display case.

The room oozed power, privilege, secrecy. Lucinda pictured the meetings with General Hashemi at the head of the table, giving orders in his gentle tone, being briefed, barking reprimands, but they were mere impressions, hints. No more. The room yielded Lucinda no facts.

She closed the door behind her.

The second door on the right of the landing was also unlocked, and the moment she entered Lucinda knew this was what she was looking for. It was General Hashemi's private study.

She took a step forward and froze. Surely the General would have some sort of alarm. A motion detector, a laser, pressure pads under the carpet. Something.

But it didn't matter, did it? After all, Lucinda was a guest and she was just having a look around. And the doors were unlocked. Her invasion of Hashemi's private, inner sanctum made the excuse feel pretty thin, but she could run with it.

The study had the same dimensions as the meeting room. Recessed shelving filled with books covered every inch of wall space.

To the left of the door was the flora section, book after book in Farsi, Arabic, English, French and Italian on plants, gardens, herbs. *The Gardens of the Loire Valley*, *Italian Villas and Their Gardens*, *The English Kitchen Garden*.

To the right of the door, the fauna section. Another multilingual array of books on every aspect of the animal kingdom. Books on the preservation of threatened species, how to create wild habitats. A pamphlet on the Persian leopard, which, as far as Lucinda could tell, had been authored by Hashemi himself.

She walked into the middle of the room. On her right was a fireplace, presumably backing onto the one on the left in the meeting room.

It was surrounded by a semi-circle of two high-backed, brown Chesterfield chairs and a Chesterfield sofa. Between them, a coffee table, and on the coffee table a single book. Ibn Wahshiyya's *Book of Poisons*, written in the ninth century.

Above the fireplace was a painting. Two metres long, a metre wide.

Twelve men were sitting cross-legged in a V formation facing forwards. They all wore brown cloaks and green keffiyeh headdresses.

The twelve Shia Imams.

The Imam at the front, at the apex of the V, cradled a fork-tipped sword in his lap. Imam Ali. Lucinda assumed the two on either side of Imam Ali were his sons, Hasan and Hussein. She didn't know which was which, nor did she know the names of the other Imams in the painting.

Eleven of the twelve stared at her, proud, handsome, warrior-like. Chiselled cheekbones. Thick, dark beards. Thick, dark eyebrows. The twelfth Imam, at the back on the left of the V, had no features at all. A bright light shone where his face should have been.

Lucinda had a cursory look at the shelves on either side of the fireplace. On the right, literature and philosophy. Plato, Descartes, Spinoza, Kant. The complete works of Shakespeare in English and Arabic. Camus. Sartre.

To the left of the fireplace, history. Oriental, occidental. Military history, east and west. Lucinda shook her head and turned her attention to the length of wall behind Hashemi's desk.

Every book was in either Arabic or Farsi. If she had been in a public library, Lucinda would have stumbled into the Islamic religious and education section.

Multiple editions of the Koran filled several shelves all on their own. There was a tenth-century history of Islamic prophets and kings written by Abu Jafar al-Tabari. Thirty volumes, at least, thought Lucinda, all bound in dark brown suede and printed on rice paper. There were several versions of the Nahj al-Balagha, the teachings and sermons of Imam Ali.

Lucinda could have spent hours poring over the books in Hashemi's library, moving from shelf to shelf in a random journey through subjects and centuries.

Instead, she turned and sat at the General's desk. The surface was bare. No telephone, no pen holder, no pens. Not even a pencil. Just an expanse of green, polished leather. But there were two sets of four drawers built into the desk's support, left and right, and a two-handled drawer in the middle.

Lucinda pulled back the middle drawer. She found the pens and pencils, and the rest of the stationery items most people left on top of their desk. General Hashemi's mind was too tidy, too precise, for that.

In the top left drawer, she found a single book. An old school exercise book that had been used as a diary. Lucinda flicked through the pages, looking at some of the dates. Halabja, 1988. She put the diary back.

The second drawer contained two maps. The first was a map of Europe, A3 size, folded in four, blank on the back. Across the top of the map, in ballpoint pen, were the words Operation Hidayah.

Lucinda's heart skipped a beat. She scanned the map. Four cities had been ringed with the ballpoint.

London, Birmingham, Manchester, Barcelona.

So, Hashemi planned a minimum of four attacks. Or rather, at least four cities were being targeted.

Lucinda hoped the information she and Jake had recovered during the raid on Abu Issa's compound had led to the positive identification of the five UK suspects. But she didn't recall anything in the material on Barcelona, and she was certain they hadn't missed anything.

Why Barcelona? That seemed random. And if Barcelona, why no other European cities? Maybe it was a question of logistics, opportunity, the right assets in the right place at the right time. Go with what you've got.

The second map was of the Middle East. There was no writing on it at all. Just a thick, black line stretching in a series of zigzags from Tehran to the city of Latakia on Syria's Mediterranean coastline. It followed existing roads. From Tehran into Iraq at a town called Khanaqin. Down towards Baghdad, then up, turning west before Mosul. Into Syria. Deir ez-Zoor, not far from Abu Issa's compound. Was that relevant? Lucinda doubted it. Down to Damascus via Palmyra and up through Homs to the coast. A second line broke off from Damascus to Beirut.

There it was, right in Lucinda's hands. Iran's grand plan to control the heart of the Middle East and gain unfettered access to the Mediterranean. She had no idea how far the plan had progressed, but she was staring at the road, the supply route, the artery of Tehran's strategy.

How much of it was Tehran's plan and how much of it was General Hashemi's?

Lucinda put the maps on the desk and opened the third drawer on the left. She took out a wad of four documents, each bound in a folder with a transparent plastic cover, black ring binding, and thick, black card at the back.

Her Farsi wasn't good enough to make sense of the detail, but it was obvious they were financial accounts. Quarterly reports, as far as she could tell, of an organisation called the Ahl al-Bayt. And according to the most recent report, the Ahl al-Bayt had made an operating profit of over four hundred million dollars in the last quarter.

The Ahl al-Bayt. Hashemi had used the name yesterday. But when? In what context? Lucinda wracked her brain. The People of The House. Aisha was jealous of them. The Ahl al-Bayt were Imam Ali, his wife Fatima and their sons, Hasan and Hussein.

Lucinda dropped the report on the desk.

Hashemi had gone rogue, branched out on his own. Either that or the Supreme Leadership of Iran had created a secret organisation within its own secret organisation. Possible, Lucinda supposed, for plausible deniability purposes. But more likely in Lucinda's view was Hashemi had gone into business for himself. And a very profitable business it was too, comprising terrorism, people trafficking, extortion and narcotics.

It made perfect sense. Hashemi was obsessed with the history of the Shia, their disenfranchisement, their rightful claim to the Prophet's legacy. The stories, the paintings, the sword.

The Ahl al-Bayt was the first Shia family. It was also a criminal organisation run by General Hashemi making well over a billion dollars a year.

If only she had her phone. Any kind of camera. Lucinda would remember the key information in front of her, but if she couldn't get a message out soon, she would miss a lot of the detail.

She reached for the bottom drawer on the left. It was empty.

The first drawer on the right of the desk contained military orders of battle. There were lists of Shia militias, chains of command, disposition, location, equipment. This was exactly the sort of detail she wouldn't be able to retain. Fuck it.

The second drawer was full of maps, pictures, technical drawings and a series of reports. All on the Mosul Dam. Sentences jumped out as Lucinda flicked through the reports. "In light of the massive humanitarian impact a Mosul Dam failure could have," read a report commissioned by the United Nations. "The most dangerous dam in the world," was the dramatic headline of a report by a German engineering company. And if that wasn't bad enough, the US Military Army Corps of Engineers wrote in a report dated 2010, "water flow through the foundation is already compromising the central core of the dam that will lead to catastrophic failure if not remediated."

Lucinda had to get this information out sooner rather later.

She opened the third drawer. Empty.

She opened the fourth and final drawer.

Her heart stopped.

Lucinda took out a single sheet of paper. It was a black and white scanned copy of a passport page. Ann Edmunds's passport, scanned by the receptionist at the Hotel Royal Victoria in Tunis last Tuesday. The quality was poor, the photograph was grainy, but it was unmistakably Lucinda's own face staring back at her.

For the second time today, Lucinda prayed there was someone up there watching. She had to send a signal. And fast. She needed to be extracted and General Hashemi needed to be stopped.

Lucinda put the various documents back in their respective drawers, certain each was going back in the correct drawer, but equally certain Hashemi would notice the disturbance. Time was of the essence.

The first part of the plan was simple. Get outside and send a signal. After that, she wasn't so sure. Hashemi knew who she was, so she had to get out. She could figure out an extraction plan later.

Escaping on horseback didn't seem so ridiculous after all.

Lucinda left the study. The click of the latch seemed to echo through the house as she closed the door.

Halfway down the landing, Lucinda noticed the door to the meeting room was ajar. She knew she had closed it. She turned to the door and paused, her hand motionless over the handle.

'Come in, my dear, have a seat.'

'Ali,' said Lucinda, entering the meeting room, 'what a lovely surprise. I didn't expect you back so soon. I was having a little tour of your wonderful house.'

'Sit,' ordered the General.

Hashemi was in the sixth seat on the left of the V, nearest the window. The place reserved for the mysterious, faceless, twelfth Imam. Lucinda took a seat at the head of the table.

'Do you know how they killed Imam Ali? They sent spies and assassins.'

'Ali…'

Hashemi raised a hand. 'It was Ramadan in the year 661, the year forty in the Islamic Hijri calendar. Ali was attacked on his way back from praying at the mosque in Kufa. The assassin struck a blow to his head with a poisoned sword, and thus Ali became the first of many of the Shia Imams to die by the hand of an assassin.

'But to the end Ali remained a man of peace. "If I live," said Ali, "I shall consider what to do with this man. If I die, then inflict on him blow by blow. But none shall be killed but him. Do not plunge into the blood of Muslims." Ali died and the assassin was executed.'

'General,' said Lucinda, 'why are you telling me this?'

'And the hand that directed the assassin? None other than Muawiya, son of Hind the Liver Eater. Muawiya, who had been ruler of Syria for twenty years and who coveted the Caliphate.

'Hasan and Hussein washed their father's body, rubbed it in herbs and myrrh, and dressed him in three funeral robes. As per Ali's wishes, they tied his body on top of a camel and let the camel roam free. Where the camel stopped, there Ali would be buried.'

General Hashemi walked to the window and spoke to the lake.

'The camel walked for half a day, conscious of its sacred burden. Six miles from Kufa, on top of a barren, sandy rise, the camel came to a stop and knelt. There the boys buried their father.

'The burial place was to remain a secret, Ali wanted no memorial, but in time a shrine was built and a town sprang up out of the barren desert. Najaf is the name of that town and to be buried in its holy soil is what every Shia desires.'

Hashemi turned to Lucinda. 'The cemetery at Najaf, Wadi-us-Salaam, the Valley of Peace, is the largest cemetery in the world. It covers over one thousand five hundred acres and contains the bodies of more than five million Shia Muslims.

'Najaf is one of the great holy cities for the Shia because of its connection with Ali. The clay tablets we call the Turbah that we place in front of us on the ground and touch with our foreheads when we pray should be made either from the soil of Najaf or the other great holy city, Karbala.'

'General, I still don't see...'

'Spies and assassins, my dear. Spies and assassins. Tell me, what is your real name? Ann, Lucinda, or something else?'

Lucinda looked at the General.

'Lucinda,' she said.

'It suits you.'

'How long have you known?'

'I suspected from the moment I saw you. But I wanted to understand why you saved my life.'

'I don't really understand myself, General.'

'I know that now. It was instinct. Simple, complicated, human instinct.'

Two guards the size of houses appeared and stood either side of the door.

'These gentlemen will escort you to your room.'

General Hashemi walked to the wall and pressed a hidden lever. The secret door to Hashemi's study, concealed in the oak panelling, opened.

'What a shame we became adversaries, my little Humayra. Inevitable, I suppose. Drinks will be at seven for dinner at seven-thirty.'

CHAPTER NINETEEN

The Last Supper

Her reflection in the mirror was no help.

Lucinda had spent the entire afternoon locked in her room thinking how she could escape, or at least get a signal out. But the windows were locked, and the shutters outside the windows were locked.

Every idea Lucinda had was more fanciful, more ludicrous, than the last. If they had been entered in the Grand National, she wouldn't have given any of them odds shorter than 250-1. No sooner did a new idea occur than it fell at the first, and Lucinda dismissed it, ending up back at the same, inescapable conclusion.

Hashemi wasn't going to let her go. She had to kill him before he killed her.

The door opened and one of the guards nodded it was time to leave.

They walked behind her on the stairs. If she managed to grab the pistol holstered on the first guard's hip, the second guard would have plenty of time to disarm or kill her.

She couldn't outrun them, not in these heels. And even if she could, where would she go? At seven in the evening, half-naked in Givenchy, on the shores of Lake Darbandikhan?

'You look beautiful, my dear.'

General Hashemi was standing by the drinks table in a small, intimate sitting room on the ground floor. He was dressed in a dark grey suit and black polo-neck sweater. His socks matched his suit and he wore a pair of black suede loafers.

Hashemi handed Lucinda a glass of champagne. 'A Louis Roederer Cristal. 2009. I'm told it tastes like satin.'

'General,' said Lucinda, taking the glass, 'the British Government knows I'm here. You can't possibly hope to get away with this.'

'Your Ambassador met with the Iranian Ambassador in Baghdad this morning, Miss Spark. He got precisely nowhere. Unless the British are planning a full-scale military assault on my home, which would be unwise given the battalion of troops stationed outside, you are my guest for the evening.'

Lucinda took a sip of champagne. She had never tasted anything quite like it. A blend of Pinot Noir and Chardonnay, the grapes had been picked on exactly the right day, probably the right hour, perfect in their ripeness. A delicate yet supple mixture of fruits stroked her palate. Apple, orange, peach. And the finest of bubbles danced on a smooth satin surface.

She decided to change tack.

'General, we know about the attacks in the UK and Spain. We have the names and phone numbers of all the terrorists. They are being monitored as we speak and will be arrested before they can inflict any damage. You won't achieve anything. Better to tell us exactly what your plans are. Why you are doing this?'

'So impatient for the end game, my little Humayra. I will explain everything, don't worry, but we have time enough and there is one more story to tell. It is the greatest, most tragic story of all. It is our Passion Story. When you hear it, you will understand. And I want you to understand.'

General Hashemi dropped two pieces of ice into a glass of cordial and sat in an armchair by the fireplace. Lucinda took the chair opposite.

'If the seeds of the fitna were sown on the Prophet's death and watered at the Battle of the Camel, it was at the Battle of Karbala that the fitna was set irrevocably in stone. Karbala, the historic battle that led to the creation of Sunni and Shia, and the schism that has plagued Islam for fourteen centuries, and plagues us still.

'Muawiya tricked Ali's eldest son, Hasan, into signing an accord whereby Hasan renounced his rightful claim to the Caliphate. According to the terms of the accord, Hasan was to succeed Muawiya on the latter's death, but Muawiya had Hasan murdered, poisoned by his own wife, no less. Muawiya now had the deaths of two Imams on his hands, driven as he was by his lust for power. A top-up, my dear?'

'No, thank you,' said Lucinda.

'Ten years later and forty-eight long years after the death of the Prophet Muhammad, Muawiya was himself dead and the title of Caliph passed to his son, Yazid.

'The people were tired of the oppression, the corruption, and Yazid only promised more of the same. They turned to Hussein, the younger son of Imam Ali and grandson to the Prophet. Letters of support arrived from all over the Islamic world, begging Hussein to release the oppressed from their bondage. The Kufans alone promised Hussein twelve thousand men. Once again, Iraq was to be the battleground.'

Lucinda finished her champagne. Could she smash the glass, launch herself at the General, and inflict a fatal wound before the guards reacted? Possibly, but it would be her final act and she wasn't ready to give up on a way out just yet.

'Shall we eat?' said Hashemi, getting up. 'We have fish for dinner.'

The General escorted Lucinda into the dining room, followed by the two guards.

'Please, have a seat, my dear.'

Lucinda glanced at the stainless steel knives and forks on the table.

'Do not think of doing anything foolish.' Hashemi nodded in the direction of the guards. Both had settled at ease, a couple of metres behind Lucinda, arms in front of their bodies, their left hands holding their right wrists, their right hands holding a pistol.

'It's a little difficult to eat dinner under armed guard,' said Lucinda.

'A circumstance of your own making. Would you like wine with your meal, or perhaps you would care to continue with the champagne?'

'I will stick with champagne.'

'Good.'

The chubby maid bustled in, clutching the Cristal. She was dressed to serve. A white blouse was working overtime to contain her voluminous breasts, and a black, knee-length skirt was also on a double shift, straining at the seams. She filled Lucinda's glass.

General Hashemi draped a napkin over his left thigh. 'Hussein set out from Mecca in September 680 with seventy-two warriors and their families. There is still today much debate as to whether Hussein knew his fate. Whether he genuinely hoped to gather an army and win the Caliphate, or whether he knew the outcome was inevitable from the start.

'There should be no debate. Hussein knew. Of course he knew. His is the greatest sacrifice in the history of Islam.'

The maid reappeared with several dishes, which she lined up on the table. A whole fish was dressed head to tail in a rainbow garnish.

'Trout,' said Hashemi, 'stuffed with pomegranate paste, walnuts and various herbs. Covered with spices and baked for sixty minutes. Garnished with strips of hardboiled egg yolk and egg white, shredded carrot, cauliflower, purple cabbage and pickled cucumber. Allow me.'

Hashemi filleted the fish.

'Istishhad,' he said. 'Martydom, the greatest, most selfless act of all. Hussein sacrificed himself for the Prophet, for the Ahl al-Bayt, for the purity of Islam. He sacrificed himself for the people so they could be reborn. Much like your carpenter.

'Help yourself to potatoes and salad, my dear,' said Hashemi, placing a piece of fish on Lucinda's plate.

'Muawiya,' he continued, 'evil and lustful though he was, was an astute leader and he foresaw the danger. He warned his son Yazid on his deathbed of the power martyrdom conveys. "Hussein is a weak and insignificant man, but the people of Iraq will not leave him alone until they have him rebel. If that happens and you defeat him, pardon him, for he has close kinship to the Prophet and a great claim." Wise words, which Yazid would fail to heed.

'As Hussein marched towards Kufa, the ranks of his army swelled, but a messenger arrived in camp one night and told Hussein the twelve thousand Kufans he had been promised would not materialise. They had been bought off with money and fear.

'News spread through the camp, and those that had joined Hussein melted away, leaving only the original seventy-two warriors.

'Undeterred, Hussein continued his march, but twenty miles from Kufa those very same Kufan troops that had promised themselves to Hussein blocked his path and would not allow him further passage. Fickle the dog-like Kufans had proven themselves again.

'Hussein addressed them, saying, "If you break your covenant with me, you have mistaken your fortune and lost your destiny, for whoever violates his word, violates his soul. The goodness of the world is in retreat and what is good is now bitter".'

Hashemi lingered over the words and repeated them. 'The goodness of the world is in retreat and what is good is now bitter.'

'Unable to enter Kufa, Hussein turned north and at dusk he camped on a desert bluff overlooking an immense plain in the land of the two rivers, the Tigris and the Euphrates. It was the first day of the month of Muharram and Hussein would travel no further.'

Lucinda picked at her fish, searching for options. Hashemi refilled her glass.

'Four thousand troops were sent to surround Hussein and his seventy-two men. Their commander, Shimr, had a simple plan. Cut off the water supply and starve Hussein into surrender.

'What happened at the Battle of Karbala over the following ten days is seared into the mind of every Shia Muslim to this day. The most iconic images and legends of Shiism were born, and they continue to be celebrated, commemorated, mourned.

'There is Qasim, the Prophet's nephew. He married Hussein's daughter in the camp, knowing death would come. The marriage was never consummated, and as soon as the ceremony was over Qasim demanded he be allowed to go out and face the enemy in single combat. He approached Shimr's lines wearing his wedding tunic and pearl earrings. He was cut down.

'There is Abbas, Hussein's half-brother, who wore two white egret plumes atop his chain mail helmet. Abbas made a break through enemy lines in the dead of night to get water. He filled a goatskin but was ambushed on the way back. He killed dozens of Shimr's men before his right arm was cut off. He fought with his left, exclaiming, "This is why God gave us two arms".

'After seven days without water, Hussein's infant son was so weak from dehydration he could no longer cry. Hussein approached the enemy, held his son in the air, and begged Shimr to show the women and children mercy. A single arrow was the reply, an arrow shot straight into the neck of the child as he lay in Hussein's outstretched hands. Hussein prayed to Allah to accept his child's sacrifice, and the blood of the infant defied gravity and flowed upwards to heaven.'

Lucinda pushed her plate away.

'You don't seem to have much of an appetite, my dear.'

'I'm not really in the mood, General, and there are other matters I would like to discuss.'

'Patience. All in good time. The eve of the final day came. Hussein gathered his remaining warriors and begged them to leave, absolving them of all obligation. They refused to abandon him. One said, "By God, if I knew I was to be burned alive and my ashes scattered, and then revived to have it done to me again a thousand times, I still would never leave you. How then could I leave when what I now face is a matter of dying only once?"

'Hussein simply replied, "We belong to God, and to God we shall return."

'The eve of the battle when Hussein gathered his followers is the start of Ashura. Every year the Shia faithful commemorate the events in a series of passion plays called the Taziya. They are for us what your York Mystery Plays are for you, except, of course, few in your Godless world have any idea.

'That night, Hussein took off his chain mail, anointed himself in myrrh and dressed in a simple, flowing, white robe.

'The battle took place the next day on the tenth of Muharram. One by one the remaining warriors went out to meet their deaths. One by one they were slaughtered. By midday, only Hussein remained. He mounted Lahik and charged the enemy lines, his hair and robe flowing as Lahik galloped majestically towards death. "By God," said one of Shimr's men, "I have never seen his like before or since. The foot soldiers retreated from him as goats retreat from an advancing wolf."

'Volley after volley of arrows rained down. Lahik was hit again and again, yet still he charged with his master astride, sword aloft.'

General Hashemi raised his right arm, a tear in his eye.

'Hussein was struck by an arrow and fell from Lahik. The enemy gathered. A knife, a sword. In all, thirty-three slash wounds. Shimr's cavalry rode over the body, trampling Hussein into the dust of Karbala. Lahik, still alive, bowed and dipped his forehead in his master's blood. He returned to the tents of Hussein's female relatives, beat his head on the ground, and there this mighty Arab stallion died.

'They decapitated Hussein and they decapitated every one of his seventy-two warriors. Their heads they put in sacks. Hussein's, they put on a lance.'

Hashemi refilled Lucinda's glass. The guards were immobile behind her.

'One infant son of Hussein survived. He became the fourth of the twelve Imams.'

The chubby maid cleared the plates. There was nothing Lucinda could do.

'A shame you did not eat much fish, but please, have some fruit. And join me in a glass of syllabub, sweetened with honey. It will allow me at least to digest my meal.'

Hashemi sat back in his chair. 'And this, my dear, is what I want you to understand. Do you know what happened to the Imams?'

'No, General, I do not,' said Lucinda.

'At first the Caliphs of the Ummayad dynasty tolerated them, as the Imams immersed themselves in theology, not politics. But in time the Ummayads were ousted by the Abbasids.

'The Abbasid Caliphate is considered a golden age in Islam. They built a new capital on the banks of the Tigris, known originally as Medinat as-Salaam, the City of Peace, but it soon became known by its Persian name "gift of God", or Baghdad.

'Science, literature, philosophy flourished. You will know *The Book of One Thousand and One Nights* which was compiled during this time.

'A golden age it may have been, but the Abbasids felt threatened by the descendants of the Prophet. The seventh Imam was kept under house arrest and died in prison in Baghdad. The tenth and eleventh Imams were imprisoned in Samarra and are entombed in the shrine there.

'The twelfth and final Imam, the last rightful heir to the Prophet Muhammad, Peace Be Upon Him, was born in Samarra. He is the Mahdi, the one who guides divinely. When he was five, he descended into a cave underneath Samarra and went into occultation. There he became a source of light, hidden from view. We know him as Al-Muntazar, the Awaited One, and he will return on judgement day. And when he returns, he will be accompanied by Fatima, who will hold the heart of her son Hasan in one hand, and the severed head of her son Hussein in the other.'

Lucinda looked at the General. 'And when is judgement day?' she asked.

'All the Imams belong to the Ahl al-Bayt, and so do I, my dear. My destiny is to clear a path for the Mahdi, to set the conditions for his return.'

'By blowing up European cities and killing innocent people? That's absurd, General, pointless. You sound like Muawiya to me. And anyway, I told you, we know who the terrorists are. We have broken Hakim Nasri's north African network. It won't work. Your judgement day will have to wait.'

'You disappoint me, my dear. You are in possession of information which will enable you to disrupt some of the attacks in the UK. That is an inconvenience, I admit. But minor. The attacks are a sideshow, part of a message to remind you we can reach you in your homes. To persuade you to stop interfering in our affairs, to stop invading our lands, to leave us alone.

'It is a message we will repeat for years to come and it is getting easier to send. The world's population is growing. And where does it grow? In areas blighted by conflict, famine, in areas

198

that offer no hope, no end to the cycle of despair. There is an inexhaustible supply of young men willing to sacrifice themselves. It is a tide you cannot hope to stem. You cannot win. This war will never end.'

A sideshow. What did the General mean by a sideshow?

Lucinda screwed her eyes shut. She had a headache and was nauseous.

'The dam,' she said. 'You're going to blow Mosul Dam.'

'Brava, my dear. Brava.'

'You will kill tens of thousands of people.'

'No. I will kill hundreds of thousands of people. Perhaps as many as five hundred thousand. At this time of year, the dam has over 10 billion cubic metres of water. I will unleash a tsunami, a flood of biblical proportions. Mosul will be under twenty metres of water in three hours. The city must be purified of the filth that defiled it during the so-called Islamic State Caliphate.

'Bayji, Tikrit, Samarra. All flooded. The banks of the Tigris will burst all the way to Baghdad, and within four days the Abbasid capital will be under four metres of water.'

'You're mad,' said Lucinda. 'And you will kill thousands of Shia as well as Sunni.'

'Istishhad,' said the General. 'Martyrdom. Sacrifice.'

'When? When are you going to do this?'

'That is a present which must remain a secret.'

Lucinda felt sick to her stomach. Waves of nausea crashed over her. She had a pounding headache. 'What did you give me?' she asked, looking at the glass of syllabub.

'Gamma-hydroxybutyrate. GHB. What you would call a date rape drug. Rather prosaic, I'm afraid. I wanted to make something for you myself, something special, but you gave me no time.'

Lucinda put her hands on the table and tried to stand, but her body was a dead weight. She couldn't focus. Her head was spinning.

'Before you pass out, my dear, I want to tell you two things.'

General Hashemi stood, fastened the top button of his jacket, and looked Lucinda in the eye. 'First, you are going to be treated to a little Shia hospitality to teach you a lesson. You should never have interfered in the affairs of men. And second, you needn't worry about disrupting the attacks in the UK. I have something much better than a handful of suicide bombers. I have you. Can you imagine the impact, the outrage, when the world watches the decapitation of an MI6 officer streamed live on the internet? You, my little Humayra, will be the star of the show.'

Lucinda grabbed a fork and willed every muscle to obey her. She crashed unconscious to the floor.

CHAPTER TWENTY

Cut to the Quick

An expanse of solid ocean stretched beyond the horizon. A single gull skirted an invisible sky, its screeching caws echoing inside the edge of consciousness. In the distance, on the sea, she could see herself, and then she was herself, perspective shifting from third to first person, dreaming that she was dreaming.

Lucinda forced herself awake. She blinked several times, the eyelashes of her right eye brushing against her hair, which cushioned her head on the hard surface.

Her senses rose one by one, not yet joined up, signalling obfuscated messages to her brain.

She smelled dust and concrete.

She licked her lips to wet her mouth.

She tasted heat and fear.

Her neck was stiff and her head pounded.

Lucinda stretched her hands, splaying her fingers. She flexed her ankles. Her senses communicated a new pain, a tightness. She opened her eyes wide and saw that her left wrist was bound. A trail of rope came into focus, snaking away from her wrist.

A primal instinct brought full consciousness flooding back in an instant.

She was naked.

Lucinda pushed herself into a sitting position, checked her body for injuries and scoured the room.

It was empty. Her best guess was that she was in a self-contained, one-storey building, a warehouse. It had a smooth concrete floor, scarred with different-sized tread marks. A forklift, a van, maybe a medium-sized truck too. Windowless, whitewashed walls on three sides. At the far end, a grey sliding metal door. Three banks of strip lighting, twenty-seven bulbs in all, ran down the length of the ceiling plinking a bare, unnatural light.

Lucinda got to her feet. Both wrists and both ankles were bound with nylon mountaineering rope. The knots were simple, unprofessional, but tight. She followed the rope from her right wrist along the floor and up to a rusty, brown metal pulley hanging from a hook in the ceiling. There were four pulleys on four hooks, equidistant above her. The ropes from each of them looped down to hooks on the two side walls. Lucinda pulled at the rope attached to her right wrist. The pulley whined and the slack curled on the floor beneath her. After three pulls the rope was taut.

The grey sliding doors rumbled back on their rails, a harsh, metallic sound filling the warehouse. Daylight poked its head inside, but made no impact on the LED strips, and it retreated, afraid to enter the room.

Four men in combat fatigues walked in single file and took up positions at each of the hooks. Lucinda put her right hand on her left shoulder, covering her breasts, and held her left hand between her legs, but not one of the soldiers looked at her. Instead, they grabbed the ropes and started to pull. Lucinda dropped to the floor to stop her legs being pulled from under her. The ropes tightened, biting into her wrists and ankles as her arms and legs were stretched in opposite directions and she was lifted off the ground. With each pull of the rope and each whine of the pulley, her body jerked up six inches. Her shoulders felt like they were about to be pulled from their sockets.

The soldiers tied off the ropes to the hooks on the walls.

Lucinda was suspended in midair, three feet off the ground, her arms and legs pointing to the four points of the compass.

Naked. Spreadeagled. Defenceless.

Measured footsteps grew louder as they approached. Lucinda looked up and saw a bear of a man. He wore the same combat fatigues as the soldiers, but with a different rank insignia. Lucinda couldn't make it out. In his right hand he carried a bottle filled with a clear liquid, and he had a stick of some sort tucked under his left armpit.

Colonel Farrokzhad stopped in front of Lucinda, his groin a foot from her face. He put the bottle on the floor and undid his belt buckle.

He pulled the buckle.

The tail of the belt flicked through the trouser loops as it was released. Frrp. Frrp. Frrp.

Farrokhzad dropped the belt on the ground.

He undid the button of his trousers.

'Please, don't do this,' begged Lucinda.

Farrokhzad moved out of her field of vision and stood behind her, between her legs. Lucinda felt a giant, rough hand touch the back of her left leg. It enveloped her thigh and grated like sandpaper as it moved down over her calf.

Lucinda closed her eyes and tried to retreat into the darkest, most distant corner of her mind. A hiding place where no one could find her. Not even Louisa. Where her body was no longer part of her, where it became no more than a shell, a vessel, a host to carry the real part of her. The part that mattered. The part that would refuse to be hurt.

A sharp, stinging pain whipped across her back. Lucinda cried out in agony and opened her eyes. She could see his legs. He was standing on her left side. Before Lucinda could work out what was happening, he whipped her again.

She fought to reorganise her mental defences for a different kind of pain. Her first thought – this would hurt like hell. But that was a lot better than what she thought was going to happen. Should she try to relax her whole body, or tense up? She tried to relax, but her body ignored her command and tensed in anticipation of the next blow.

Colonel Farrokzhad felt nothing but disgust for the object beneath him. Touching her had made him feel dirty, but he knew how to terrorise the vulnerable. He had made a career out of it. He would happily have beaten the bitch to death, but General Hashemi had given him strict orders. He whipped her again, bringing the bamboo cane down with three-quarter strength.

Every sinew in Lucinda's body strained, every nerve screamed. She could feel the nodes of the cane cut into her skin. How many blows was that? Three? Four? How many more? She tried to concentrate on the beads of sweat which dripped off her forehead and splashed in dusty pools on the concrete floor.

She breathed in and out through her mouth, trying to slow her heart rate, to impose some kind of control over her body. Another blow slashed across her back. Another. Each strike more painful, more vicious than the last. Another. Lucinda let out a piercing scream, the loudest scream she could. In agony, in defiance.

Colonel Farrokzhad smiled to himself and whipped her again. It was always the same. A futile attempt to resist, to show strength. But everyone broke. Sooner or later. One final whip, the ninth, and this one he would give full strength.

Lucinda turned her head to the sliding doors, willing Jake to burst in with a Delta Force team. Another savage blow rained down, slicing her back, cutting her open.

There was no sign of Jake. All she saw was her tormentor, in front of her again, picking up the bottle.

Colonel Farrokzhad twisted off the cap and poured half a litre of vodka over the bitch's back. One final animal scream and she passed out. They always did.

CHAPTER TWENTY-ONE

Edge of Reason

'You talk, you die.'

Lucinda was lying on her front in a confined space. It was pitch black. Her whole body ached and her back was on fire. There was a strong smell of diesel and the steady groan of an overworked engine. She had no idea how long she had been out or how long she had been cooped up in the mobile coffin.

The floor was corrugated metal and at least six feet long. She could lie straight without her head or feet touching the ends. When she pushed her arms out she could touch the sides. The fake floor of the vehicle which was the roof of the coffin was a foot above her. She could move, but it would be an effort to turn over. That was a blessing, her back hurt so much.

'You talk, you die.' The voice had a heavy Arabic accent.

The engine changed its tune and the vehicle slowed to a stop. The scent of cool night air relieved the diesel fumes. The driver had wound his window down. A checkpoint. Lucinda strained to hear the conversation. She thought she heard the words "papers" and "Anbar", but she couldn't be sure. And just like that the cool night air disappeared and the diesel fumes returned to smother the black void. As the vehicle accelerated, it hit a pothole and bounced her off the floor. Her back and head smacked into the plywood roof and Lucinda welcomed back the warm embrace of unconsciousness.

They could have driven one hour, they could have driven ten hours. She had no idea. The vehicle was stationary, engine idling. A metal gate swung open and the vehicle reversed. She heard voices. Anxious. Hushed.

The back doors of the vehicle opened and Lucinda was dragged out by her feet. She crumpled on the ground.

It was still dark.

'Where am I?' she asked.

'Get her inside now. And you, don't say another fucking word.' The accent was English, southern. Not London, but somewhere close by. Two men took an arm each and hauled Lucinda to her feet. They half-walked, half-carried her inside. The house was in darkness, but one of the men used the torch on his mobile phone so Lucinda could discern images, snatch impressions of the space inside. The place was a mess. Mattresses on the floor, clothes discarded, empty cups and glasses. They dragged her through a kitchen into a small room at the back of the house. There was a large hole in the floor. The man with the phone shone the light through the hole.

'Downstairs,' he said. A second English accent.

Lucinda edged down a metal staircase with a single, cylindrical railing. Ten steps. When she got to the bottom, she was blinded by a sudden light and instinctively covered her eyes.

'Don't move,' said the second voice. She blinked herself used to the light, which came from a single bulb dangling from a piece of white flex. The voice followed her down the stairs. He was wearing a balaclava.

Whoever they were, they had excavated the underneath of the house and carved a subterranean cave system out of the sandstone rock. A mishmash of wooden support struts and beams had been constructed to prevent the house from collapsing. It looked like a gold mine from the Old West. Directly ahead of Lucinda was a tunnel. The bulb cast a dim light down the first few metres, but it was impossible to tell how long the tunnel was or where it might emerge. On her right in front of the stairs was a makeshift door, a square sheet of metal welded to two poles with a rudimentary stable lock on the outside. There were two more metal doors on her left.

The second voice threw the bolt on one of the left-hand doors.

'Inside,' he said. Definitely English. And Lucinda detected a hint of sympathy in his voice. Almost apologetic.

The open door revealed a cell. A five feet by five feet cell hewn from sandstone and shale.

'What's your name?' asked Lucinda.

'Please, inside.'

'OK. OK. Thank you,' she replied. Lucinda ducked her head and entered the cell. The door was bolted behind her, shutting out all but a shaft of light.

Lucinda pushed at the door. It rattled and gave a little. It wouldn't take much to force if the moment came. She looked around her new room. From one confined space to another. It was impossible to stand upright so she sat on the damp floor. She tried leaning against the wall, but her back screamed in agony.

'Anyone else down here?' she asked.

Silence.

Lucinda drew her knees to her chest and wrapped her arms round her legs. Only now did she realise she was wearing the blue cotton pyjamas from General Hashemi's house and that she had wet herself during the journey. She was filthy, exhausted, and in agony. Severe agony.

She must have slept because she woke lying on her side. Her back throbbed, flashing out pulses of pain as regular as her heartbeat. Every muscle in her body ached. Even the simple act of breathing hurt.

A slither of light crept into the cell and Lucinda heard footsteps on the stairs. She stood up, back and neck stooped, and closed her eyes to listen. The bolt on one of the metal doors, the door on the other side by the stairs, was opened for a moment and then closed. No words exchanged.

The door to her cell was unlocked and the rest of the light from the bare bulb trickled in. A man in a balaclava stood in front of her with a bucket of water and a plate.

'Hi,' said Lucinda.

'Please, no talking.' The second voice. He passed the bucket over the threshold and held out the plate. Plain rice.

'Thank you. I'm starving.'

'No talking,' the voice repeated. 'It makes him angry.'

'Sorry,' whispered Lucinda. 'What's your name?'

The voice looked over his shoulder. 'Hazim,' he whispered in reply.

'Thank you, Hazim. I'm Lucinda.'

'Eat,' said Hazim and closed the door.

Lucinda scooped the rice off the plate. Boiled, no seasoning, no nothing. She wolfed down three mouthfuls. She needed the fuel, she needed to start the process of mending her body, to find some strength, however meagre, for whatever lay ahead. She finished the rice and splashed her face with water from the bucket. She washed the back of her neck and ran her wet fingers through her hair, combing out the worst of the knots. Food and water. She felt a little bit of strength returning.

More footsteps on the stairs and the bolt to the door of her cell was opened again.

'Put this on.' It was the first voice, angry, firm. He tossed the clothing at Lucinda and she looked at it in horror, recognising in an instant its terrifying significance. It was an orange jumpsuit.

'I'm not putting this on,' said Lucinda.

'You have one minute. After that, for every minute you don't put it on, I will break one of your fingers.' The first voice pointed a pistol at Lucinda.

This couldn't be right. Lucinda had had dinner with General Hashemi two nights ago. She didn't get any sense he was going to blow the Mosul Dam imminently. And his plan was to have Lucinda executed on the same day. It was a measured, meticulous plan, the General's plan. Surely it needed time to implement. What had gone wrong? It couldn't be now.

'Put it on!'

Lucinda stepped into the legs of the suit. 'I can't get my arms in. There's not enough space.'

'Do it out here.'

Lucinda emerged from her cell cradling the upper half of the orange suit in her arms. She stood up straight and looked into the voice's jet-black eyes. 'You're too much of a coward to even show your face.'

The voice smiled and pulled the balaclava off his head. 'My name is Younis,' he spat. He pressed his pistol against Lucinda's forehead. 'Put it on. Now!'

Younis had a wispy, dishevelled beard and shoulder-length, frizzy black hair. His eyebrows just met in the middle above the bridge of a thin, bony nose which looked as though it had been broken several times. He couldn't have been more than mid-twenties.

He grabbed Lucinda by the shoulders and pushed her up the stairs. Hazim and the third man were waiting for her in the kitchen. Both wore their balaclavas and were armed with AK-47s.

They led Lucinda outside. Electricity cables sagged from a line of poles on the far side of the high fence which gated the compound. It was mid-morning, maybe ten, ten-thirty. Warm, but not yet hot. A blue sky was filtered yellow by the desert sand. A sandstorm was on the way.

'Get on your knees.'

'You don't have to do this, Younis,' said Lucinda. 'You're obviously British. We can work with the–'

'Get on your knees!' Younis raised his pistol.

She stared into the jet-black eyes, out of options, nowhere to go. Defiance was all Lucinda had left. 'There is no fucking way you are going to make me kneel. Shoot me now, but I am not giving you the satisfaction of beheading me, you fucking animal.'

'I thought you might say that.' Younis looked at the third man and said, 'Omar, go get him.'

Hazim shifted his feet and said, 'Younis, we can't do this. They'll see us. They're up there.'

'Shut up,' rebuked Younis. 'I told you, they can't watch us all the time. The first drone passes early in the morning. It's long gone. There's a satellite pass around 2 pm, and a second drone flies by in the afternoon. They're like clockwork these stupid infidels. We're fine. Just do as you're told.'

Two men came back out of the house. 'Good,' said Younis, 'bring him over here. This is Kirit Masuda.' Younis nodded once and without a word Kirit knelt, head bowed, a broken animal obeying his master's command.

'We captured Kirit almost two years ago. He is thirty-five. A journalist.'

Younis took a mobile phone out of his pocket. 'This is his wife, Fumiko. And their two daughters. Beautiful, aren't they?'

Lucinda looked at Kirit. His beard was unkempt and his straight black hair covered his collar and ears. He wore a threadbare white T-shirt and stained blue jeans. He was barefoot. Kirit returned Lucinda's gaze, but there was nothing in his eyes. No soul, no spirit, he was defeated.

Omar held his AK-47 an inch from the back of Kirit's head.

'This could be Kirit's lucky day,' said Younis. 'Now I have you,

I don't need him. I can ransom him and he could be back with his family in no time. You have the power to save Kirit.'

'And how do I know you won't kill him after you've killed me.'

'You don't. All you know is that if you don't get on your knees right now, Omar is going to blow Kirit's head off in front of you. You want to take that to your grave or do you want to give his daughters a chance to see their father again?'

Lucinda dropped to her knees. 'You bastard,' she said.

Younis moved behind Lucinda and zipped her hands behind her back with a plastic tie. 'OK,' he said. 'Hazim, let's go.'

Younis put his balaclava back on. Hazim pressed record.

Lucinda stared beyond the yellowing sky. She could see her mother, her father, Louisa. In her mind's eye.

Younis grabbed a handful of her hair and yanked her head back. He drew a six-inch serrated knife from its sheath and held it in front of Lucinda's neck, his jet-black eyes staring into the camera.

The blade glinted in the sun.

CHAPTER TWENTY-TWO

Unfinished Business

Colonel Fernando Alvarez glanced at the display of his mobile phone and sighed with heavy heart. The window for the first of Maria's three daily calls was fast approaching.

It was already 8.47 am and Alvarez had witnessed nothing out of the ordinary since he had parked up two and a half hours earlier. Just everyday scenes. Vignettes of life being repeated all over the country. Dogs lifting their legs against lamp posts and taking their reluctant owners for a walk. Parents hustling their children out of the house, taking them to the park, to sports practice, keen to make the most of a Saturday off. Old folk, some arm in arm, some alone, hobbling down the street past his parked car, waving good mornings to one another, returning home sometime later with a newspaper or groceries. That would be him soon enough.

Yep. Nothing unusual to report.

Alvarez took a sip from the paper coffee cup he knew was empty and looked in the rearview mirror at the reflection of the quiet suburban street that stretched away behind him. Not a peep of activity from Number 35, the house he had under surveillance.

No movement in or out. The curtains were closed, keeping the world at bay, hiding a secret. Alvarez would bet his life on it.

The phone rang. 9.01 am. Maria was up early today.

'Where are they?' she screamed. 'That barren bitch has stolen my children again. I'm calling the police. Why do you let her do this, Fernando?'

'Maria, the kids are at football practice. Ines dropped them off this morning. You know…'

'I want my children,' Maria screamed in reply.

Alvarez flicked to autopilot, listening to Maria's rants, saddened, wanting to help, but knowing there was nothing he could do. She would shout and scream some more, he would fail to calm her down, and eventually he would end the call the same way he did every day. 'I'll be home soon. Stay where you are, Maria. I'll be home soon.'

Alvarez hung up and tossed the phone onto the dashboard.

At home, Maria would be banging on the main door of the house, screaming at poor Ines to give her back her children. Ines would be inside, in the kitchen, calm but with no intention of opening the door, waiting out Maria's daily tirade, understanding why Alvarez wasn't there to help, but wishing he was. She had never said it, but she felt let down. Another small crack in the mirror of their marriage.

Maria and her two children had moved into the converted garage in the summer of 2008, five months after her husband was killed in Afghanistan. Major Ignacio Alvarez, stationed in Herat as part of the Spanish Army's support to NATO, had just left a meeting on capacity building with his Afghan counterpart when a massive car bomb exploded inside the military compound. Thirty-five dead. Among them Ignacio, Colonel Fernando Alvarez's younger brother, his legs blown clean off, his face disfigured beyond recognition. The coffin was closed at the funeral.

Maria's slide from grief through despair into full-blown alcoholism had been gradual, held up by the support of her extended family, not least Colonel Alvarez and Ines, but she was on a one-way journey and once she reached bottom, she stayed there, with no hope of return. Alone, incapable of accepting help. Alvarez had tried everything, and in the first few years there had been moments of optimism, but those had long since been snuffed out, and almost every day of the past six years had played out in the same inevitable, soul-destroying way.

The conversion had gone well and the two-storey maisonette was almost finished when Maria moved in. The only problem was the garage had been converted for Alvarez's parents-in-law, not his brother's widow. But what could they do? They had to support Maria and the children. Ines understood and her parents weren't that frail back then.

A flicker of movement in the rearview mirror distracted Alvarez. The electric gate to Number 35 slid open and a blue Volkswagen Golf poked its nose out. Alvarez had gambled, parking between the house and the quickest route to the highway. The Golf turned left, picked up speed and passed Alvarez. The gamble had paid off.

Alvarez looked straight ahead and pretended to be on his mobile phone, so he only caught a glimpse of the driver out of the corner of his eye. But there was no doubt. Fahd El Idrissi was behind the wheel of the Golf.

Idrissi turned right onto Ronda Doctor Ferran. Alvarez followed, forty metres back, shaking his head. He just wasn't buying it. Idrissi had no discernible source of income yet he was living in a decent, middle-class neighbourhood. The gates to his house were electric for God's sake. This was a man who had fought for ISIS in Iraq, lived in Fallujah and Mosul, and now here he was back in Spain, free to move around wherever and whenever he liked.

Idrissi crossed a roundabout and stayed on Ronda Doctor Ferran.

Well, not exactly free. The Spanish authorities had kept a close eye on him for six months after his return, but he was no longer deemed a threat and all Idrissi had to do was register at his local police station once a week and that was that.

If that wasn't bad enough, some were praising Idrissi as a textbook example of rehabilitation, a success story of how to integrate former terrorists back into society. A local newspaper had even run a feature. Idrissi worked for a charitable Islamic foundation and gave weekly talks at the local mosque on the dangers of radicalisation. He was paying his dues to society.

No, Alvarez wasn't buying it. He had interviewed Idrissi his last day on the job before taking disability, and he saw something in Idrissi's eyes. A darkness. An unforgiving soul. This man wouldn't change his ways. He couldn't.

Alvarez's former colleagues at the Guardia Civil were more than happy for him to keep an eye on Idrissi. Alvarez was one of them. An insider. Trusted. Spain's economy was in no better shape than the rest of Europe's, and that meant austerity. And austerity meant cuts. Even if they wanted to keep Idrissi under police surveillance, the Guardia lacked the resources.

Idrissi took the first right at Plaça Italia onto Via Europa towards the highway. Once he crossed the Plaça Franca, it was a simple choice. Left to Barcelona or right up the coast.

Alvarez had followed Idrissi a hundred times and he had to admit he had little to report. No suspicious meetings, no suspicious purchases. But his surveillance was necessarily sporadic, and his gut told him today would be different. During his weekly coffee meeting catch-up with former colleagues, Captain Benitez had told him the British authorities had increased the UK threat level to Critical. That was the highest level. An attack was imminent. They had also issued a generic warning to all major European partners of possible attacks on mainland Europe. Nothing concrete – there seldom was – but something was in the air.

Idrissi drove over Highway 32, looped back on himself at the junction and took the on-ramp in the direction of Barcelona. It may have been a Saturday, but the road was still busy, the traffic flowing at eighty to a hundred and twenty kilometres an hour. Idrissi sat in the slow lane, well within the speed limit. Alvarez was three cars back.

Thirty kilometres to the city.

Alvarez's phone rang. 9.38 am. The second call always came in half an hour to forty minutes after the first. And at least the second call was easier to take.

'Fernando, I am sorry. Please forgive me. It's just so difficult. You know I don't mean to be horrid to Ines. She has done so much to help. I couldn't go on without you two.'

Guilt. Contrition.

'Maria, it's fine. Don't worry. I just wish there was something more we could do to help.' Some days Alvarez would push and suggest he go with Maria to see the counsellor. It depended as much on his mood as hers.

'I promise I will make it up to Ines,' said Maria. 'I'll bake some biscuits today and take them over. You have been so kind to me.'

They passed Les Carts shopping mall on the right. Alvarez moved into the middle lane and checked on the Golf. Inside lane, five cars ahead, ninety kilometres an hour.

'That would be lovely, Maria. I will be back soon and we can have coffee.'

Two calls down, one to go. But for Alvarez, the third call was the hardest of all.

The Golf pulled into the middle lane to overtake a pair of slow-moving trucks. Imposing, six-axle trucks, both with the same red livery, traveling in tandem and laden with freight out

217

of France. Idrissi passed them at a steady hundred kilometres an hour and indicated back into the slow lane.

Alvarez thought it unlikely Idrissi had noticed his tail, but he didn't want to take the chance. He accelerated and moved into the fast lane.

Up ahead was a major junction where Highway 32 split. Keep going straight and it became Highway 20 which skirted around the north of Barcelona. Bear right, then left under Highway 20, and the road became Highway 31 which led to the heart of the city.

Alvarez guessed Idrissi was headed to the city centre. He overtook the Golf and took the right fork. When he emerged from the underpass, he slowed, hoping his second gamble of the day had paid off.

After what felt like an eternity but couldn't have been more than a minute, Alvarez breathed a sigh of relief. The Golf was coming up behind him, expanding in the rearview mirror. Alvarez slowed some more and another minute later Idrissi passed him.

The timing of Maria's third call was unpredictable. It could be anywhere from forty-five minutes to six hours after the second call, and it depended on two factors. Whether Maria needed to go out to buy more alcohol and how black her despair was on that particular day.

Alvarez didn't drink so he had spoken at length to the counsellor to try to understand the generic behaviour patterns of an alcoholic. What he learnt just filled him with his own despair. Some days Maria would fight off the first drink for as long as possible. She would prowl around the house searching for distractions, walk in and out of the kitchen opening and closing the fridge, cursing herself, the call of the bottle getting louder and louder as she became increasingly irascible. It was a battle she was doomed to lose.

Other days Maria would pour a glass straight away, conning

herself that today she would pace herself, that today she was in control, that today she would only have a couple of drinks. One now. One at lunch. And maybe one in the evening.

And on the bleakest days of all, she would dive headlong into the bottle with no thoughts at all other than to disappear into its warm anaesthetising embrace.

The terrible truth was that however she got there, the result was always the same. Alvarez allowed himself a wry smile as he thought of his grandmother's alcohol aphorism for the thousandth time. One is sufficient, two is too many, three is not nearly enough. How right the old girl was.

Alvarez followed Idrissi over the Rio Besos and continued on the highway until it turned into the Gran Via de les Corts Catalenes, one of Barcelona's main arterial routes pumping traffic into the heart of the city. The Golf turned right into Carrer de la Independència and then left into Carrer d'Aragó.

Alvarez looked up and knew where Idrissi was going. He thought about calling the Guardia but decided to hold back for now.

The towering sandstone spires of the Basilica of the Sagrada Familia twisted and turned to the sky, basking in the morning sun. Idrissi turned right onto Carrer de la Marina and slowed the Golf right down as he drove by the three porticos of the east-facing Nativity façade. Antoni Gaudi's Gothic masterpiece was still unfinished almost a hundred years after his death – only eight of the eighteen planned spires had been completed – but the Nativity façade was finished in 1930 and it bore the greatest hallmarks of its designer. Elemental life burst from the carved sandstone celebrating the natural world. The branches and leaves of the tree of life spiralled up towards the façade's four spires, each dedicated to one of four apostles.

Idrissi hugged the Basilica, turning left along the north side of the church and then left again past the west-facing Passion façade. Carved images portrayed the Last Supper, Judas's betrayal, the crucifixion, the ascension, each framed daily against a setting sun and a darkening world, exactly as Gaudi had planned. Giant columns straddled the portico pointing to four more spires dedicated to four more of the apostles.

The one-way system prohibited a left turn at the southwest corner of the Basilica, so Idrissi boxed round the next block and took a left into Carrer de Mallorca, driving past the Glory façade, completing his square of the Sagrada Familia. Alvarez was certain it was a recce for a future attack. Today was not the day.

Confirming Alvarez's suspicions, Idrissi drove on straight for a few blocks and then turned back on himself, eventually rejoining the Gran Via de les Corts Catalenes, heading back to Highway 31.

Alvarez needed to report this to the Guardia. He needed to pick Maria's kids up from football practice. And he needed to get home in time for lunch.

A wave of tiredness crashed over Alvarez. He felt half the man he used to be. His brother was dead, there was nothing he could to do to help Maria, and her two beautiful children were a constant reminder of the one thing he had never been able to give Ines.

His phone rang. It was the third call. The hardest call. Maria would be in tears, bereft and distraught. A cocktail of grief, despair and self-pity stirred by the alcohol.

In the distance, Idrissi continued on Highway 31, the Golf retracing its morning steps. Alvarez let him go and turned left at the Rio Besos heading north, heading home.

Maybe he could at least avenge his brother.

Alvarez answered his phone.

CHAPTER TWENTY-THREE

Cellar of Death

The rubber teeth of the fake blade rippled across Lucinda's throat.

'Don't worry, bitch, your time will come. And soon.' Younis put his boot in Lucinda's back and kicked her to the ground. He unsheathed his real knife and cut the plastic zip tie, freeing her hands from behind her back. He turned to Hazim and Omar. 'Get them inside.'

Hazim helped Lucinda to her feet. Her world was suspended, spinning, in chaos. She didn't know where she was. Her heart was pounding her chest at over a hundred and fifty beats a minute. She was numb and shaking uncontrollably.

'I'm sorry. I'm sorry,' whispered Hazim as he opened the door to Lucinda's cell. Without a thought, she entered, grateful for the comfort of darkness. She didn't hear the metal door bolt behind her. She collapsed to the floor, drew her legs up into her chest and lay there. Motionless. Terrified.

She had to get her heart rate down. She breathed in through her right nostril, held her breath for a few seconds, then breathed out through her left nostril. In through the left, hold, out through the right. She repeated the cycle, counting sequentially every time she breathed out through her right nostril. She counted to sixty.

Lucinda imagined sitting among the avenue of beech trees that stretched up the lane above her childhood home to the top of the hill. She was on the bank staring out over her favourite field, looking down on the farmland valley below. It was May and she was surrounded by a thousand shades of green.

The majestic trunks of the giant beech trees stood guard, their interlinking canopies wrapping her in a blanket of protection. Dark green gorse bushes, forever in yellow flower, dotted the undulating pasture. In the valley below, the winter wheat was standing tall, waiting patiently for its golden transformation under the summer sun. The fields and headlands were dissected by symmetrical tramlines.

Lucinda had never experienced a moment of such sheer terror in her life. She had been subjected to violent interrogations and put in multiple stress positions during her training. She had even been waterboarded. But nothing could have prepared her for the mock execution.

Her body had stopped shaking and her breathing was mostly under control. Lucinda stripped off the jumpsuit and threw it in the damp corner of her cell. She crawled to the entrance and put her hands against the metal door.

'Kirit, can you hear me? Kirit? Talk to me.'

Silence. Not a word from the cell by the stairs.

'Kirit,' repeated Lucinda. 'We have to help each other.'

Nothing.

Lucinda wasn't surprised. When she looked into his eyes before the mock execution, all she saw was emptiness, a black void where humanity used to be. Kirit Masuda was a broken man, his spirit destroyed by the cruelty of incarceration. She couldn't imagine what he had gone through. An ISIS prisoner for the best part of two years. Or the worst part, rather. Two years of savage captivity. Kirit had no doubt suffered his own mock executions, been beaten and tortured, starved and humiliated, moved from location to location. What did that do to a person?

Was the destruction of your identity gradual, a slow diminution, day by day, the pain and humiliation eating away at your soul like a canker, destroying the last vestiges of hope until one day you no longer knew who you were? Or was it sudden? Your resistance holding out against the torrent of terror for as long as possible only to be swept aside in a final terrifying assault against which you were defenceless?

Lucinda didn't know and she had no intention of finding out.

'Kirit, don't worry. I'm going to get us out of here.'

Footsteps rattled down the metal stairs and a few seconds later the bolt to her cell was thrown back.

'Here, I have some food for you. Rice and vegetables. Some bottled water. And an empty bucket.'

'Hazim, I know it's you. I recognise you, so you may as well take off that balaclava. And thank you for the food.'

Lucinda knelt by the entrance to her cell and took the plate of food. Boiled potatoes and carrots on a bed of rice. Hazim looked over his shoulder to the stairs and removed the balaclava.

'Where are you from, Hazim?'

'Woking.'

'How long have you been here?'

Hazim looked over his shoulder again. 'I can't talk to you.'

'Hazim, it's OK. It's just a minute. I can get you back to Woking, Hazim. I know you don't want to be here. There is a way back. Trust me.'

'Shhh.' Hazim paused. 'There's no way back for me. Not now.'

Lucinda lowered her voice to below a whisper. She had to draw him in. 'There is, Hazim. I can get you back, away from Younis, away from here. Home. But you have to trust me and we have to work together.'

'Hey! What are you doing down there?' Younis's voice shot down the stairs and echoed off the sandstone walls.

'Nothing,' replied Hazim. 'I'm just on my way back up.'

Lucinda grabbed Hazim's arm. 'Think about it, Hazim. For both us. I can get us out. I promise.'

Hazim bolted the door and Lucinda heard him climb the stairs. He switched off the light and she ate her food in the dark.

There weren't many, but Lucinda did have a couple of options. She was confident she could get Hazim onside. Everything about the way he talked, the way he looked, the way he carried himself, told Lucinda he had had enough. Hazim had come to the end of his journey in the crumbling Caliphate and he wanted out. That much was clear. Maybe it was because the Caliphate was dead that he wanted to go home. Or maybe he had lost his will some time ago, disenchanted by the reality of the failed ISIS utopia. There could be any number of reasons. And it mattered, because it might help her turn him.

The problem was it would take time. And time was in short supply. Lucinda didn't know how long she had, but it was going to be measured in days, not weeks.

That led to the second, more direct, option. Overpower Hazim when he came with food. Again, she was confident she could do it. But one of the problems with this option was that Hazim didn't have his weapon with him when he brought a meal. That might make it easier to overpower him and keep Younis from hearing, but Lucinda needed a weapon. Should she climb the stairs and hope to find the AK by the entrance to the cave complex or should she take her chances and go unarmed down the tunnel and see where it led?

Climb the stairs. High risk, but the obvious choice. It was quantifiable. The tunnel option had no certainty at all.

Lucinda's decision, precarious though the outcome may be, imbued her with a sense of control. She would give it the rest of the day to try to turn Hazim. She hoped that would give her two, maybe three, opportunities. If that didn't work, and she was far from convinced it would given the time constraints, it was Plan B first chance she got the following day.

The sudden sound of gunfire split the air. Rapid gunfire. Fully automatic. Large calibre. The house above shook to its foundations.

A slither of light slipped through the door to Lucinda's cell and someone ran down the stairs.

'I'll fucking kill them!' screamed Younis.

The door to Kirit's cell was opened and there was another burst of gunfire. An AK-47. No doubt about it.

Lucinda had no time to think. The moment was now. She stood up and the second she heard the bolt thrown back she launched herself at the door, forcing it open with all her strength. It caught Younis full in the face and before he could regain his balance, Lucinda was out of the cell and tackling him to the ground. Younis dropped his weapon as he fell and Lucinda jumped on top of his body, knees either side of his chest. She managed to pin his right arm to the ground with her left leg.

But his left arm was still free and he lashed out with a punch, catching Lucinda square on the temple. She dug her fingers into his eyes, scratching, gouging, ripping wildly. Younis screamed in agony and threw another punch at Lucinda. The blow knocked her off balance, but she stayed strong on top of him. If he threw her off, they would be on level terms. She had to keep her advantage.

Younis stared at Lucinda, blood and hatred streaming from his eyes. He grabbed her hair and pulled, arching and bucking his back, desperately trying to shake her off.

Lucinda put her left hand on his throat and squeezed as hard as she could. With her right hand she reached down Younis's side. He launched another left hook, but Lucinda saw it coming and managed to sway out of the way. She felt the handle of his knife

225

and pulled it out of its sheath. She used her left to block his next flailing punch and plunged the knife into his chest.

Younis yelled out in pain and in the second he took to register the wound, Lucinda took the knife out of his chest and stabbed him again. Younis yanked at Lucinda's hair, but his strength was starting to fail. She stabbed him again. And again. Multiple times, screaming in a wild frenzy, but still able to hear the awful crack of splitting bone with each stab of the knife. She watched the light drain from his eyes. His body fell limp.

Lucinda rested her hands on Younis's shoulders, bowed her head, and breathed. She was dripping in sweat.

Before she could move, she heard footsteps emerging from the tunnel. She pulled the knife out of Younis's dead body and in one swift movement threw herself at the new attacker with a primal scream from the depths of her soul. She didn't care if it was Hazim or Omar. She wasn't going to die today. Not in this subterranean hell.

Jake D'Souza grabbed Lucinda's wrist, disarmed her, and spun her round so her back was pressed against his chest, her arms pinned.

'It's me. Jake. It's OK. You're safe.'

'Let go of me. Let fucking go of me,' she cried.

'OK, OK, I'm letting go.' Jake relaxed his grip and Lucinda broke free, stumbling forward. She reached for the metal railing of the stairs, bent over, and vomited.

Jake took a step towards her. Lucinda held out the palm of her hand. 'Don't. Don't touch me.'

'It's OK, Spark. It's over. It's over. I'm gonna pour some water in your hair.' Jake took a bottle of water from a side pocket of his trousers and poured it through her hair, brushing out flecks of sick.

Lucinda wretched, puking up a burning stream of yellow bile. Jake swept her hair back, holding it off her face. 'It's done, Lucinda. It's done. You're safe now.'

Jake looked through the door of the cell by the stairs and got on the radio. 'We need a body bag down here. Yes. Just one.'

'His name was Kirit Masuda. That bastard killed him. Get me out of here, Jake.'

CHAPTER TWENTY-FOUR

Rules of the Game

'I've got to get the information out now.'

'Don't worry. I've already sent the headlines. The rest will wait till morning. We've got more important things to do.'

'Like what?' Lucinda asked.

The flight back to Erbil in the Black Hawk had passed in a daze. Jake wrapped her in a blanket and Lucinda regurgitated as much of the information General Hashemi had told her as possible. She struggled to make herself heard over the noise of the engines, but she told Jake about Hashemi's plan to blow the Mosul Dam, about the attack in Barcelona, about the Ahl al-Bayt. She tried to keep the information succinct and in a logical order, but it came out in fragments, inarticulate details tripping over each other in her confusion. And now she couldn't remember exactly what she had told Jake and what she hadn't. But she remembered the screaming pain across her back and she remembered he gave her a painkiller. Something strong.

'You're coming back to my place. I'm gonna get you drunk and clean those wounds.'

'Jake, I'm serious. I've got to speak to London.'

'No, you don't. Not yet.'

Lucinda was exhausted. She had no more fight left inside her and she didn't want to be alone.

Back in his trailer, Jake poured a Jack and coke. Half and half, with four cubes of ice. 'Here,' he said, 'take a big hit on that.'

Lucinda took a small sip. The strong taste of the Jack chased with the cold fizz of the coke felt good. She took a large gulp. Then another.

'That's better,' said Jake. He took her glass and topped it up.

'Now, take your top off and lie face down on the bed.'

'Not the most romantic proposition I have ever had.'

'Stop fooling around, Spark, and do as you're told.'

Lucinda turned her back to Jake and started to unbutton the stained pyjama top. She had been wearing the pyjamas for two days and they were as filthy as she was. Lucinda remembered she had wet herself and was embarrassed. Everything hurt. 'Jake, I can't undo the fucking buttons.' She started to cry.

'Don't worry, Spark. All you have to do is drink.' Jake took a pair of scissors from a medical bag and cut the pyjama top up the back. He peeled the two sides off and they slid down her outstretched arms, exposing her naked back.

'Jeez, that's nasty,' he said.

'Cut the pants off too. They're disgusting,' said Lucinda.

Jake cut down the side of Lucinda's pyjamas from the hip all the way to the bottom of the leg. They dropped to the floor and Lucinda stepped out from the crumpled, dirty cloth. She was naked.

'I'm going to take a shower first.'

'OK,' said Jake, 'but don't get any water on your back. It'll hurt like hell if you do. I'll clean it up after. Finish your drink and I'll make you another.'

Lucinda downed the rest of her Jack and limped off to the shower. Her back still hurt, but the pain wasn't sharp anymore.

It was a dull, uncomfortable throb. Jack and the pain killer were doing their job.

Lucinda washed her hair as best she could, but it was difficult as every time she raised her arms she felt the wounds on her back opening. She winced and swore.

The hot water hit her chest and ran down her body. She scrubbed herself all over and watched the swirl of dirty brown water disappear down the plughole.

'Here, take this,' said Jake, when Lucinda walked back into the room. She had patted herself dry and wrapped a towel around her waist. She covered her breasts with an arm. She took the Jack and coke.

'Right, lie down on the bed and let's get your back cleaned up.'

Lucinda took another sip of Jack and lay down on Jake's bed. She covered her bottom half with a sheet and held the glass of Jack in her right hand.

'How did you find me?' she asked. 'And I thought you were in the States.'

'I turned the plane round the minute I heard General Hashemi had you. Somewhere over Germany, I think. As for finding you, our friend Abu Issa was a little taciturn to begin with, but he became quite talkative in the end and gave up the names of a number of ISIS safe house locations. We had twenty-four-hour coverage all along the Iraq-Syria border. That's where you were, by the way. Took longer than I wanted to find you, but we got you in the end, Spark.'

'Don't think I'm not grateful, but why didn't the Brits come get me?'

'Ah, well, kinda slipped my mind to tell 'em. I wanted to come get you myself.'

Lucinda smiled. She tilted her head to take a sip of Jack, spilt a little on the sheet, and put the glass on the bedside table.

'How bad is my back?'

'You've got nine separate wounds. All roughly the same length. Twenty-five, thirty centimeters long. There are a couple of pretty bad ones, and one's bleeding a little now. Who did this to you?'

'One of General Hashemi's goons. A big guy. But he never said a word. It was a cane of some sort. What are you going to use?'

'Nothing, I'm just going to clean the wounds with room-temperature water and cotton wool. It's a myth that alcohol sterilizes a wound. And creams and Vaseline just add to the pain. Plain old water is best. Then I'll just put on a light dressing and we'll keep checking over the next few days to make sure it doesn't get infected.'

Jake tipped water from a bottle onto a cotton wool ball. 'I'm going to start at the bottom right of your back, and I'll keep telling you where I'm going so you can try to manage the pain.'

He dabbed the worst wound at the bottom. Lucinda winced. 'Fuck,' she said and took a hit of Jack.

'You'll get used to it,' said Jake. And she did. Jake had a deft touch and moved in a slow, methodical way up and down her back. She was able to predict where the next dab would be and that helped her track and control the pain.

The alcohol relaxed her and she felt warm and safe lying on the bed.

'Do you want to talk about it?' asked Jake.

'I don't know,' said Lucinda. 'I've never killed anyone before.'

'And you want to tell someone close to you. Your father, mother, a brother, a sister. You want to be wrapped up in the warmth of your family. To go back. But you know you can't.'

'I don't know. I don't know what I feel.'

'I do. I've been there. And I'm the one you need to talk to. If you want to talk. When you want to talk. Not because I'm me, but because I'm here and I do the same shit you do. And you have to protect your family. You can never tell them, Spark.'

Jake wetted another piece of cotton wool and continued dabbing clean the wounds on Lucinda's back. Gentle, slow, meticulous. He looked at her back, the curves of her skin, the nape of her neck, her wet hair splayed over the pillow. Beaten and bruised, she was the most beautiful, perfect thing he had ever seen.

'And I'm supposed to get used to this? Used to killing people?'

'Here's the deal, angel, and you might not like it, but it's how it is. That man was an evil man. He hurt you and killed God knows how many people. In a vicious, horrible way. He had at least a dozen beheadings to his name. He deserved to die. You did the right thing today. And the hard fact is, if you want to stay in this game you will have to kill again. Hopefully not often, but you will, and you have to be prepared to.'

'And what does that make me, Jake? What will I become?'

'It will make a part of you, a large part of you, hard and distant and unforgiving. But you will be alive, doing your job. And hey, look on the bright side, you will become like me.'

Lucinda laughed. 'Make me another drink, D'Souza,' she said.

'You wanna know the moral of the story, Spark? Whatever happened in that cellar, you've got to harness it to make you stronger. If you don't, it'll kill you. And the best way to start that process is to talk about it with someone who understands. OK, that's the wounds washed. I'm going start applying the dressings now.'

Jake took a sip of his drink. 'And you don't need to talk about it now. Whenever you're ready, but don't leave it too long. Take it from someone who knows. Not dealing with it is wasted time. Dangerous time.'

Lucinda closed her eyes. She had never talked about it before. Not even to Louisa. She had kept it wrapped deep inside all these years. But now, for the first time, she felt ready. And it was Jake she wanted to tell.

'It was a beautiful summer's day. It was supposed to be our time.'

CHAPTER TWENTY-FIVE

Slings and Arrows

'It was a Thursday. August 2nd, 2012. We were excited, full of hope, and still on a high. Kim, Emma and I had been for our run and were discussing tactics over breakfast.'

'Tactics?' Jake unrolled a length of dressing and cut off a strip.

'You are looking at the scarred back of an Olympic athlete.'

'Really? Awesome. Which sport?'

'Archery.'

'Archery?'

'Everybody says it like that. A slight question mark in their voice, tinged with a little disappointment. Archery doesn't sound cool. It's not a headline sport. Not like athletics or rowing or cycling.'

'Don't be so defensive, girl. I didn't say it like that at all. To be an Olympic athlete in any sport is pretty cool.'

'It's OK. I was like that before I tried it. My dad dragged me and my sister to the local club one summer holiday. We were twelve. I will never forget it. I fell in love with archery immediately. And the funny thing is, Louisa didn't. It was the first time in our lives we had a separate interest.'

'Louisa's your twin sister?'

'Yes. And we were inseparable. We still are, in our own way. But we both found a different interest that summer. It gave us an individuality we had never felt before, yet at the same time it deepened our bond. It's a twin thing. Anyway, that's not the point.

'The moment I shot that first arrow I was hooked. It's an incredible sport. The perfect mix of individual and team.'

Jake laid the first piece of dressing along one of Lucinda's wounds and bit off a piece of surgical tape. Lucinda winced a little as he taped the dressing to her shoulder blade.

'Sorry,' he said. 'I'm being as gentle as I can.'

'It's OK,' said Lucinda.

'Go on,' said Jake.

'In some team sports, like football, or soccer for you,' Lucinda lingered on the first syllable of "soccer", Americanising it, 'you can have a bad individual performance and the team can still win. Archery is one of those sports where there's no hiding. If you play badly as an individual, you lose as a team.'

'What's the format?' asked Jake. He only needed little prompts to keep her mind occupied.

'There are a number of disciplines, but in the Olympics it's seventy-metre recurve. The target is seventy metres away and the tips of the bow curve away from the archer. It's called a recurve bow. And it's an outdoor competition.

'You might not have to be as fit as a one-hundred-metre runner, but you need strength, poise, precision, intense concentration, total control of your breathing and judgement of the conditions. You are on your own, but part of the team.

'The women's division is dominated by the South Koreans. They are on a different planet. They've won every team gold since Seoul in '88. But we medalled. We won the bronze. The first British women's team to medal in Olympic archery history.'

'You're an Olympic medallist, Spark? Now that is awesome.'

'Yes. We won bronze on the Sunday. Kim, Emma and I. The individual competition followed the team event a few days later. Emma and I were knocked out in the first round – no disgrace by the way, I lost to the Mexican girl who went on to win silver – but Kim got through to the final day. How are you doing back there?'

'Three dressings done,' said Jake. 'Take a breather.' Lucinda took a sip from her Jack and put the glass back on the bedside table.

'You want me to top that up?'

'No,' said Lucinda, 'I think that's enough. Thanks. Sportsmen and women are superstitious people at the best of times. After the bronze, Kim, Emma and I ran the same route every morning. We ate the same thing for breakfast every morning. We had to keep our routine exactly the same every day for luck. Down to wearing the same socks.

'We left the Olympic Village just after 7 am. It was already sixteen degrees and a clear blue sky. That's a beautiful summer's day in London. There was that buzz, that buzz of excitement and anticipation on the bus as we drove to the venue with about thirty girls and various coaches from the other competing nations. Kim and I were sitting together four rows back on the left-hand side. I was by the window. Emma was in the seat in front of us.

'The journey was about an hour. We drove round the north of London and came down through Holloway and Camden, not that that will mean much to you. But to get to Lord's we had to skirt round the north side of Regent's Park.'

'Lord's?' asked Jake.

'The venue for the event. Lord's is one of the most iconic sporting venues in the UK. It's a beautiful place. Known as the home of cricket.'

'Cricket. I know about cricket. That's baseball for old men, right? Takes like a week to play and half the time no one wins?'

'Funny, D'Souza. Very funny. Maybe one day I'll take you

to a game and educate you. Anyway, that's where the archery was being held. We stopped at a set of lights between Regent's Park and Primrose Hill. I found out later it was 7.47 precisely. A beaten-up, blue transit van pulled alongside us at the lights. I was chatting with Kim. Emma was turned towards us holding the back of her seat, not wanting to miss out. I don't know why I looked over at the driver of the van, but I did. And he was looking straight at me. Dark, ugly eyes, black pools filled with hate. He smiled at me, muttered to himself, and closed his eyes.

'There was a blinding white flash and a huge explosion that blew the bus sideways. Sometimes I see the whole thing in slow motion, the windows of the bus shattering in a ball of light and flame, shards of glass flying in a vacuum, bodies being sucked sideways, backwards, forwards. How much of it I remember and how much I have filled in over the years, I really don't know.'

Lucinda's voice was distant. She no longer felt Jake's touch on her back.

'I guess I blanked out for a bit. A few seconds, a minute, I don't know. There is so much I don't know, so much I can't piece together. The not knowing haunts me.

'When I came to, Kim was slumped in my lap and I was covered in blood. Her blood. Her body was twisted like a corkscrew. She was looking up at me. Half her face was missing, cut to shreds. I felt for a pulse, but knew it was useless. I just sat there holding her in my arms. I don't know how long for. At some point the emergency services came and took her away from me.

'It's the eyes I can never forget. In my dreams, I see Kim's, questioning, beautiful, dead. In my nightmares, I see his, sometimes looking at me from the van, sometimes staring up at me from Kim's lifeless body, smiling.

'They said later it wasn't that big a bomb. Fifty, maybe seventy pounds of explosives. A miracle more people weren't killed, they said. That meant nothing to me. Kim was dead, so were six other girls and two coaches. And the driver. Emma lost her left arm and an eye. We haven't spoken for six years. Multiple lives ruined by a random act of madness. And that's supposed to be a miracle?

'You run the whole thing through your head, endlessly, searching for answers you know won't come. Why didn't we catch an earlier or later bus? Why that bus on that day? Why did I get on the bus before Kim and take the window seat? What were we doing that meant I got on the bus first? Why didn't we sit further back?'

'Why did she die, not you?' said Jake.

Lucinda opened her eyes and hauled her mind back to Jake's trailer.

'I know, I get it. You can spare me the survivor guilt psychobabble. I've lived it a thousand times. I've asked myself those questions a thousand times. Banal, stupid, pointless questions. It is what it is, I get it. But it doesn't change the fact that Kim is dead, that she was twenty-two years old, beautiful, driven, and had everything taken away in the prime of her life. And as time passes, I ask those stupid, banal questions less and less, and I hate myself for it.'

Lucinda raised herself up with her left hand and reached for her glass of Jack.

'You won't get any psycho bull from me, Spark. Just remember the moral. What happened in London, what happened in that cellar, it's part of you. Embrace it and it'll make you stronger. Don't and it'll kill you. It's that simple.'

'Why do you think I joined the Service?'

Jake got up from the bed and poured himself a drink. 'How bad were your injuries?' he asked.

'Hardly a scratch. You see the little dint on my temple?'

'I'm looking at it right now,' said Jake, sitting back down on the bed. 'I noticed it the first time I saw you.'

'Kim saved my life. She took the brunt of the blast. Her head must have smacked sideways into mine, the point of her sunglasses banging me on the temple. A permanent reminder every time I look in the mirror, not that I need one.'

'Well, it's your only imperfection, Spark. Physical imperfection at any rate.' Jake finished applying the final dressing and looked down Lucinda's back. 'And right now, I'm speaking from a position of some authority.' He put his hand on her buttock.

Lucinda smiled into the pillow. 'I'm going to have some nasty scars.'

'You'll have a couple, but most of it will clear up.

'Anyway, I've got another small scar from the attack.'

'Oh yeah? Where?'

'Maybe one day you'll get to see it. But I don't think tonight.'

Jake leant forward and kissed a dressing covering one of Lucinda's wounds. Then he kissed her on the back of the neck.

Lucinda was asleep.

CHAPTER TWENTY-SIX

The Day After Tomorrow

'I smell coffee. Good coffee.'

'Well, good morning, beautiful. You do indeed, but fuck knows if I'm doing it right. I don't even know what this thing's called.'

'It's called a moka, and you're doing fine.'

'And you, how are you doing?'

'Everything hurts like hell. I didn't even notice the pain in my head yesterday where I got punched, but it's pounding like mad this morning.'

'That's a good sign,' said Jake.

'Really? How's that?'

'It means the pain on your back isn't all-consuming. Your brain's got space to think of other stuff.'

The coffee percolated into the top half of the electric moka.

'It's ready,' said Lucinda. She sat up in bed as Jake brought a cup over.

'This is Vergnano,' she said, taking a sip and looking up at Jake. 'Where did you get this?'

'Diplomatic pouch has its advantages. I was planning to get

239

some stateside, but I had to turn around to save your sorry ass, remember? Airborne buddy of mine stationed in Italy bagged it over. By the way, I've been meaning to ask you something. It's been on my mind all night. If your bus got attacked on the way to the finals, how come the Mexican girl won silver?'

'They decided to go ahead with the competition, so they rescheduled. To send a signal. We won't be terrorised. You won't win. The world's athletes united against terror. It was the right thing to do, but I don't want to talk about it anymore. We've got work to do, D'Souza. We've got to stop General Hashemi. I've got to go to the house and send a report. Can I borrow some clothes, Jake?'

Jake sat on the edge of his desk and shook his head. 'That's gratitude for you. Some of us have been busy while you've been sleeping it off, babe. Here,' he said, picking up a small rucksack and putting it on the bed. 'I went to the house early this morning and picked up some clothes from your closet. I also brought your laptop. Met some dude called Elliot. He gave me a new phone for you. Sounded kinda pissed. Said he had to upload new software seeing as you left the last one in enemy hands. Asked you to be a bit more careful with this one. I didn't like the guy. Hair was too greasy.'

Lucinda swung her feet off the bed and put her hands on the edge of the mattress. The room spun. 'Fuck,' she said.

'OK, take it easy, Spark. One step at a time. Let's do this together. You dictate and I'll type. I'll even spell in Limey.'

Lucinda smiled. 'OK. Give me the phone.'

Jake tossed the phone on the bed and fired up the laptop.

'Looks like I need your thumb print and a password,' he said, turning the screen of the laptop to Lucinda. She pressed her thumb on the sensor and typed in her password. Jake took the laptop to his desk.

Incoming messages pinged one after the other on Lucinda's

phone. Emails, SMS, instant messages. A constant flurry of different pitched beeps competing for her attention. She didn't want to open any of them.

'You sound like a wanted woman,' said Jake.

The work ones were from Laird and Varma in London and Hollister in Baghdad. Most of them were out of date, given the events of the past few days. She ought to make contact, but as soon as she did, they wouldn't leave her alone, and she didn't want to deal with them right now.

Her dad, mum, and Louisa had all sent messages. They had no idea what had happened to her, but they felt her silence.

Lucinda thought about the last week and wondered if there was one ultimate cause that had set the resulting effects in motion. Was it the raid on Abu Issa's compound? Was it the bomb at the Jeddah IDP camp? Did it matter?

She thought about General Hashemi, his study, the V-shaped table, racing Alima through the oak forest. She thought about Imam Ali, Aisha, the Battle of Karbala, the twelve Shia Imams. She thought about the Givenchy dress and the dinner. She thought about the warehouse and being beaten.

She thought about the cave and Kirit.

She thought about Younis and killing a man.

Time to get dressed. Lucinda dug a T-shirt, a pair of knickers and a pair of jeans out of the rucksack. She dressed, emptied the moka, and put another pot of coffee on.

You can never tell them, Spark.

Jake was right. Lucinda sent three short messages telling her parents and Louisa she was up to her eyeballs in work and promising to call them soon.

It will make a part of you, a large part of you, hard and distant and unforgiving.

Lucinda opened a message from Miles Cavendish. 'God knows what you've been through. I'm here. Miles.'

'Let's do this,' said Lucinda. 'Open up the CX Report template on the desktop.'

'Whatever you say, ma'am,' said Jake.

Lucinda poured herself a coffee and started dictating.

CX Report

Intelligence Grade: A

Source Reliability: 1

Executive Summary

- Major General Ali Hussein Hashemi leads a criminal organisation called the Ahl al-Bayt

- General Hashemi is planning terrorist attacks in London, Manchester, Birmingham and Barcelona

- General Hashemi plans to destroy the Mosul Dam, resulting in estimated casualties of up to half a million people

- The codename for the attacks is Operation Hidayah

- The attacks will be coordinated

- The date of the attacks is not certain...

- General Hashemi is overseeing the construction of a road from Tehran to Syria that will give Iran (and Hashemi's Ahl al-Bayt) direct access to the Mediterranean

- It is not clear whether the Iranian regime is complicit in the Ahl al-Bayt or whether General Hashemi is acting independently. The latter is the most probable

- The Ahl al-Bayt made a net operating profit of over four hundred million dollars in the previous financial quarter

- Criminal activities of the Ahl al-Bayt include terrorism, people trafficking, extortion and narcotics

- General Hashemi is obsessed (and driven) by the rift between Sunni and Shia Islam, and believes his destiny is the restitution of Shia primacy in the Islamic order

'Pretty punchy summary. All we need now is the date,' said Jake.

'He told me.'

'Well, it would be nice of you to pass it along. It's kinda important, Spark.'

'Not in so many words, but I asked him. What the hell did he say?'

Lucinda drained the moka and drank the last of the Vergnano.

'He talked about the twelve Imams, about the twelfth Imam, the Mahdi. Judgment day. I asked him when it was going to be.'

'Yeah, and what did he say?' asked Jake.

'He said something about it being a present which must remain a secret.'

Lucinda pulled up a chair beside Jake. 'Give me the laptop,' she said.

Lucinda opened a search engine and started typing. She hit the return button and scanned the results. She clicked on two of the links but went back to the search engine and started typing again, her fingers flying over the keyboard. She clicked on another link.

Lucinda swivelled the laptop to Jake.

'15th of Sha'ban in the Islamic calendar,' she said. 'Or May 1st. That's the date the Mahdi was born.'

'That's the day after tomorrow,' said Jake.

'I'm going to send this now. I can get to the rest later.' Lucinda put the date in the Executive Summary and attached it to an email. She typed Laird's and Varma's addresses in the "To" field and put Hollister on "Cc". She marked the email "Top Priority" and hit send.

'That should be good enough for us to convince the Iraqi Government to arrest General Hashemi, or at least kick him out of the country. He can't be allowed anywhere near the Mosul Dam.'

'42nd Brigade Asaib al-Haq took over security of the dam yesterday morning,' said Jake.

'But Asaib al-Haq are a Shia militia. The dam is supposed to be secured by the regular Iraqi Army.'

'You and I know that half the Shia militias report directly to General Hashemi. They're his own private army. But technically, they all come under the Iraqi Ministry of Defense. So right now, Asaib al-Haq are the regular federal authorities. And that's not all. We have imagery intel that General Hashemi arrived at the dam last night.'

CHAPTER TWENTY-SEVEN

Call of Duty

'What time is it?'

'Time for you to stop playing that game and practise again.'

Aziz put the console of the PlayStation 4 on the table and picked up the AK-47. He had never held a real gun before. The cold metallic black of the barrel was scratched and the wooden stock was scarred with age. The weapon scared him.

The man Aziz knew only as Faisal said, 'Now, remember, when you take the gun out of the bag tomorrow, it will have a magazine attached and the safety catch will be on. What do you do?'

Aziz held the pistol grip in his left hand and tried to pull back the charging handle. It didn't budge.

'No,' said Faisal. 'We've been through this. What's first?'

'The safety,' said Aziz. 'I'm sorry.'

'Don't be sorry. Concentrate.'

Aziz flicked the safety catch down two notches and ratcheted back the metal handle.

'Good,' said Faisal. 'The safety all the way to the bottom so you're on semi-automatic, not fully automatic. You're ready to shoot.'

'I shoot the whole magazine, then I put in the next magazine.'

'Practise.'

Aziz held the butt against his shoulder and pulled the trigger again and again, firing imaginary bullets, until Faisal said, 'Empty. Reload.'

Aziz tilted the weapon forty-five degrees with his left hand and released the magazine catch with his right. He put the first magazine on the table and picked up the second. He dreaded this part.

The curved magazine of the AK-47 was difficult to put in place. He struggled to find the fit, his hands shaking.

'Take your time, Aziz. Front part in, then snap back and up. It's easy.'

The magazine clicked into place. Aziz pulled back the charging handle.

'Good,' said Faisal. 'Then you shoot the whole second magazine. And remember, when you change magazines, you leave the safety off. Like you did just now. It's easy, Aziz. Again.'

Faisal took the weapon, flicked the safety lever to the safe position, and handed the AK back to Aziz.

Aziz repeated the drills. Safety off. Pull handle back to chamber a round. Fire, fire, fire. Take empty magazine off. Reload. Fire.

'Perfect,' said Faisal. 'Let's get some food. What do you want?'

'Pizza,' said Aziz.

'What kind?'

'I don't know. Whatever,' said Aziz.

'Aziz, you can have whatever you want.'

'Four cheeses,' said Aziz. 'Can I play the game?'

Faisal dialled a number on his phone. 'Yes,' he said.

Aziz picked up the console and went back to Mission Four of Call of Duty Black Ops III, deep inside the Singapore Q-Zone. He knew the game inside out and within seconds he was killing everything in sight.

'What time is it?' he asked, not taking his eyes off the screen.

His parents wouldn't be worried about him yet. On Mondays and Wednesdays, Aziz had cricket practice at the indoor nets and didn't get home until after seven. Every other night of the week, he was home by six at the latest.

Except Aziz hadn't been to practice for a month. He told the coaches he had pulled a hamstring, but every Monday and Wednesday morning when he left the house for school, he still took his cricket bag with him. His parents had no idea of the subterfuge.

As he played the game, Aziz had to admit that he really didn't have any idea either. He didn't know how he had ended up with Faisal in the upstairs flat just off the Ladypool Road in the Sparkhill area of Birmingham. It had just happened.

Aziz was a straight "A" student. He had flown through GCSEs and was now studying at sixth form college for his A levels. Maths, Physics and IT. He had a bright future ahead of him, and there was even a chance he would get a trial for Warwickshire County Cricket Club. He had had several nets at the Edgbaston ground and he was under the watchful eyes of the county's scouts. His father constantly embarrassed him by telling anyone who would listen that Aziz was going to be the first Muslim captain of the England cricket team. Practising Muslim, anyway.

He was happy, in so far as he knew what happiness was. He wasn't part of the popular crowd at college and he kept himself to himself, but he wasn't bullied. He just got on with his studies.

His elder sister, Naima, was at university, studying medicine. Aziz knew she was seeing a white boy, but it didn't upset Aziz. He wasn't angry. He loved his sister. And even though she hadn't told their parents, Aziz was sure they wouldn't mind either. They talked every day about the importance of integrating, of being part of British society. It was a mantra in the Malik household.

And he didn't think he had been led astray. Natural curiosity had led Aziz to research fundamentalism and jihad on the internet. It was a harmless hobby, conducted at the remote cut-off of his computer screen. Aziz wasn't interested in joining any groups, he just wanted to find out more. Discover who these people were, what drove them.

He dipped in and out of chat rooms to learn about life in the Caliphate, why people left their homes, their lives, to pursue this strange dream. Where were all the foreign fighters now the Caliphate was a distant dream? His searches led him from group to group, navigating a random, unpredictable course, until he stumbled across an online community of British Muslims demanding Sharia law in the UK. Hamid, one of the most vocal posters in the group, got in direct contact with Aziz and they started talking on the HiddenChat messaging app. It was still harmless. There was no commitment to a cause.

Hamid was aggressive and argumentative, and he challenged Aziz at every opportunity. He accused Aziz of betraying his background, of wanting to be white. Aziz disagreed; an education was important. You need to integrate. They argued back and forth. After a few weeks, Hamid suggested they meet in person, and instead of going to cricket practice for the last month, Aziz had met Hamid and his friends.

They were all older than Aziz, but he didn't think he had fallen under their influence. But he must have done. Somehow, without really noticing it. Because here he was with Faisal learning how to use an AK-47 and preparing for a terrorist attack. Tomorrow. But he didn't think of himself as a terrorist.

'I'm going to go out and get the pizza. I'll be gone five minutes. Stay here.'

Aziz didn't want to kill anyone. Maybe he could run away while Faisal was gone. But they knew where he lived. Maybe he could go to the police. But what would that do to his parents?

Aziz wanted to speak to Naima, but Faisal had taken his phone as soon he got to the flat. He had no one and there was no way out. It was inevitable. He had to do what they told him.

Faisal returned with the pizza and as they both took a piece from the box, he said, 'Right, let's go through the plan again.'

Aziz ate his first slice of pizza and picked up a second. He held it in his hand, the tip of the triangle drooping down, tied to the rest of the pizza by a string of cheese.

The plan was simple in theory. Walk to Stoney Lane and catch the number six bus. Nine stops. Get off at Park Street and walk to the Bullring Shopping Centre. Take the AK-47 and spare magazine out of the cricket bag and start shooting.

Faisal emptied a bag of cartridges onto the table and started loading the magazines. 'Twenty-five bullets in each magazine,' he said.

'I thought the AK-47 took thirty rounds,' said Aziz.

'It does, but twenty-five is more efficient. It means less weight so it'll be more accurate.'

Faisal didn't know if Aziz would buy the explanation, but he wasn't about to tell him the springs in the magazine were so old and stretched they couldn't take the pressure of a full mag. The chances of the Chinese AK jamming were high.

'What if they're looking for me?' asked Aziz. 'My parents will report me missing tonight.'

'That's the beauty of it, Aziz. They're not looking for you. They're looking for someone else. You're a clean skin. A ghost. And even if your parents do report you missing, the police aren't going to do anything about it tonight. What's another missing Paki to them? And you know the best thing, Aziz? You were born in this country. You are a second-generation British Asian. That will send a message louder than any we can send.'

Aziz took a bite of pizza.

'What time is it?' he asked.

8.22 pm. He should have called it in. He should have let them know Fahd El Idrissi was their man. But he didn't. Instead, Colonel Alvarez was standing outside Number 33 with a bouquet of spring flowers in his hand. He rang the bell and prayed the old lady hadn't gone to bed yet.

The intercom crackled into life.

'Yes?' questioned a hesitant voice.

'Colonel Alvarez of the Guardia Civil. May I come in? This is police business.'

The gate to Number 33 clicked open and Alvarez entered, shutting the gate behind him. The old lady was waiting for him at the front door. Alvarez fished out his ID.

'Señora Ferrer. Colonel Fernando Alvarez. My apologies for disturbing you at such a late hour. May I come in?'

'What pretty flowers, Colonel,' said Señora Ferrer.

She led Alvarez through a hallway back in time to a dark sitting room. The only light came from a standard lamp standing behind an armchair by the fireplace. The green shade of the lamp was fringed with gold tassels. The fireplace was laid, but not lit. In the gloom to his left, Alvarez noticed a grand piano covered with ornate silver picture frames.

'The dead,' said Señora Ferrer. 'Keeping an eye on me.'

Señora Ferrer was five feet three inches tall, wafer-thin, and fierce. Her wavy silver hair was immaculate and she was wearing a brown tweed skirt, cut just below the knee, and a green cardigan. A twin set of pearls emerged from the downturned collar of her pristine white blouse.

She took two Riedel sherry glasses from an antique cabinet and put them on a silver tray which sat in the middle of an otherwise empty, round rosewood table.

'I shall be back in a minute, Colonel,' she said. 'Make yourself comfortable.'

Alvarez didn't have time for pleasantries, but he didn't want to frighten Señora Ferrer. She was old-school and seemed imperturbable, but it wasn't every day you found out you lived next door to a terrorist.

'Fino,' said Señora Ferrer, walking back into the room, 'chilled, very pale, very dry. You will join me in a glass.'

'I'm sorry, I don't drink, Señora,' said Alvarez.

'And I don't drink alone, Colonel,' said Señora Ferrer, pouring two glasses of sherry.

'In which case, I would be delighted, Señora. May I call you by your first name?'

'My given name is Margarida,' she said. 'But you may call me Señora Ferrer. Now, it is not often I receive visitors from the Guardia Civil. To what do I owe the pleasure?'

Alvarez took a deep breath and jumped straight in. He told Señora Ferrer about Fahd El Idrissi. She didn't bat an eyelid. Instead, she explained she didn't like to pry and she had never seen the neighbour from Number 35. She minded her own business and expected others to do the same.

'So,' she said, when Alvarez had finished, 'I am living next to a terrorist who is planning to detonate an explosive device at Gaudí's Sagrada Familia. How may I help?'

'For now, Señora, please just stay here. I need to go and have a look.'

Alvarez went out through the back door to the kitchen and walked to the bottom of the garden. To his left, dividing the properties, was a six-feet-high brick wall. He stood on tiptoe and peered over. Number 35 had an empty, tarmacked back yard. So far, so good. Lights were on in a ground floor room at the back of the house, but heavy shades were pulled down over the windows. Alvarez couldn't see in, but that meant Idrissi couldn't see out.

Alvarez tightened the straps of the mini rucksack on his back and checked his old service Beretta 92 was secure in the waistband at the back of his trousers.

This was his last chance to call it in and do it by the book. The police wouldn't need any convincing. They would believe him straight away. Captain Benitez had told Alvarez earlier of the imminent threat against Barcelona passed on by the British. One phone call from Alvarez and an armed response team would be swarming all over Number 35 within twenty minutes.

Alvarez hauled himself up and threw one leg over the wall. He paused a second, turned his body, brought his other leg over, and slid down the wall into the back yard of Number 35. He crouched, and paused again, patting his back to check the Beretta.

Alvarez crabbed across the yard parallel to the house with one hand out in front of him for balance. His right knee was beginning to complain. When he was level with the lit windows, he moved forward, approaching the house one step at a time, keeping as low as his ageing body would allow.

What seemed an eternity later, but was no more than thirty steps, Alvarez was up against the wall of the house, on his knees below the windowsill, catching his breath.

A half-inch gap between the blinds and the edge of the window gave Alvarez a chance to look inside. If it went wrong and Idrissi saw him, he had the Beretta and his phone. If it went really wrong, Señora Ferrer had Benitez's phone number. Alvarez dismissed the fact his only back-up was an octogenarian by now no doubt tucking into her second glass of sherry. She was a tough old bird. She would be fine.

Alvarez got on his haunches and peered through the gap in the blinds. He recognised the back of Idrissi, but he had no idea who the second man was. He had never seen anyone else go in or out of the house.

On the floor of the kitchen were seven blue plastic oil drums.

Fifty-five-gallon drums if Alvarez had to take a guess. Idrissi and his partner worked at a table each. On the first table, there were kilo-sized packets of white powder wrapped in clingfilm. Idrissi was putting them into an oil drum.

TATP had not been in common use during Alvarez's time on the Guardia Civil counter-terrorist desk, but he knew without doubt that the cocaine-sized packets contained the explosive.

The other table was covered in rusty nails and small scraps of metal. Idrissi's partner was putting them into plastic bags and laying them on top of the white powder in the drum. A layer of powder, a layer of scrap metal.

Idrissi screwed on the top of one of the drums. He and his partner took a handle each and carried the drum out of the kitchen. Alvarez ducked down below the windowsill.

On the side facing Number 33, a garage was attached to the house. Between the garage and the property-dividing wall was a small alleyway allowing access to the backyard. Alvarez crept along the alleyway. He just needed to be quiet. There were no windows on the side of the garage to give him away.

A white transit van, hired from a local company, was parked flush against the garage door. Alvarez stopped and strained to listen. Idrissi and his partner didn't say a word, but he could hear them walk through the garage and put the oil drum in the back of the van. One of the men got into the van and slid the drum towards the front. Both men walked back into the house.

Alvarez waited.

And waited.

Five minutes later, he heard footsteps inside the garage and another drum was loaded on the van. He had counted seven drums in the kitchen, and in all likelihood Idrissi and his partner had already loaded several in the van before Alvarez had climbed the fence. Alvarez reckoned on a minimum of five hundred pounds of explosives.

This was it.

Alvarez took the Beretta out of his waistband and put it on the ground in front of him. He loosened one of the straps of his rucksack and slid his arm out. He unzipped the rucksack, reached in, and took out a small, magnetic bomb.

He waited for the next drum to be loaded on the van and the two pairs of footsteps to recede back into the house. He crept forward until he was level with the van and lay on his back. He pushed the timer switch and reached in under the bottom of the van.

The bomb jumped out of his hand and attached itself to the underside of the van with a resounding clank. Alvarez sucked breath in through his teeth and turned his head.

The timer was set to three minutes. Three minutes until the bomb exploded, detonating the TATP in the van.

Alvarez thought about scrambling over the side of the wall by the house, but if they were close to loading another drum in the van, he might make too much noise. Better to retrace his steps. Alvarez crept back along the side of the alleyway.

When he heard the footsteps back in the garage, he tiptoed round the side of the house to the kitchen and walked away from the light.

He got to the wall at the end of the backyard.

Two minutes.

As Alvarez was about to climb the wall, he realised he had left his Beretta behind. Too late for that now. Alvarez scrambled over the wall and headed back to Señora Ferrer's kitchen door.

'You were gone an awfully long time, Colonel. I was about to call it in, as you police folk say,' said Señora Ferrer. 'Is everything all right?'

Despite his time on the counter-terrorist desk, Alvarez was no explosives expert. He knew the explosion would be big, but he had no idea how bad the damage would be. Logic told him that with the doors of the van open, the main part of the blast would be directed into Number 35. Idrissi and his partner shouldn't stand a chance. As for the collateral damage, Alvarez hoped it would be no more than the neighbours' windows and a car or two parked nearby.

One minute.

'Come with me, Señora Ferrer.' Alvarez led her back into the sitting room, the room furthest away from Number 35. 'There's going to be a loud explosion. There may be some damage to your property, but don't worry, the Spanish authorities will pay for everything. Come here and sit with me on the floor, Señora.'

Alvarez helped Señora Ferrer to the floor and sat down next to her by the piano.

Thirty seconds.

Alvarez thought of his brother, Ignacio, killed in a foreign field. A family destroyed. This at least, Alvarez could do for his brother.

Señora Ferrer reached for Alvarez's hand and said, 'Rather exciting, isn't it? And Colonel, you may call me Margarida.'

Five seconds to go.

CHAPTER TWENTY-EIGHT

Forward and Rear

Built between 1982 and 1985 by order of former Iraqi President Saddam Hussein, Mosul Dam is the fourth largest dam in the Middle East. Its clay core stands one hundred and thirteen metres high. Sloped, earthen embankments on either side of the core have an eight-hundred-metre cross-section at their base.

The dam is 2.21 kilometres long, and at maximum capacity it can hold over eleven billion cubic metres of water, arresting the natural flow of the River Tigris to provide hydroelectric power, drinking water, and irrigation for the people of northern Iraq.

Mosul Dam is a feat of 1980s engineering to make any Middle Eastern dictator proud. There is only one problem.

The dam was built on a water-soluble rock foundation of gypsum and anhydrite. It is inherently unstable, shifting millimetre by millimetre as the bedrock dissolves and sinkholes appear. Repair works had to begin before the original construction was even completed. Grouting via cement injection is required twenty-four hours a day to plug the holes which form under the dam.

This essential maintenance slowed following the US

invasion in 2003. Not surprising, given the total collapse of Iraqi infrastructure that brought the country to its knees. Worse was to come in 2014 when the Islamic State took control of the facility for ten days. Work stopped completely.

Overnight, Mosul Dam became the single most strategic target for the Coalition to regain and it wasn't difficult to see why. Were the dam to fail, a humanitarian catastrophe would ensue. A giant tsunami would be unleashed, sweeping down the Tigris river valley all the way to Baghdad.

Within three hours, the city of Mosul would be engulfed by a twenty-metre wave. A ten-metre wave would consume the town of Bayji. Tikrit – Saddam Hussein's home town – Samarra, and all the other towns and villages on the Tigris south of Mosul would be swept away by the path of the tsunami. Four days and four hundred kilometres later, a four-metre wave would crash through the centre of Baghdad, wiping out much of the Iraqi capital. Conservative estimates put the number of dead at five hundred thousand and the number of displaced at four million.

For the past two years, the Italian engineering company Fratelli Fontana SpA have been leading efforts to stabilise the dam. In addition to plugging the holes in the rock foundation, Fratelli Fontana have been pumping cement to a depth of a hundred metres below the core to create a cement curtain to shore up the failing dam. One million cubic metres of cement is required to do the job. It will take six years to complete. And it is not a permanent solution. It is a patchwork of plasters to cover a leaking wound. In the hands of ISIS, Mosul Dam was a weapon of potential mass destruction. Today, the dam remains a timebomb that could still devastate Iraq.

'Spark, you have a visitor,' Elliot shouted up the stairs.

Lucinda closed her laptop. She didn't need to read any more.

'Thanks,' she said, walking into the sitting room. 'Have you seen Dave today?'

'No, he went out early this morning. I've no idea when he'll be back.'

Lucinda turned to the visitor.

'Mike Evans, ma'am. SAS.'

Mike Evans was a very different creature to the six-feet Delta Force monsters Lucinda had met on the Erbil military base. Evans was small, five feet seven at the most. He was ferret-like, lean and wiry, with flecked hair. His tan leather skin looked like it could blunt a knife.

'If you don't mind, ma'am, I'll get straight to the point.' There was a soft Welsh lilt to Evans's accent. 'We're working closely with the Americans. They'll take the dam. I'm leading the assault on General Hashemi's house at Lake Darbandikhan.'

A four-man SAS team would raid Hashemi's house to retrieve the documents Lucinda had found. Security was minimal now that the General had left, so a four-man team with air support was deemed sufficient. Lucinda gave Evans a detailed layout of the house, focusing on the second-floor library. That was the only room the team needed to target.

'Thank you, ma'am. I am authorised to ask if you would like to accompany us on the raid.'

'No. I'll be going to the dam.'

Evans shifted in his seat. 'Your superiors thought you might say that. If you don't want to accompany my team to the lake, I am instructed to tell you to take the next flight home.' Evans held up his hand. 'I'm only the messenger, ma'am.'

Lucinda paused. She stood up. 'Thank you, Mike. You can let yourself out,' she said.

Lucinda went upstairs to her room. She had been avoiding her email because she knew she would get dragged into the office politics, reined in by the incessant restraints a rear headquarters always imposes on its forward operators.

And sure enough, there it was. An email from Cristine Laird

thanking Lucinda for her work, offering her the opportunity – London offering her the opportunity no less – to accompany the SAS team on the Darbandikhan raid, otherwise Spark was to "take the next available flight home and report to the office for a full debrief. Travel will be sending you an e-ticket in due course".

Lucinda slammed shut the lid of her laptop and paced the room. 'Fuck you,' she said, 'fuck you, you bitch. There is no way.' She stood over the desk, opened up the laptop and started a new mail. 'No fucking way,' she muttered to herself.

Lucinda deleted the draft and changed into her maritime blue 5.11 Spitfire shirt and black 5.11 Fast-Tac cargo pants.

Fifteen minutes later she burst into Jake's trailer without knocking.

'Those bastards. Those utter bastards. Did you have anything to do with this?'

'Whoa, slow down, Spark. What are you talking about?'

'They want to send me home. I am not going. I am not leaving now, not after everything that's happened. What did you tell them?'

'Hey, I didn't say a word. I got no dog in this fight. But I can understand where they're coming from.'

'What the hell is that supposed to mean?' spat Lucinda.

'Listen,' said Jake, 'this is not a simple raid on a small compound in Syria. This is a full-scale Special Forces assault on a heavily-defended piece of major, critical infrastructure. It's gonna be a fight. And like it or not, Spark, you are not trained for combat operations. Besides, you've been through the ringer in the last week. You've done your bit. You need to get some rest, heal up.'

'And leave things to the professionals?' Lucinda glared at Jake, who slumped into his chair and smiled.

'Goddammit, you are one contrary piece of work, Lucinda Spark.'

'Jake!'

'OK, OK. I may have a spare seat. If you play nice. And on one condition.'

'What's that?' asked Lucinda.

'You stick to me like glue and do exactly what I tell you, when I tell you. If you don't, I'll shoot you myself.' Jake got up and went to his desk. 'And while we're at it, you may as well have one of these. Just in case. Try to hang onto this one. They don't grow on trees.'

Lucinda put the transmitter pen in the sleeve pocket of her shirt. 'Thanks, D'Souza. And don't worry, I'll play by the rules. What's the latest?'

'It's not good. Let's walk and talk. We've got a brief to go to.'

Lucinda and Jake walked out of his trailer into the warm night air. It was 11 pm and twenty-one degrees. Summer was coming. Night-time temperatures wouldn't see twenty degrees again for five months.

'We reckon on eight hundred troops at the dam. 42nd Asaib al-Haq are there, so too are the regular Iraqi Army unit. They stayed. That means their commanding officer is in the pay of General Hashemi. And we've got another problem. There's an Italian company up there working on the dam.'

'Fratelli Fontana,' said Lucinda.

'Yeah. They have four hundred and fifty Italian Carabinieri looking after them. Or had. They are now under armed guard, locked down in the contractor camp below the dam. So we're gonna have to get them out too. This whole thing's getting messier by the minute.'

They cut across Dorsey Square. The basketball court was deserted, but lights were still on in the shops around the square.

'No time for coffee,' said Jake, nodding in the direction of the Green Beans. 'There is one bit of good news, though. Hashemi's not yet ready to blow the dam.'

'How do we know that?' asked Lucinda.

'We got intel coming direct from the Fontana chief engineer. He is being held in the Control Room against his will. Being forced to tell Hashemi where best to place the explosives. Guy named Paolo Rosati. Seems pretty switched on. He gave up his smart phone but managed to hide his backup. An old Nokia, so at least we know the battery won't die. Rosati's been sending text updates when he can.'

'Hashemi's only had a day. How can he be anywhere near rigging enough explosives to blow the dam?'

'Easy. It's not as if he's planning a controlled implosion of an apartment block on the Upper East Side. He wants to cause as much destruction as possible. All he needs are the explosives, detonators and several hundred meters of det cord. And all that is readily available in this country, particularly if you're the commanding officer of the Iranian Quds Force. And he doesn't need to do any drilling to emplace the explosives. It's already been done. A grouting gallery runs the length of the dam at the bottom of the core. That's where Fontana inject the cement and they have drilled over two thousand bore holes that go down a hundred metres or more. Our experts and Fontana agree. With the right amount of explosives in the right place, Hashemi can cause enough movement in the rock foundation to collapse the dam. He's using shaped charges with PETN explosive, and Rosati reckons Hashemi will be ready to blow the dam by early morning.'

They passed the helicopter bays by the landing zone. Apaches, Black Hawks and Chinooks nestled together in the bays, protected by a vertical blanket of T-WALLs.

'What's the plan?' asked Lucinda.

'We're about to find out, but there's no time for any of your British subtlety. We're going to do this the American way. Full frontal. Loud and proud. Right, let's do this. After you, Spark.'

Lucinda recognised many of the men in the briefing tent from

261

the raid on Abu Issa's compound. Master Sergeant O'Neill seemed to take up half the room on his own. She saw Weisz, Cobb, Mathis and Cortez. They nodded greetings to Lucinda and D'Souza.

And at the back of the tent on the right, sitting alone, she recognised Mike Evans.

'Hi,' said Lucinda. 'Paige Turner, CIA.'

Evans's expression hovered somewhere between a smirk and a smile.

'Mike Evans, SAS. A pleasure to work with the Americans, ma'am.'

Lucinda took a seat next to Jake. Monitors and whiteboards at the front of the tent were covered with imagery of the dam from every conceivable angle and height. Satellite images, aerial reconnaissance photographs, pictures taken at the dam itself.

Panoramic images depicted the dam in its entirety, some taken from in front, some taken from the reservoir side, some taken from a bird's eye view, slap bang above the middle of the dam.

Close-up shots showed the width of the road across the top of the dam and the two earthen embankments either side of the clay core. On the west side were the four power generators for the hydroelectric plant and the two bottom outlets, capable of discharging 2,600 cubic metres of water a second. On the east side of the dam was the main spillway with five massive, hundred-metre tall, concrete outlet gates through which a torrent of water could flow at 13,000 cubic metres a second. A road bridge, supported by the elliptical concrete columns of the gates, ran over the top of the spillway. Beyond that was the emergency spillway, gravity-operated should the water in the reservoir ever reach three hundred and forty metres above sea level.

There was close-up imagery of the Control Room on the east side of the dam between the spillway and the start of the dam itself. Below the Control Room, built into the side of the dam, was the lift shaft that descended all the way to the grouting gallery a hundred metres in the darkness below.

The gallery itself was a cylindrical tunnel, three metres wide and three and a half metres high. Pipes and electrical cables ran the length of one side of the tunnel. Lucinda counted at least four grouting rigs, and in one of the pictures she could make out some of the bore holes through which the cement was injected.

Delta Force Squadron Commander Lieutenant Colonel Bosman entered the tent and strode to the briefing podium. He commanded the room.

'OK, gentlemen. Listen up. Time is short.'

CHAPTER TWENTY-NINE

To God We Belong

First light. Two AH-64 Apache attack helicopters flew fast and low, away from the rising sun. The downforce from their rotor blades left a ripple effect on the water, an evidence trail following the Apaches all the way to Mosul Dam.

Behind them, keeping pace at one hundred and fifty knots, three MH-60 Black Hawks transported the Delta Force assault team. Twelve thousand feet above them, an AC-130 gunship descended to its combat altitude and waited for the command to engage.

Lucinda knew the dam would be impressive, but as it rushed towards her at 2.8 miles a minute, its true scale became clear. It loomed out of the retreating night sky, a sprawling concrete giant holding back the waters of the Tigris. The imagery at the briefing didn't begin to do the dam justice.

'Fire when ready,' commanded Master Sergeant O'Neill over the radio.

Miniscule figures darted back and forth across the top of the dam like crazed ants desperate to escape a poison trail as the AC-130 sprayed 25mm shells from its GAU-12 Gatling gun. Its job was to destroy or tie down Asaib al-Haq defensive positions and create an inner perimeter for the Delta assault team to penetrate.

Close protection for the team was provided by the Apaches. They peeled off left and right, hovering either side of the dam, sleek birds of prey, noses down, the windshields of their eyes scanning for targets.

The lead Black Hawk headed for the middle of the dam to drop off the first Delta callsign, Golf-1. They would attack the Control Room from the west. The second Black Hawk carrying Golf-2, Spark and D'Souza, banked left towards the main spillway so they could attack from the east. The Golf-3 team would land near the contractor camp below the dam and liberate the detained Carabinieri. That was the plan.

'RPG,' yelled Jake over the radio.

From the circular guard tower jutting out over the reservoir, a soldier emerged with a rocket-propelled grenade perched on his shoulder. He aimed at Golf-1 as it came in to land.

'Take that hostile out now,' ordered O'Neill.

One of the hovering Apaches marked its prey and loosed a Hellfire missile. Two seconds later the tower was obliterated, but the RPG was already in the air. The Black Hawk pilot from the 160th Special Operations Aviation Regiment took evasive action, banking hard right.

He was too late. The RPG punched through the tail rotor, forcing the helicopter into a wild spin. The pilot fought to regain control as the Black Hawk pitched and spun. He killed the power and dropped the helicopter hard, crash landing on top of the dam.

Golf-1 looked to have made it, but it was teetering on the edge and before any of the team could extract, the helicopter tipped over and started to slide down the earthen embankment, fifteen thousand pounds of heavy metal and human flesh forced to obey the inexorable law of gravity. Lucinda watched in horror as the Black Hawk flipped nose to tail. The spinning rotor blades smashed into the embankment and splintered like matchsticks. The helicopter exploded.

Master Sergeant O'Neill and his Delta Force team plunged to the bottom of the dam in a ball of fire. They didn't stand a chance.

'Golf-1 down, Golf-1 down. Golf-3 continue as planned.' Sergeant First Class Cortez took command. 'Get us on the ground now,' he shouted to the pilot of Golf-2.

The Black Hawk landed east of the spillway and the Golf-2 team exploded out of the helicopter, laying down suppressing fire in a one-hundred-and-eighty-degree arc. One of the Apaches covered their six.

Reinforced concrete Jersey barriers, eighty-one centimetres high, were staggered across the length of the spillway bridge road. They were there to deter vehicle-borne improvised explosive devices, slowing traffic through a series of enforced chicanes, but they provided perfect cover for Golf-2.

Cortez and his team reached the first barrier on the bridge. He looked back and gave Jake the OK. 'Stay with me, Spark, and keep your head down,' said Jake. They jumped out of the helicopter and ran to Cortez's position. The Black Hawk lifted off.

The plan had been to attack the Control Room from two fronts. Golf-1 from the dam, Golf-2 from the spillway. It hadn't survived first contact and now Golf-2 had to do the job alone. A double layer of T-WALLs provided heavy fortification around the Control Room and the Delta team was already taking fire. Both Apaches strafed the target with their chain guns, tearing off chunks of concrete and forcing the Asaib al-Haq defenders back into their redoubt.

'Move,' commanded Cortez. Mathis ran ahead and took cover behind the next Jersey barrier. As he provided covering fire, the rest of the team moved up. A barrier at a time. Jake and Lucinda kept twenty metres back, following in the team's cleared shadow. The Golf-2 team was level with the second gate on the spillway bridge, but there were still three gates and sixty metres to go before the Control Room. Progress was slow.

'Move,' commanded Cortez. Weisz took point, moving quickly in a crouched position, the butt of his Heckler & Koch 416 carbine tight against his shoulder. Five metres from the column marking the third spillway gate he jerked right and fell to his knees. A round fired from the Control Room had severed the femoral artery in his right leg. Cortez was alongside side Weisz in seconds, dragging him to the protective safety of a Jersey barrier. Cortez grabbed a tourniquet from his med kit and bound it tight, two inches above the bleeding wound in Weisz's leg.

'Shit,' said Jake.

'What now?' shouted Lucinda.

'Blow the whole fucking Control Room.'

'You can't do that, it'll take us hours to get through the rubble.'

'Tell me something I don't know, Spark,' said Jake. 'I'm gonna go get Weisz. Stay here. Keep your head down. OK?'

Lucinda put her hand on Jake's shoulder. 'Cover me,' she said. Before Jake realised what was happening, Lucinda was up and sprinting along the spillway bridge towards the Control Room, hugging tight to the left wall.

'Fuck,' said Jake. 'Cover fire. Cover fire. Everything you've got,' he called into his radio.

Lucinda sprinted past Cortez and the injured Weisz. The two Apaches sprayed the Control Room, destroying the remains of the outer T-WALL. The AC-130 gunship targeted anything hostile that moved. Lucinda covered the eighty metres of the first four spillway gates in ten seconds flat. When she reached the start of the final gate, she ducked down behind a Jersey barrier to catch her breath. She looked back, but couldn't see Jake.

Golf-2 would continue to try to infiltrate the Control Room from the main access point, but she had no idea how long it would take, and time was something they didn't have.

There was another way in.

Lucinda took two deep breaths and jumped up onto the wall of the spillway bridge. She no longer heard the Apaches. She didn't even know if she was being fired at. All she knew was she had twenty metres to run. And then jump.

The lift down to the grouting gallery was built into the side of the dam below the Control Room. Lucinda had to cut the corner and jump across the last section of the spillway. She guessed it was a five-metre jump and a ten-metre drop. Should be fine and the target area was a large concrete pad next to the lift.

Lucinda leapt off the ledge and arched her back, pulling at the air with her arms and legs like a long jumper. She didn't dare look down at the base of the spillway a hundred metres below. All her energy was focused on making the landing pad.

In the final seconds of flight, Lucinda bent her legs and tucked her body to break her fall. She hit the pad hard, rolled twice and came to a sudden stop, smacking into the wire mesh of the lift with her knees. She scrambled round to the front of the lift, slid the metal door shut, and pushed the green button on the yellow control panel. She had made it.

The lift jolted into action, clattering and clanking, groaning metal reluctant to start its journey. But within seconds it picked up speed, dropping down the enclosed shaft at ten metres a second, carrying Lucinda into another world. A pitch black, cold, damp world.

The fight above receded into distant cracks of thunder as Lucinda descended into the darkness. Metre by metre, she disappeared deep into the bowels of the dam.

A dim light punctured the blackness below Lucinda's feet and the lift began to slow. Journey's end. The lift shuddered to a halt. Lucinda slid open the metal door, her right hand on the pistol grip of her holstered Glock.

In front of her was the grouting gallery, running the length

268

of the dam at the bottom of the clay core. Lights, caged in metal cases, ran the length of the curved walls in a gentle V-shape, appearing to meet at some distant point. Lucinda walked down the tunnel.

Water dripped from fissures in the gallery wall. A grouting rig stood idle. Hundreds of pipes dotted the tunnel floor, poking out five inches above ground as far as the eye could see. They were the boreholes through which Fratelli Fontana pumped the cement to keep the dam alive.

Lucinda shivered. The dank tunnel reverberated in the silence.

Bright yellow cables disappeared down some of the boreholes, snaking their way a further hundred metres down through the gypsum foundation. Detonator cord. At the end of which lay the shaped charges of PETN explosive primed to tear the bedrock apart and destroy the dam. Lucinda was standing on hundreds of kilogrammes of explosives. Above her, billions of cubic metres of water.

Even if she had a knife, Lucinda wasn't sure cutting the det cord was a good idea. And trying to cut it with a jagged piece of metal lying on the gallery floor seemed to her an instinctively bad idea. She had to track the cord back to the source. That was where General Hashemi would be.

Lucinda followed the gathering trails of cord back towards the lift. They led left into another tunnel. Lucinda turned and ran straight into a human brick wall. She took a step back. And instantly recognised the beast of a man who had stood between her legs and stroked her thigh with his sandpaper hands. The man who had beaten her. Colonel Farrokzhad.

Lucinda went for her Glock, but Farrokzhad smacked it from her hand like a plastic toy. He lunged forward, but Lucinda managed to sidestep him. He was quick for a big man, but Lucinda was quicker.

Farrokzhad had his own pistol, but he left it holstered. He

stood and stared at Lucinda, smiling. A heavy triangle of sweat darkened his khaki shirt from neck to navel. Watery beads dripped from his forehead. He lunged again. Lucinda moved back and away. She transferred her weight to her right leg and kicked with her left. Hard, connecting with Farrokzhad's midriff. He didn't budge. She kicked again, and this time he almost caught her leg, knocking her off balance.

Farrokzhad lunged at her again, but Lucinda ducked past his approaching bulk. She punched him in the kidneys as hard as she could, but he didn't notice the blow. He just turned and stared at her, still smiling.

Lucinda knew she had more stamina than Farrokzhad and would be able to wear him down, but how long that would take and what she would do with him when he was punched out, she had no idea. And she didn't have the time to find out. She had to break the deadlock. She had to get to the Control Room.

An idea. An insane idea. If it went wrong, it would be her last. Legs astride, Lucinda beckoned Farrokzhad with her right hand. That wiped the smug smile off the bastard's face. Farrokzhad took a step forward, and instead of backing away as he expected, Lucinda leapt at him. Farrokzhad's natural reaction was to catch her. He wrapped his arms around Lucinda's body and started to squeeze. He had her in a bear hug, a vice-like, steel grip. The breath was being squeezed from her body and the muscles in her back were cracking. Lucinda put her left hand on Farrokzhad's chest and pushed herself back. She could feel her ribs being crushed, the wounds on her back opening up. She didn't have long.

Farrokzhad looked at her, triumph in his eyes. He would snap her spine in a matter of moments. Stupid little bitch. Her last, fatal mistake. And this time the General had given the right order. Kill her.

With her free hand, Lucinda pulled the transmitter pen from the pocket of her left sleeve and flicked off the lid. She held the pen tight in her fist and drove the point as deep as she could into Farrokzhad's neck, aiming for and finding his carotid artery.

Lucinda yanked the pen out and a fountain of blood spurted from the punctured artery. A confused look crossed Farrokzhad's face, but he squeezed harder. Lucinda put both her hands on Farrokzhad's chest and pushed as hard as she could, desperate to find some breathing space, praying that Farrokzhad would weaken before he crushed her to death.

The blood pulsed out of his neck and his grip began to slip. Farrokzhad dropped to his knees, Lucinda still in his arms. As soon as her feet touched the ground, she kneed him in the chest and forced herself free from his dying embrace.

Colonel Farrokzhad covered the gaping wound with his hand, blood still leaking out, but slowly, in a trickle. The pressure of life had gone and his heart beat for the final time. Lucinda fell back against the tunnel wall and looked at the dead beast. She picked up her Glock and followed the cord.

No wonder Farrokzhad had been sweating. The yellow det cord led up a precast concrete tube, like a huge inverted drainage pipe. Completed during the original construction phase, it had been the only way to access the base of the clay core before the lift was put in and the grouting gallery was built. It was at an angle of ten, maybe fifteen degrees, which would make the climb a little easier, but a little longer. How much longer, Lucinda didn't know. This was no time for Pythagoras.

Metal rungs were set into the concrete a foot apart. An imperial climb and Lucinda's limbs were already aching. She put her left leg on the bottom rung and started the ascent to the Control Room.

The det cord was tied together in bundles of six and attached with a plastic tie to the metal ladder every nine or ten rungs. There were eight bundles. Forty-eight separate charges. And those were just the ones Lucinda knew about. It was more than enough to blow the dam.

To focus her mind, Lucinda counted each rung on the ladder. She stopped to rest when the count reached twenty-eight. The top of the tunnel seemed no closer and the bottom was barely any further away. Lucinda took a deep breath and carried on.

The muscles in her forearms and shoulders began to scream in complaint. Her fingers hurt and were losing their grip. The buildup of lactic acid burned deep into her thighs, robbing her of strength. She was exhausted.

Lucinda stopped to rest again. She reckoned she must be almost halfway. She put her right arm through a rung and held on with the crook. She dropped her left arm by her side and shook the pain loose. She did the same with her leg, flexing her ankle, and then repeated the process on the right side of her body. Lucinda closed her eyes and went through her Olympic training routine. She thought of Kim and the early morning runs. The hours spent in the gym. She cricked her neck and hauled herself up the ladder.

The 5.11 shirt stuck to her back and she had to wipe the sweat from her hands every couple of steps, but at last Lucinda could feel a draft of warm air from above. No more than ten rungs to go. And she heard gunfire. Muffled gunfire of the fight on the dam above.

The pre-mission briefing hadn't contained any imagery of the concrete tunnel so Lucinda didn't know what to expect when she got to the top. She paused with her hands on the final rung and raised herself up on tiptoes so she could see out. She was still underground. In front of her was a flat expanse of compacted earth covered in wooden duckboards. Fifteen metres beyond the duckboards was a large, square, prefabricated plastic container with Perspex windows. A set of metal stairs ran from the far side of the container up to a room above. The main Control Room.

Lucinda climbed out of the tunnel and crept towards the corner of the container, staying away from the windows. The duckboards moved as she crossed them, but the sound of wood on compacted mud was drowned out by the gunfire.

The container was a bunker. A secure, secondary command centre providing operational redundancy for the dam's bottom outlets and spillway.

Lucinda peered through a side window. At a desk with his back to her, was a uniformed soldier. In the middle of the room, a man was bound to a chair by his wrists. Paolo Rosati, the Fratelli Fontana chief engineer. And standing in front of Rosati, in the full military dress uniform of the IRGC Quds Force, was Major General Ali Hussein Hashemi. Lucinda ducked back into the shadows.

The fighting on the surface sounded intense, but there was no sign of panic on Hashemi's face. Golf-2 must still be some way from breaching the Control Room. Lucinda traced the bundles of yellow cord from the concrete tunnel along the duckboards to a hole in the bottom of the container. They culminated inside a large, gunmetal grey junction box on the floor. A solitary, thick, black cable ran from the other side of the junction box to the back of an open briefcase on the desk. The uniformed soldier's back blocked much of her view, but Lucinda could see a screen in the open top of the briefcase and part of a keyboard in the bottom. A toggle switch with a red safety cover was attached to the keyboard.

The control panel for the explosives.

It had to be now.

Lucinda crouched below the level of the window and drew her pistol. She crept along the side of the container and tried the door. It was unlocked. She counted to three, burst into the room, and fired twice at the soldier's back. He slumped to the floor. Lucinda turned her gun on Hashemi. His hand was on his sidearm, but he hadn't managed to draw it in time.

'Don't move,' shouted Lucinda. 'Don't you fucking move.' Lucinda walked further into the room and, with her pistol trained on General Hashemi, she kicked the soldier to check he was dead.

Without taking her eyes off the General, she said, 'Rosati?'

'Yes,' Rosati replied.

General Hashemi took a step towards the Italian engineer, his hand still on the grip of his pistol. 'Hello, my dear,' he said.

Two more steps and Rosati would be between the General and Lucinda, a human shield that would strip Lucinda of her advantage.

'I said don't move, General, and I mean it.'

'And what will you do, my dear? Shoot me?'

Lucinda fired. Centre mass. Double tap. Hashemi dropped to the ground.

Lucinda looked at Rosati and pointed to the briefcase. 'Can you make it safe?'

'Yes,' he said.

Lucinda ripped the tape from his wrists. 'Do it.'

General Hashemi was lying on his back, blood oozing from his chest, seeping into the shirt of his pressed uniform. 'You cannot possibly win, my dear. The time of the Mahdi is upon us.' He struggled for breath. 'We belong to God, and to God we shall return.'

Lucinda put her foot on General Hashemi's chest and gripped the Glock with both hands. She aimed the muzzle between Hashemi's eyes.

'Where you're going, General, God is dead.'

Lucinda pulled the trigger.

CHAPTER THIRTY

Home Truths

Lucinda Spark cracked three eggs into a mixing bowl and whisked them lightly with a fork. She added a twist of sea salt and cracked pepper. Into a small, nonstick saucepan on a low heat she dropped a knob of butter. When the butter had melted, she added the eggs, stirring continuously with a wooden spoon.

With the eggs still runny, but on the turn, she killed the heat and stirred for another thirty seconds, essential to ensure the right consistency. Lucinda spooned the scrambled eggs onto a plate, where they joined two rashers of crispy bacon, and poured herself a second shot of Vergnano from the moka. It was good to be home.

Lucinda had been flown straight to the UK in the back of a cavernous C-17 Globemaster transport aircraft. She had the entire plane to herself. The decision to fly her out of Iraq had been made so fast she barely had time to say goodbye to Jake. She searched for him on base and found him by the basketball court on Dorsey Square, thirty minutes before wheels up.

'What, you're leaving? Already?' he said, an obvious tinge of disappointment in his voice.

'Yes,' she said. 'Orders. Given I was the one who killed

Hashemi, my bosses want me out now. I can't even get my stuff from the house.'

'Orders, huh? Not your greatest strength. At least let me give you a ride to the airhead.'

Jake drove Lucinda in the armoured Lincoln Continental. They made conversation, but that's all it was. Awkward, stilted conversation.

'I guess this is it,' said Jake, when they pulled up at the airhead.

'I guess so,' said Lucinda. 'Jake…'

'Come here, Spark.'

They hugged, holding each other across the bench seat of the Lincoln.

'I should go,' Lucinda whispered into Jake's ear.

Jake put his hand on the side of Lucinda's face and stroked her cheek with his thumb. His touch was warm and soft. He kissed her on the lips.

'Go,' he said.

Lucinda got out of the car and walked away. It didn't seem right it had to end this way. She stopped and looked back.

Jake had a broad grin on his face. 'Yo, Spark,' he yelled, 'we did it!'

Lucinda smiled and walked into the terminal building.

She hoped their paths would cross again, but as she turned left out of the house on Maunsel Street and right into Horseferry Road, Lucinda had other things on her mind. It was her second day back in the office and she had a decision to make.

Early-morning commuters keen to avoid the worst of the rush hour queued in coffee shops for their morning latte. Some bought sandwiches and salads, knowing they would be chained to their desks for the entire working day.

Newspapers racked on a stand outside a newsagent competed for their attention. "Coordinated Terror Attacks Thwarted", read the headline of one. "Terror Plot Foiled", read another. And a third, "Brummy Mall Cop Hero".

Lucinda tightened the belt of her brown, wool-blend trench coat. It was a nothing sort of a day. The sun couldn't be bothered to come out to reflect the mood of a grateful nation and there was no sign of rain in the milky-grey clouds.

She grabbed a double macchiato from Gianni's and walked to the Vauxhall Bridge Road bus stop. She sat on the low concrete wall by Henry Moore's abstract bronze and replayed the conversation she had had the previous day with Sir Philip Colville-Browne, C, the head of Britain's Secret Intelligence Service, and her ultimate boss.

Lucinda had been ordered to C's office first thing that morning. No meeting with Laird. No meeting with Varma. Straight to the Chief, do not pass go. She didn't like the sound of that. It was most unusual. Back in London, her actions in Iraq already seemed a world away. A high-stakes world with no rules. Here, in the heart of the British establishment, rules were the foundation of government on which the architecture of Whitehall was built.

Daisy Thorn, Sir Philip's personal assistant, didn't inspire confidence when Lucinda asked her what mood the boss was in. 'A little tetchy, to be honest,' was the reply. Lucinda didn't have time to probe further. The phone on Daisy's desk rang.

'You can go in now,' said Daisy. 'Good luck.'

Sir Philip was sitting behind his mahogany empire desk below the four paintings commemorating the Duke of Marlborough's victories in the War of the Spanish Succession.

'Quite a time you've had of it, Spark,' said Sir Philip, motioning Lucinda to sit. 'How are you?'

'All things considered, sir, not too bad.'

'Good. Before we get down to business, you may be interested to know what's been happening back here.'

'Yes, sir.'

'We interdicted all five individuals identified in your original report. The police and Security Service have recovered significant

277

intelligence that will have a material impact on those who seek to do us harm. The sixth terrorist, Aziz Malik, was a ghost, but thankfully he did little damage.'

'What happened, sir?'

'He walked into the Bullring Shopping Centre in Birmingham and took an AK-47 out of a cricket bag. He shot out two shop windows and then his rifle jammed. He dropped it and ran. Scared of his own shadow, as luck would have it. Dumb kid. Well, quite a smart kid as it turns out. God knows how he got caught up in all this. A security guard apprehended him and he's now in police custody.'

'And the explosion in Barcelona, sir?'

'The official line of the Spanish authorities is two terrorists were killed when the explosives they were loading onto a van for an attack on the Sagrada Familia detonated prematurely. TATP is notoriously volatile, but I suspect there may be more to the Spanish explanation than meets the eye. Never mind. Two terrorists are dead. Now,' said Sir Philip, picking up a dossier on his desk, 'to more personal matters. Your conduct.'

Lucinda braced herself for what was to come and started preparing a defence. "Ends", "justifies", "means", were the only words that came to mind.

'You have shown a flagrant disregard for the chain of command, wilfully and consistently disobeying direct orders from your superiors, at times ignoring them completely. You acted selfishly, putting yourself and others in harm's way. You engaged in unauthorised, covert operations with the CIA, potentially jeopardising our strategic relationship with the US intelligence community. And that is just the tip of the iceberg. Your actions, Spark, could be construed as foolhardy in the extreme.'

Sir Philip tossed the dossier on his desk and swept back his errant fringe. Lucinda shifted in her chair. The wounds on her back throbbed.

'On the other hand,' continued Sir Philip, 'it could also be said you have shown a healthy disregard for authority, admirable decision-making abilities, and considerable initiative. All this while acting with minimal support behind enemy lines at great personal risk. Your actions have without doubt saved many lives both in this country and Spain. Not to mention hundreds of thousands of lives in Iraq. What,' said Sir Philip, 'do you know about Military Intelligence?'

'I'm sorry, sir?'

'Military Intelligence, Spark. The MI numbers.'

'Er, not much, sir. During the First and Second World Wars our security services were organised in military intelligence sections. There were at least ten separate sections at one point, I think. But today, in popular parlance at least, only two remain. MI5 and MI6.'

'Do they not teach history anymore?' lamented Sir Philip. 'You are partly right. What I am about to tell you, Spark, is top secret. You are to tell no one. And when I say no one, I mean neither your family, nor your colleagues. Understood?'

'Yes, sir,' said Lucinda.

'There is a third Military Intelligence section in existence today. MI9. It is a highly specialist organisation comprising the most capable individuals we have in MI6, MI5 and our Special Forces. The cream of the crop, you might say. MI9 currently has eleven active personnel. I would like you to become the twelfth.'

Lucinda said nothing.

'We can get into the details later, should you accept. But for now, I will say this. MI9 is an extra level of protection at the very pinnacle of our security services. Teams are put together on a case by case basis to deal with a specific threat. An operative might work alone or as part of a unit. Flexibility and operational independence are key to its success. You have already met one serving member of MI9.'

Lucinda paused and said, 'Mike Evans. He led the SAS raid on Hashemi's house at Lake Darbandikhan.'

'Yes,' said Sir Philip, 'and his opinion of you was favourable. Training is extensive and exhaustive. Once complete, you will be fitter than you have ever been, stronger than you have ever been, and an expert in just about every military and intelligence discipline you can imagine. Questions?'

'Thank you, sir,' said Lucinda, unsure where to begin. 'How would my role change? Would I still do the same job?'

'Nothing changes. On the surface at least. You would carry on in the same role as now. There would, however, be occasions when we needed a particular, specialist response to a national security problem. That is where the men of MI9 come in.'

'How many women have served in MI9, sir?'

'You would be the first.'

Sir Philip looked at his watch. 'For a young agent at the beginning of her career, Spark, you have shown exceptional attributes and strength of character. MI9 has a unique role in the defence of the realm and I believe you would be a good fit. You would become part of a close-knit family with an unshakeable bond. MI9 is the highest calling in our business.'

'Yes, sir,' said Lucinda, her mind bursting with more questions.

'You do not have to decide immediately. I told you to tell no one, and let me remind you that includes your colleagues. There is, however, one man from whom you may seek advice. That is all, Spark. And well done.'

'So,' said Miles Cavendish at dinner that evening, 'he asked you to join The Unit.'

'The Unit?'

'MI9.'

Miles refilled their glasses with the 2008 Clos de Litanies Pomerol. Le Boudin Blanc in Shepherd's Market was one of Lucinda's favourite restaurants, and it was the perfect place for her first dinner back in London. The warm, cozy atmosphere was like a comfort blanket.

'What can you tell me about it, Miles?' asked Lucinda.

'For a start, it was my idea. I wanted to call it the S&M club, after David Stirling and Paddy Mayne, the founding fathers of the SAS. Not surprisingly, that didn't fly. We created MI9 in the aftermath of 9/11, which was without doubt the greatest intelligence failure of the modern era. The intel community was out of date, unprepared, stagnant, and handcuffed by bureaucracy. We had to get back to the pioneering spirit of the North African Campaign in World War II. Flexible, dynamic, intelligence-led operations. And the best way to do that was to create a specialist unit drawn from the very best of our intelligence services and Special Forces.'

'How does it work?' asked Lucinda.

'Amazingly well,' said Miles. 'In exceptional circumstances, C, the head of MI5, and Director Special Forces agree on a course of action to meet a particular national security need and get permission from the Prime Minister to carry it out. Of course, the PM doesn't officially sign off on anything. There has to be plausible deniability.'

'What do you think, Miles?'

'Did Sir Philip say you would be part of a close-knit family, a band of brothers with an unshakeable bond?'

'Something like that,' replied Lucinda.

'Well, that's true. But think about it carefully, Lucinda. What he didn't tell you is that if you go down this road, you will never be more alone. And this is the sort of alone you can never shake.'

Lucinda sat on the wall by the Vauxhall Bridge Road bus stop and thought about Sir Philip's offer and what Miles had said. A number 87 bus squealed to a halt behind her and spilled another tranche of commuters onto Millbank.

This is the sort of alone you can never shake.

Lucinda looked through Henry Moore's abstract bronze across the Thames to the MI6 building and took a sip of her macchiato. It was cold.